BLANCANALES YANKED THE BERETTA FREE AND RAN FOR THE ALLEY

He could hear the vehicles screeching to a halt behind him. Turning, he saw a burly guy climbing out of the backseat of the SUV, a shotgun in his hands.

Blancanales raised the Beretta and squeezed off three quick shots. One of the Parabellum slugs lanced into the guy's right shoulder, jerking him around before a second round drilled his chest. His finger pulled the trigger in a death reflex and a blast thundered out of the shotgun's muzzle. Another of Escobar's gunners was coming around the other side of the truck, pistol drawn. Blancanales fired off two more shots and the guy ducked behind the hood.

Blancanales darted a few yards into the alley. He heard the sound of rubber squealing against pavement and assumed more were coming for him.

What had ignited all of this? Had Ortega given him up? If so, Escobar had probably gone to ground already. That'd make him all the harder to find.

If Blancanales even lived through the next few minutes.

DON PENDLETON'S

STONY
AMERICA'S ULTRA-COVERT INTELLIGENCE AGENCY
MAN ®

REVOLUTION
DEVICE

A GOLD EAGLE BOOK FROM
W RLDWIDE ®

TORONTO • NEW YORK • LONDON
AMSTERDAM • PARIS • SYDNEY • HAMBURG
STOCKHOLM • ATHENS • TOKYO • MILAN
MADRID • WARSAW • BUDAPEST • AUCKLAND

This book is dedicated to the intelligence professionals killed or injured in a suicide attack at Forward Operating Base Chapman, Afghanistan, in 2009. God keep.

Recycling programs for this product may not exist in your area.

First edition December 2013

ISBN-13: 978-0-373-80442-9

REVOLUTION DEVICE

Special thanks and acknowledgment to Tim Tresslar for his contribution to this work.

Printed in U.S.A.

REVOLUTION DEVICE

PROLOGUE

Kinshasa, Democratic Republic of Congo

"What brings you to Africa?" Blake Pearson asked.

One of the men—slim, his black hair shaved down to stubble—looked up from the tablet computer on his lap, his right eyebrow cocked, lips pressed together in a bloodless line, and stared at Pearson for several seconds.

"Business," the guy said. He cast his gaze back to his tablet and fell silent again.

Pearson, the newly installed ambassador to the Democratic Republic of Congo, nodded at the top of the man's head and bit down on a pointed reply.

The three men were twenty minutes into what Pearson considered an excruciatingly quiet ride through the capital. A former oil executive, Pearson had spent the past several years as a diplomat. His connections in Riyadh, Saudi Arabia, had made him a good fit for a diplomatic post there. After three years, the White House had tapped him to serve as ambassador to Iraq. His command of Arabic and his connections in the Gulf region had made him a natural choice for that job, too.

When the State Department underwent a post-election game of musical chairs with its Middle Eastern operations, Pearson had found himself without a seat when the music stopped. He'd blanched when his superiors offered him a post in central Africa as a consolation prize. Initially he refused the post because he knew so little about the country or the region. The secretary of state countered that, like his previous posts, the DRC had oil, which made it critical to U.S. interests. They needed someone with his diplomatic and business credentials to man such a significant post.

He'd always been a sucker for flattery so here he was in the Congo.

Today's to-do list included personally traveling to N'Djili Airport, one of the country's largest airports, to pick up his two companions and ferry them back to the Embassy. The last-minute request had come in a cable from a high-level State Department official and it had seemed shrouded in mystery from the start. The man who'd just spoken had introduced himself as Mr. Jacob.

Jacob had introduced his fellow traveler—a rangy guy, his pale skin mottled with freckles—as Mr. Taylor. Both apparently had left their first names back in the United States, because when Pearson asked the question, Jacob changed the subject. He simply asked to be taken to the Embassy so they could discuss some "critical issues best not mentioned in the open."

Pearson guessed the two men were CIA or maybe military intelligence. He'd met enough of each during his time in the Middle East to know when spooks were around. Maybe the Lord's Resistance Army, which had operations in the country, was planning to raise some hell. Maybe some mid-level al Qaeda operative was drifting through the country. Whatever the issue, he'd know soon enough. They'd refused to discuss it until they arrived at the Embassy.

In the meantime he just needed to sit here, in the air-conditioned comfort of his limousine, while the sphinx brothers studiously ignored him and instead stared at their computers.

The longer the ride took, the more his irritation grew. He was, after all, the U.S. ambassador. Between private meetings, lunches and dinners with dignitaries, an occasional grip-and-grin photo shoot and the like, his days usually stretched well past the twelve-hour mark. He'd been forced to cancel a slate of appointments to retrieve his new visitors. For his troubles, he'd been treated to a nearly uninterrupted view of their scalps and stony silence.

Lucky him.

He could only imagine what other joys the day held for him.

JULES NMOSU PULLED the vibrating phone from his pocket and brought it to his ear.

"Yes?" he asked.

"They should be at your position in five minutes," the other man said. "You know what to do when they get there, right?"

"I do," Nmosu said.

"Then do it," the caller said and hung up.

Nmosu scowled and slipped the phone back into his pocket. Of course he knew what to do. He'd been planning this operation for months, since shortly after the new ambassador, Blake Pearson, had come into the country.

For a diplomat, Pearson had proved himself skilled at alienating all the wrong people in the country. From the moment he'd arrived, Pearson had taken a hard line with several local rebel groups, including Nmosu's militia.

Nmosu had wondered for some time whether he'd succeed in killing Pearson. The man wasn't reckless. Nmosu guessed his years in Iraq had taught the ambassador the value of watching his ass. He constantly was surrounded by State Department security agents or contractors. He always traveled in armored vehicles.

Then Nmosu had found a benefactor who had changed everything. The man was at times arrogant, controlling and condescending. But he wanted Nmosu to succeed. He wanted to see Pearson dead, though he refused to say why. Nmosu cared little about the man's motives so long as he kept the weapons, money and advice coming.

He stopped at a small shop where meats, nuts and coffee were sold and stared at the display window. In the glass, he could see at least a partial reflection. He was tall and rail-thin. The skin of his face was drawn tight, to the point where his bones seemed on the verge of poking through. His eyes were sunken and marbled with little red lines. He'd always been unnaturally skinny, but also strong, speedy and aggressive. As a boy growing up in Uganda, he'd excelled at soccer and his well-meaning parents had filled his head full of stories about how one day he would play the sport professionally, or at least get a scholarship, maybe at a famous American or British university.

That plan hadn't worked out so well for him.

His father had a run a meat shop, similar to the one in front of him. One day, a pair of Ugandan soldiers had entered the store and first began taking food from the shelves and then helping themselves to the money in the register. Nmosu's old man had fought back, telling them to stop.

They'd rewarded his bravery by firing round after round from their AK-47s into the elder Nmosu. The barrage of 7.62 mm rounds had chewed through his stomach, his chest, his back, like dozens of blades punching through stretched paper. By the time the soldiers had finished their work, his father's torso had been ground up like the meat he sold. He'd been dead on the spot.

Though it'd been decades, the image of his father's bullet-riddled corpse crashing to the floor, the strobe-like flashing of the rifle muzzles, ran through his mind, again and again. It was like a ghost following him through life, rattling chains so often to get his attention that he no longer paid attention to the intrusion. It just flashed across his mind's eye—a shredded corpse slamming against the floor—and went away.

At the time of the shooting, he'd been lucky enough to pass out. The sheer terror he'd felt and the truth of what he'd seen had been too much for his young mind to bear. He'd come to later in a hospital. Someone, another mysterious benefactor, had brought him to the hospital.

After that, the plunge into despair had been fast and sharp. The family had lost the store and their father's meager income. The soldiers had accused the old man of attacking them, leaving them no choice but to cut him down with a withering barrage of autofire.

Nmosu had denied this. He'd told his mother the truth. She'd been horrified, but not by the truth. No, what had terrified her was her son's insistence on telling the truth. After all, honesty wouldn't buy them justice, but would instead brand a target on their backs.

It had been at that moment that he'd realized he was alone. If he wanted something in life, whether it was justice or power, he'd have to get it himself. Fortunately, it also was the time when he'd realized there was no justice in the world, so go for the power instead.

That had been the allure of the LRA for him. He cared little about the group's philosophy, beliefs and political agenda. He cared even less about their paper-thin pretensions of Christianity. They had the power of life and death. That had been enough to buy his allegiance. That he got to keep the best women from the villages they raided, to plunder their food and other possessions, was a bonus.

The lust for power had, in fact, driven him to leave the LRA and launch his own group.

And now this American, with his tough talk, wanted to dismantle what he'd built. Nmosu wouldn't stand for that. He glanced at his watch and smiled. In just a few minutes he'd show the United States he was here to stay.

THE HUMVEE SLOWED, taking Pearson's attention from his phone, where he'd been checking emails. Immediately his grip tightened on the phone and his heartbeat kicked into overdrive. Looking up, he glanced through the vehicle's side windows and saw the cars and trucks in the neighboring lane also slowing to a crawl before stopping altogether.

Peering through the windshield, he could see that the lead escort vehicle had stopped a few yards short of an intersection. A uniformed police officer was gesturing for them to stop. Looking past the officer, Pearson could see a red sedan, its front end crumpled, standing in the intersection, balancing on its passenger's side. A black van, steam rolling out from its engine compartment, stood a few yards away, its tattered front end turned toward the oncoming traffic. Uniformed officers milled around the intersection, a couple trying to direct traffic away from the accident scene.

It's just a wreck. Pearson forced himself to take a deep breath and hold it for a couple of beats before exhaling.

"You all right?"

Pearson looked over at his fellow passengers and saw Jacob eyeing him.

"Fine," Pearson said.

"You were in Iraq, right?"

"Yes. Fourteen months almost to the day."

"Car slows down there, you start thinking roadblock. Then you start thinking, which crazy militia is blocking the road? After that it's, am I about to become a hostage or star in some freaky al Qaeda snuff video? Am I right?"

"Very much so."

"Understood," Jacob said. "I spent a couple of years there. Did a lot of traveling."

"In the Green Zone?"

The corners of Jacob's lips turned up into a cold smile. "Too civilized for the work I did."

"Which was?"

"Something we'll talk about at the Embassy." He turned his attention back to his tablet computer.

"Of course," Pearson muttered.

He turned his attention back to his phone. Scrolling through his email's inbox, he saw that six more messages had arrived in less than a minute, a couple from the administrators in Foggy Bottom, two from his staff at the Embassy, one from an old contact in Baghdad and one from his wife, Kathleen. His first inclination was to read and respond to the business-related emails first, relegating his wife's message to the lowest priority. Catching himself, he tapped his index finger on her email. Just then, the Humvee lurched forward, rolling a few feet before veering into a right-hand turn.

"The police officer directed us to turn," the driver called over his shoulder.

Pearson acknowledged the man with a nod. He knew they could drive a few blocks north past the accident and roll back onto the road they'd just left.

He read the email from his wife: We miss you. Be careful. Attached was a picture of the twins, both clad in their bathing suits, the waters of the Embassy's pool sparkling behind them.

Blake—his blue eyes wide and his gap-toothed grin even wider—stared directly into the camera. Ashley, her smile more tentative, eyes narrowed with curiosity, was reaching a small hand toward the lens. Pearson smiled at the picture.

Losing his first marriage had been a sucker punch that'd left him reeling. He hadn't seen it coming, though in retrospect he should have. He'd resigned himself to the life of a divorced workaholic, somehow too defective to pull off a career and a marriage. Meeting Kathleen had changed that for him and he was grateful to have a second chance at a family.

The Humvee slowed again. Pearson glanced up and saw another police officer directing them to make a left-hand turn. The driver complied and seconds later they were headed in the direction of the Embassy again. Pearson typed a reply: Miss you 2. Home soon.

He then turned his attention to his other emails.

"Hey," Jacob said, "why isn't the cop directing anyone else down this street?"

A cold fist of fear buried itself in Pearson's gut. He looked over his shoulder and saw the escort car trailing behind them, but no other vehicles. Further on, he could see the police officer standing at the end of the street, waving other vehicles on.

What the hell?

He whipped his head back toward Jacob and Taylor and saw both men reaching under their jackets. A Diplomatic Security Service agent sitting in the front passenger's seat was also hunting for his sidearm.

"Stop, it's a trap!" Jacob yelled at the driver.

The driver stomped the brakes and Pearson felt his body being pulled forward, torso straining against the seat belt. Rubber squealed against the weathered pavement. The ambassador clenched his jaw and pushed his feet against the floorboards, bracing himself in case the escort car pounded into them. When the hit didn't come, he exhaled deeply. Casting a look over his shoulder, he saw through the rear window that the third vehicle had come to rest just inches from his own Humvee.

Pearson saw that Jacob and Taylor had brought out weapons from under their coats. The ambassador, who'd spent the past decade surrounded by security details, recognized the weapons as micro Uzis.

"Back up! Back the hell up!" Jacob shouted.

The driver had his phone pressed to his ear and was speaking rapidly into it.

"Back up, back up," he said, his voice taut. "Questions later! Just back up!"

Pearson's mind began to race through the possibilities. Was this a kidnapping? An assassination attempt? Hell, were they just paranoid? Maybe the police had isolated them for their own protection. Maybe, though his gut told him otherwise.

Looking over his shoulder again, he saw the vehicle behind them jerk once before it began backtracking toward the location of their last turn. Peering past that vehicle, he saw a second officer join the one who'd sent the diplomatic caravan rolling down this street. Both were carrying assault rifles, not unusual for police in the DRC's capital. One of the officers began to raise his rifle. Shit, Pearson thought, the bullets wouldn't pierce the specially made SUV's armored hide, but gunshots could turn an already tense situation into something deadly. It could cause the drivers, understandably, to run down the officers, all over a misunderstanding. Aside from two people dying needlessly, such an even would embarrass the United States and heighten tensions between the countries.

Knowing he couldn't allow that to happen, he turned back to Jacob and Taylor.

"Let me talk to them," the ambassador said. "They may have sent us down here for a reason."

Jacob shook his head emphatically. "They have something to say, they can cable the Embassy. For now, they can get the hell out of our way!"

THE WHITE BACKUP lights on the Humvee closest to Nmosu flashed before it jerked into motion. The African tensed, but kept his assault rifle's muzzle angled toward the ground. Those riding in the convoy obviously sensed something amiss. He didn't want to fuel their suspicions by reacting aggressively.

His free hand slid into his pocket and his long fingers curled around a second mobile phone—a disposable model that had been supplied to him. He brought the phone into view and entered the first four numbers of a five-digit detonation code for an IED.

The middle car, the one that contained the ambassador, was halted near a red Renault parked at the curb.

From the corner of his eye, he saw the man beside him raise his assault rifle and draw a bead on the convoy.

"What are you doing?" he snapped. His hand lashed out and he knocked away the weapon's muzzle. "I've got this."

The man glared at him, but Nmosu ignored him. He'd deal with the moron later—and, judging by the mood Nmosu was in, the LRA—after he made sure the convoy couldn't put any more distance between itself and the Renault. With his thumb, he pressed the final button in the detonation sequence.

An ear-shattering explosion rent the air, drowning out the normal sounds of the neighborhood. Thick columns of orange-yellow flame lashed out at the diplomatic vehicles, enveloped them, while the shaped charges and pieces of razor-sharp shrapnel battered and shredded the skin of the vehicles. The force shoved the ambassador's Humvee hard to the left before thrusting it onto its side; the inside engulfed in flames. Fire tore through the vehicles for a few seconds before reaching the gas tank in the one furthest from Nmosu, igniting another explosion that yanked the Humvee from the earth, flipped it a quarter turn in mid-air before it crashed back to the ground, flaming wheels and other debris breaking loose and skittering across the ground.

The closest Humvee had most of its front end ripped free by the blast, leaving it crippled. The Renault's engine had struck the State Department vehicle's roof, crumpling it like paper. The panes of bulletproof glass, webbed with cracks, came loose from the frames and crashed to the ground.

Nmosu, with the other LRA gunner on his heels, jogged toward the carnage. As he neared the killzone Nmosu's lips widened into a grin. A wave of heat slammed into him and brought him up short. He spotted one man, flesh rent by shrapnel, clothes smeared with blood, crawling from the vehicle's interior. He didn't recognize the man, but assumed he worked for the U.S. State Department or some other American agency.

The African raised his assault rifle and sprayed the man with a quick burst from the weapon. The man jerked under the onslaught, only falling still after Nmosu eased off the trigger. Nmosu circled the vehicle and found another man, his battered body caught in the seat belt. The injured American shuddered as pain coursed through his body, his face contorted with agony. The LRA gunner swung the rifle barrel around and put the man's face in his sights. It'd be an easy shot, one that'd put the man out of his misery. Nmosu would have the satisfaction of making another up-close kill. Shaking his head, he lowered the weapon and walked away from the vehicle.

Nmosu wished he had time to stay, to watch the man die. Unfortunately he had no time for such indulgences. He could hear the wail of sirens growing louder in the distance. Once the authorities realized what had transpired here, the place would be crawling not only with local police and soldiers, but also FBI agents, helicopters and drones. The CIA likely would be involved and the NSA would start sweeping up every phone call on the continent.

The sound of footsteps from behind startled Nmosu and caused him to whip around, raising his weapon as he did. A man dressed in tan khaki pants, brown loafers and a sky-blue button-down shirt was approaching him.

In an instant Nmosu recognized the man. He relaxed slightly, though the man's presence perplexed him.

"I didn't expect you to come here," Nmosu said.

"I wanted to admire your work," the other man said.

Nmosu grinned. He turned and looked again at the flaming wreckage.

"It worked perfectly," he said. "Better than I imagined."

"Yes."

"But we'd better go."

"Please, stay," the other man said. Nmosu felt something cold and hard press against the back of his head. What? Before he could turn around, blackness swallowed his world.

HOSSAN AHMADAH TURNED from the dead African sprawled in the street and briskly walked away from him. He stuffed the Makarov pistol in a holster beneath his jacket and moved to the nearest alley, used the narrow passage to get to the neighboring street. He did this a few more times and, within the span of a couple of minutes, had put several blocks between himself and the blast site.

He walked another block until he saw a weathered white van parked along the curb, its engine idling. As he neared it, the side door slid open and he climbed through it. Within a minute the driver eased the vehicle into traffic, driving for half an hour to a large warehouse.

The van rolled into one of the bays. The side door slid open again and Ahmadah slipped out, this time dressed in jeans and a polo shirt. He'd left his other clothes and the gun inside the van. The van's remaining occupants would dispose of those things and destroy the vehicle.

He crossed the warehouse's concrete floor to a second bay, where a faded red Renault stood waiting. He slid into the driver's seat and pulled down the sun visor. A set of keys dropped into his palm. He slid a key into the ignition, brought the engine to life, and drove the car from the warehouse.

It took him two hours to arrive at to his safehouse, in part because he'd taken evasive measures to prevent being followed.

Entering the house through the back door, he found himself inside a cramped kitchen. Pocketing the keys, he turned the dead bolt and punched the alarm code into a keypad on the wall. Though the house was small, he had taken the time to memorize the floor plans and found the back bedroom easily. A single-size bed stood against one wall. Crossing the room, he knelt next to the bed, reached beneath and felt around until his fingers grazed the smooth plastic of a briefcase handle. Clutching the handle, he dragged out the case, set it on the bed, opened it and withdrew an encrypted satellite phone. He punched in a number and waited. After two rings, a man's voice answered.

"Yes?" the man said.

"It's done," Ahmadah said.

"All of it?"

"Yes."

"Good. Many things are about to change."

The line went dead.

CHAPTER ONE

"Grab a seat, gentlemen," Hal Brognola said to the three Able Team warriors as they entered the War Room.

Brognola, the director of Stony Man Farm, America's ultra-secret intelligence and counter-terrorism agency, was sitting at the oval-shaped table that filled most of the room. A cup of coffee and a glass ashtray sat on the table at his right elbow. The sleeves of his dress shirt were rolled up to the middle of his forearms. His tie was pulled loose from his unbuttoned collar and dark half circles rimmed his eyes.

Hermann "Gadgets" Schwarz, the team's electronics expert, lowered himself into a seat directly across from Brognola, who acknowledged him with a nod. Rosario "Politician" Blancanales moved to the coffeemaker and began pouring coffee into a white disposable cup.

Carl "Ironman" Lyons, decked out in faded jeans and a loud Hawaiian print shirt, leaned against the wall just inside the door, his arms crossed over his chest. The former Los Angeles Police detective's mouth was creased into a scowl. His blond hair was mussed and his shirttails, the fabric webbed with wrinkles, had been pulled loose from his jeans.

Blancanales moved to the table, selected a seat next to Aaron "the Bear" Kurtzman and lowered himself into it. He punched Kurtzman, the leader of the Farm's cyber team, in the bicep.

"Don't start something you can't finish," Kurtzman said, grinning.

"Like this coffee you made?" Blancanales said.

"Words hurt, fella," Kurtzman replied.

Barbara Price, the Farm's mission controller, moved around the table, handing out folders to the Able Team warriors. When Price handed a folder to Lyons, she paused, narrowed her eyes and gave him an appraising look.

"You too restless to sit?" she asked.

"Hell, yes," Lyons said. "Been cooped up here for days. No mission. No leave. A guy can only spend so much time at the shooting range. Then he starts to get edgy."

"Carl," Price said, smirking, "you've been here less than forty-eight hours."

"So? Forty-eight hours in an ultra-secret facility? Might as well be forty-eight days. You guys are killing me!"

Rolling her eyes, Price released the folder and moved toward her seat next to Brognola. Shaking her head, she muttered, "Drama queen."

An unlit cigar jutted from between the big Fed's lips. Leveling his gaze at Lyons, Brognola plucked the cigar from his mouth.

"You need some action?"

"Yeah," Lyons said.

"You're in luck," Brognola said. "You're about to get it in spades."

A laptop sat on the table in front of Brognola. He tapped a couple of keys and a white projection screen lowered from the ceiling with an almost inaudible whir. While he waited, he put the cigar back into his mouth. A ceiling projector clicked on an instant later and filled the screen with a disturbing image.

Lyons turned his attention to the screen and saw the remains of three vehicles, their steel frames twisted, tires and upholstery vaporized by intense heat, wisps of oily black smoke wafting up from the charred metal. Water had pooled in several places on the pavement, a leftover from the efforts of firefighters to douse the blaze. Several people, mostly men, decked out in uniforms Lyons didn't recognize, were moving around the scene.

"This is—or at least was—a diplomatic convoy in Kinshasa, the capital of the Democratic Republic of Congo. That is before it was blown all to hell by an improvised explosive device."

"Was this the ambassador and his entourage?" Schwarz asked. "I read about this yesterday."

Lyons muttered, "Apple polisher."

Without turning around, Schwarz raised his hand and gestured at Lyons with his middle finger.

Brognola scowled.

"I'm about to give you two a time out. Right after I stick my foot up your asses," Brognola growled. "Hermann, to answer your question, yeah, this is that blast. This particular photo came from the news wire services, in fact, so you may have seen it on the internet. But here's one you may not have seen."

Brognola punched a couple of buttons and another picture flashed on the screen. A black man, wearing the same uniform as others at the accident scene, lay sprawled on the ground. His head was turned, the right side of his profile visible. A crimson pool had spread over the pavement around his head. An assault rifle lay just out of reach of an outstretched hand.

"Meet Jules Nmosu," Brognola said.

"I don't recognize the uniform," Lyons said. "He a cop or a soldier?"

"That's a police uniform," Brognola said. "But he's no cop."

"So he's indulging in a little cos-play?" Schwarz asked.

"Cos-play? What the hell is that?"

"People make costumes and— Never mind, Hal. You need to leave the Farm once in a while. Seriously."

"Tell me about it. Anyway, Nmosu's a ranking officer with the Lord's Resistance Army. As you can guess, his specialty is assassination and he's wanted in several African countries, including the DRC. He also had his hand in several other atrocities, including village massacres and the trafficking of sex slaves."

"All-around piece of shit," Lyons said.

"On his best day," the big Fed replied. "Slippery son of a bitch, too. Our intelligence services have been following him for years. Last we'd heard up until two days ago, he was in northern Uganda, making people's lives miserable. But apparently he took his horror show on the road and went back to his homeland."

Blancanales shifted in his chair. "So who killed Nmosu? Was it the cops on the scene?"

Brognola turned toward his old friend.

"That is an excellent question," Brognola said. "One we don't have an answer for at this point. We know it wasn't the police, since he was dead before the cops or the soldiers showed up on the scene. Best they can determine, it was a single round to the head. The shooter covered his tracks. He picked up the spent shell casing and dug the slug out of the ground before leaving. There were no surveillance cameras around, so we have nothing in the way of footage to examine."

"So we have zilch on this," Lyons said. "Is that what you're saying?"

"Simmer down, Carl. I'm saying we don't have all the information we'd like to have. But we're not empty-handed. The guy had no shortage of enemies. In theory, it could've been anyone, including someone with a beef against cops."

"In theory it could've been a small child playing with an assault rifle," Blancanales said.

Brognola nodded. "You get where I'm going. Since it wasn't the authorities who shot him, the most logical guess is that another LRA puke did the deed."

"Like they wanted him dead to tie up a loose end."

"Something like that. Maybe it was a loose end. Maybe Nmosu did something freaky at the scene and they thought they needed to put him down."

Lyons shook his head.

"Doesn't play," the Able Team leader said. "All they did was leave a calling card. So everyone knows the perpetrator."

"Except you're thinking like a cop," Schwarz interjected. "These guys have no real agenda. But they consider themselves a relevant movement. They probably wanted the U.S. to know they killed our ambassador. They'd consider it a shot across the bow. From what I read, Pearson was pretty vocal against the LRA."

"Fair enough," Lyons grumbled.

"I think you're on to something, Gadgets," Brognola said. "Unless Nmosu had a confrontation with another LRA fighter that turned deadly, we can assume this was planned. As best we can tell, he was hit once from behind in the head. He fell to the ground and was shot execution style in the head. If it was a heat-of-the-moment thing, the other guy likely would have shot him multiple times." Brognola slurped down some coffee, grimaced and set the cup back on the table. "There are a couple of other pieces, too. Neither is available to the public and each conflict with the other."

Lyons uncrossed his arms. Squeezing his eyes shut, he rubbed his temples with his fingertips. "You're killing me,

Hal," he said. "Is this a murder investigation or are we going to get some action?"

Blancanales smirked. "You're making his head hurt with all this talking stuff."

"Hey, I know how to investigate a murder. I'm just saying…"

"Like I said, Carl, simmer down. This stuff's important to know before you start kicking in doors and busting heads. But you will get to kick in doors and bust heads."

"Thank God," Lyons muttered.

"Carl's real problem is he hasn't been to a strip club in a few days," Blancanales said. "He needs to slap bellies, not bust heads. It's making our amigo cranky."

"Who needs a stripper for that?" Lyons growled. "I have a standing invitation from your sister."

"That's the only thing standing," Blancanales replied.

Schwarz and Kurtzman cast their eyes to the table and covered their mouths to stifle laughter.

"All right, you two," Brognola said, "give it a rest. I'm going to spend all week trying to scrub those images from my mind. Can we focus on the issue at hand? You're both nodding. I'll take that as a yes and maybe we can move on."

"So are you sending us to hunt down the guys who did this?" Lyons asked. "Please say yes."

Brognola shook his head no.

"Sorry," Brognola said.

"What, then?"

"We're sending you to Mexico."

"I can handle Mexico," Lyons said.

"We're not sending you there to party," Brognola said. "We've got real live work for you. Give you guys a chance to earn your massive government salaries."

"Shit," Lyons swore.

"But there will be action."

"I'm listening."

Brognola raised the remote control and clicked a button. A close-up of a man with a dark complexion, black hair and a thick black mustache appeared on the screen.

Lyons noticed a thin white scar on the guy's forehead, just below his hairline. His black eyes were flat and Lyons immediately recognized them as those of a killer. Both as a cop and later the commander of Able Team, he'd seen that dead-eyed look too many times to mistake it for anything else.

"Who are we looking at?" Blancanales asked.

"This is Seif Escobar," Brognola said. "You gentlemen ever heard of him?"

"Little more than a name," Schwarz said, while the other two said nothing.

"Escobar is a weapons broker based in Mexico City. He sells everything from small arms to surplus tanks all over the world. His customers include a handful of legitimate military clients, especially in Mexico and Central America. But he also sells his stuff to lots of bad guys. The Mexican cartels, the Taliban, some of the al Qaeda-linked groups in Africa. His customer list is a veritable Who's Who of people we'd like to see dead."

"Okay, I'm confused," Schwarz said. "How does a Mexican gunrunner dovetail with the assassination of a U.S. ambassador in Africa?"

"Excellent question," Brognola said. "The answer's a little complex."

Lyons intoned, "Apparently we have time to kill."

"Carl's just frustrated," Schwarz said. "You're throwing a lot of words at him."

"Hey," Lyons said.

Schwarz snickered.

Brognola cleared his throat. "Here's the deal with

Escobar," he said. "Even though we haven't been following him, some other U.S. intelligence agencies have been, especially since he has a habit of arming our enemies. They'd noticed that a couple of the front companies Escobar operates were shipping components used to make IEDs over to Africa. Until yesterday, most of the intelligence agencies found it interesting, but only mildly important. Today, it is something everyone is focused on… They found Nmosu's people had received some of the hardware."

Blancanales said, "He has a PO box?"

Price cleared her throat. "I can answer that. He has a couple of front companies of his own. And yes, Pol, they really aren't much more than PO boxes. He has a couple of addresses in Kinshasa and in a couple other cities where companies deliver the stuff he buys, whether it's fuses, magazines or spare parts for weapons—whatever. He has a group of couriers who then transfer the stuff to him. It's not sophisticated, but it works. A lot of his stuff falls through the cracks because it's so far off the grid."

Blancanales nodded his understanding. "Al Qaeda depended on a similar approach, if memory serves," he said. "Use a series of human mules and leave as small an electronic footprint as possible. It makes it a lot harder for a technology-heavy country like ours to track these guys."

"Agreed," Price said. "Fortunately for us, Nmosu and his cohort aren't as disciplined as other groups when it comes to communications. There wasn't enough information to prevent the attack beforehand. But at least there were some clues after the fact to help us deal with the situation."

"You might want to expand on that, Barb," Brognola said.

"Sure. We found a couple of phone calls between Nmosu and Hector Castillo, one of Escobar's lieutenants, dating back a couple of months. Nmosu also spoke on the phone with another number that, interestingly enough, had its roots in Iran."

"Oops," Schwarz said. "Talk about bad tradecraft. I'm sure that stuck out like a sore thumb."

"Again, after the fact it did. This person wasn't on our radar screen before all this went down."

"Right," Schwarz said.

"But now the major agencies have started tracking the number. Guess what? The owner has made calls to some bad people."

"Surprise!"

"I know, right? One of those bad guys is Castillo."

"Who also was dealing with Mr. Nmosu."

"Right."

"It could be a coincidence," Lyons said.

Price shrugged her shoulders.

"It could be," she said. "But there's a catch. One of Escobar's products, if you will, is the various dual-use components used in improvised explosive devices. He has a track record for getting hold of technology that our government tries to control through export rules and passing it along to bad people. Sometimes he buys it from employees of those companies and sometimes he purchases components illegally through a network of front companies located in the U.S., smuggles them out of the country and then sells them on the black market. And, again, it's the same components used in IEDs."

"Okay," Lyons said. He brought his cup to his lips and sipped some coffee.

"There's another wrinkle," Brognola said. "The Justice Department has been investigating Escobar for a while because of his weapons-smuggling activities. The stuff about his providing weapons specifically to the Taliban and al

Qaeda? There's a lot of evidence to prove his people have done it, especially Castillo."

"But it's harder to tie it to the big guy himself," Lyons said, nodding. "I dealt with that more times than I care to count while I was a cop. The smart ones know how to collect the money without getting their hands dirty."

"And Escobar's smart," Brognola said. "We've had a man inside his operation for a couple of years. His name's Michael Ortega. He's like Leo Turrin—he's spent most of his career working undercover. He has a good reputation in certain circles. Escobar, and scum like Escobar, trust Ortega because he's been around forever. Escobar even gave him a high-ranking position within his organization. That was stunning. Escobar's extremely paranoid, but they had mutual acquaintants that vouched for Ortega."

"So what does Ortega say about all this?" Blancanales asked.

"He didn't have any warning about the assassination, if that's what you're getting at."

"It wasn't," Blancanales said. "But that's good to know. I wondered if he's said anything about the Iran connection."

"Not specifically. But he had some other disturbing information. Apparently one of Escobar's suppliers has gotten his mitts on an unmanned aerial vehicle of some kind. Ortega hasn't seen one yet. But he's confident in what he's telling us. That's the reason we're sending you to Mexico. Escobar's connections to the killing, to Iran and possibly to advanced weaponry have the Man nervous."

"And once we verify it?" Lyons asked.

"Do what you always do," Brognola said, "and do it with extreme prejudice."

CHAPTER TWO

Mexico City, Mexico

"When's the guy coming?" Lyons asked.

Blancanales looked at his wristwatch.

"Couple minutes, tops," Blancanales said.

The group had arrived in Mexico City several hours ago and had checked into a hotel suite in the downtown, under Blancanales's alias, Alonzo Perez. Lyons was seated in the middle of a couch. His feet were hoisted onto a coffee table, right ankle crossed over left. His scowl deepened and he began drumming the fingers of his right hand on the cushion next to him.

"What's eating you, Carl?" Blancanales asked.

"Nothing," Lyons muttered.

"Bullshit."

"It's your plan," Lyons said.

"What about it?"

"It's dangerous."

Blancanales smirked. "Big change. We usually play it safe."

"You know what I mean, damn it," Lyons said. "We do a commando raid or we rough up some scumbags, we're all there. We can watch each other's back. This undercover stuff always makes me nervous."

"We've done undercover before," Blancanales said.

"Right. And the shit always makes me nervous. Real

undercover work, like when I was with the LAPD? That took months to pull together. You target someone. You set up a relationship. You build some trust. This way, you're just diving in headfirst and you have no backup."

"I have you and Gadgets."

"In the vicinity. But you're not wearing a wire. If things go wrong…"

"You'd never forgive yourself?"

"I'm going to kick your ass."

"I'll be fine."

"Famous last words."

"You're right," Blancanales said. "I can't guarantee I'll be okay. But there is something I can guarantee."

"What?"

"If something happens to me, you get my *Playboy* magazine collection."

Lyons's face reddened. "Here's a guarantee— I'm going to kick your ass."

"So you said," Blancanales said, smirking. "Still waiting."

Lyons opened his mouth to reply, but a knock at the door interrupted him.

Blancanales headed for the door. As he moved across the room, he reached underneath his jacket and set a hand on the grip of his Beretta 92 holstered on his right hip.

Lyons uncoiled from the couch and withdrew his .357 Colt Python with the four-inch barrel. He circled around behind Blancanales until he could line up a shot at the door.

Blancanales turned the knob and pulled the door open.

In the corridor stood a slender Latino, his black hair slicked back, revealing a sharp widow's peak. His slim frame was togged in brown loafers, tan slacks and a red polo shirt. In his right hand, he clutched a black suitcase.

The guy flashed Blancanales a wide smile, but it faded the instant he set eyes on Lyons.

"What the fuck?"

"You're Michael Ortega, right?" Blancanales asked.

"Yeah, I'm Michael fucking Ortega," he replied. "I heard you needed an electrician."

That was the code set up by Ortega's handlers in Washington. Nodding, Blancanales stepped away from the door and made a sweeping gesture for the Latino to enter. Ortega entered slowly. Blancanales shut the door behind him and locked it.

Lyons holstered the Colt. Crossing his arms over his chest, he glowered at Ortega.

"Sorry about the scare," Blancanales said.

"No worries," Ortega said. "Sorry about the stain on your floor."

Grinning, Blancanales nodded toward the couch. "Have a seat."

Ortega moved to the couch and lowered himself onto it. Hefting the scuffed briefcase, he set it on its side on the coffee table. According to Ortega's file, he used the briefcase to schlep around an Uzi and a couple of spare magazines for the Israeli-made SMG. Ortega was part of a special task force that fought gun trafficking in Mexico, as well as in Central and South America. Gray streaks ran through his perfectly coiffed black hair. His clothes were new and his nails manicured. Despite all this, his eyes looked sunken, bloodshot, as though he rarely slept.

"So," Ortega said, "you're looking for an introduction?"

Blancanales nodded. "And an endorsement," he said. "If you don't think it will put too big a target on your back."

Ortega snorted. "Hell, I've already been digging my grave for years. What're a few more shovelfuls of dirt before I go?"

Blancanales dropped into an armchair across from where Ortega was seated.

"You worried about getting involved?" Blancanales asked.

"Getting? Hell, I am involved. The minute I showed up here, I became involved. I've helped Escobar's people load RPGs and AK-47s onto airplanes and deliver them to narcoterrorists. I'm involved, okay? But, screw it. Leo tells me it's a big deal. It's the UAV chatter, right?"

"It is. That was a good find on your part."

"And there's a good chance, when all this is over, my cover could be blown anyway, right?"

"If we fail," Blancanales said, "the people we're going after, the ones who are left, are going to purge their ranks. If they have any suspicions about you—and I mean any— then they will kill you."

"Right after they torture me. Right, I know the drill. So give me details. What can Mr. Ortega do for you?"

"I want some face time with Seif Escobar."

"That's going to be tough."

"You can't get me an introduction?"

"Look, I don't know how much bullshit Leo floated about yours truly, but I don't have that kind of juice. I can get you a meeting with one or two of his lieutenants. I'll lie and tell them you walk on water, tell them you're a trustworthy SOB. After that, you need to work your own magic. Maybe you'll get an audience. Maybe not. Escobar doesn't set up a lot of play dates."

"Understood," Blancanales said.

"And if you do get to see Escobar, the guy's paranoid as hell. There are no surprise visits. You want some face time with him, you'd better have your back-story nailed down tight, because he'll look for holes."

"How soon can you get me in to see him?"

Ortega scowled and the creases in his forehead deepened. "Give me twenty-four hours."

ORTEGA CALLED BACK twenty-three hours and forty-seven minutes later.

The ringing of his mobile phone roused Blancanales from a light sleep. He grabbed for the phone holstered on his belt and glanced at the clock, which told him he'd been out for about four hours. He'd spent several hours studying the files on Escobar and memorizing pieces of his cover story.

Pulling himself up to sitting, he raised the phone to his ear.

"Yeah?" he said.

"It's me," Ortega said.

"Right."

"You got a meeting," he said.

"When?"

"Tomorrow," Ortega replied. "Like I said, they will want to check you out, check out your story before you see anyone."

"Will I see Escobar?"

"Hell no. You get to meet Hector Castillo, one of Escobar's lieutenants. That guy checks you out. If he feels okay about you, then you get an audience with the big guy. If not, end of story. No face time with him."

"We have other ways of reaching him," Blancanales said.

"They'll just attract more attention. Where's the meet?"

"Castillo's penthouse here in Mexico City."

"You have an address?"

"Yeah." Ortega recited the address and Blancanales committed it to memory. He'd pass it along to Stony Man Farm to track down architectural plans and other details before the meeting. He could also send Lyons and Schwarz over to conduct surveillance.

Ortega said, "Don't wear a wire. Castillo's people will pat you down. Occasionally, if they're feeling cranky, they'll throw you in the pool just to make sure any electronic devices short out. Besides, if they find a wire on you, they'll shoot you on the spot, chop your corpse into bits and feed it to Castillo's dogs."

"Thanks for the warning."

"Don't thank me. If you get killed, guess who's next on the list? I have a vested interest in keeping you alive."

CHAPTER THREE

Escobar was seated behind his desk, his feet propped up on it. In his right hand, he gripped a stubby glass with the remnants of bourbon and branch water. His head was tilted back and his brown eyes focused on the ceiling. Smoke curled up from the tip of a cigarette perched on the edge of an ashtray located just out of arm's reach.

His eyes felt gritty and his head throbbed from a lack of sleep. Nikki had kept him up well into the wee hours of the morning, his body fueled by copious amounts of bourbon and pills. Last night, he'd felt like he could go forever. This morning, Nikki had begged him to stay with her. It had taken everything he'd had to pull himself away from her so he could speak with his various lieutenants.

Thankfully, the last call of the day was almost over.

"What else do you have for me, Hector?"

Castillo's disembodied voice came out from the intercom. "Maybe a new customer."

"Okay."

"Name's Alonzo Perez." Castillo paused, apparently expecting the name to register with Escobar. "He's a buyer."

"Our customers usually are buyers," Escobar said. "That's why they're customers. The real question is, who is he buying for?"

"He's a free agent. Supplies MS-13, the Colombian drug gangs and the revolutionaries."

Escobar scowled. "I don't like free agents."

"I know."

"You can't trust people who stand for nothing," Escobar said. "You never know where they're coming from. You have no leverage over them."

"Right," Castillo said.

This was an old conversation. Escobar thought he detected weariness in the other man's voice, but he ignored it.

"So what else do we know?"

"He has a home base in Paraguay. Apparently he'd promised a load of rockets to some Colombians. They were being made in a factory in Syria. The Israelis took the place out with a missile strike. Now Perez needs to find another supplier quickly."

"He has the money?"

"Ortega says he has the money."

"Okay."

"But we're checking up on him. We have a team scanning through his history, making sure the accounts really exist."

"Make sure they weren't just opened last week, too."

"Of course," Castillo said.

Again Escobar detected weariness and maybe some irritation in his lieutenant's voice. Escobar felt his face flush and was aware of heat radiating from his neck, cheeks and forehead. He pulled his legs from the desktop and planted his feet solidly on the floor.

"You have something you need to say?" Escobar growled.

"What? No, Seif."

"You think maybe I shouldn't ask so many questions? Maybe I ought to be quiet and trust you to handle things?"

"No…"

"If that's what you're thinking, spit it out."

"It's not."

"Apparently you think you're somehow my adviser, like maybe I need you to coach me, lead me by the hand, show me how little I understand. Is that where this all is going?"

"Shit, no. Not at all."

"Maybe we're equals."

"I didn't say that." Castillo's voice sounded strained. "I didn't say any of that."

"Hell, maybe I forgot my place. I thought I was your boss, the guy whose ass is on the line. I'm delusional, right? Maybe you should just give this prick my address, all my security codes, the whole thing. Hell, why don't I send you my laptop and you can just hand it over to this jerk? Right, you're the security expert."

"It's good, Seif. I didn't mean to piss you off."

"So you're going to check this guy out, right? Not some half-assed make two phone calls and then go lounge by the pool. You're really going to make sure this guy's clean, right?"

"Sure. Of course. I've got a couple of guys running his name right now. If there's anything weird about him, we'll know it soon enough. Ortega vouched for him and you trust him, right?"

Escobar ignored the question. "Make sure this Perez is legitimate," he said. "Make sure he has money. If anything doesn't pass the smell test, you kill him, you understand?"

"Of course."

"Good," Escobar said before he hung up.

ESCOBAR STARED AT the phone for a few seconds and considered the conversation he'd just ended.

Castillo's sloppiness rubbed him the wrong way. The guy knew better than to put money before security protocol. Escobar had no problem with greed, none at all. Hell, he skimmed as much off the top of his profits as he could before he sent the money to its rightful owners. But he also knew better than to allow his greed to make him careless.

Picking up a pack of cigarettes from his desktop, he shook a cigarette into his hand, slipped it between his lips and shook his head. The stakes this time were too damn high for sloppiness. Taking the gold-plated lighter from his pants' pocket, he torched the end of the cigarette and puffed on it a couple of times until it was lit.

He tossed the lighter onto his desk, shot up from his chair and began to pace the room.

Chances were this new guy was just another customer, a gunrunner who'd lost his supplier. Fair enough. Escobar could accommodate someone like that. But he needed to be sure before he let him see how things worked. He'd gotten himself into some heavy business in the past couple of years, heavy but with the potential for a big payday if he did things right and made sure he'd left nothing to chance.

That was no problem for him. He was ballsy. But he knew better than to play things fast and loose. His childhood in Tijuana, the bastard son of a hooker, had taught him that.

His mother had been unusually beautiful, petite with glossy black hair, deep brown eyes and full lips. She'd also been unusually lazy. Gripped by poverty, Escobar could understand her decision to become a whore. But she hadn't pursued that with much energy, either, leaving them dirt poor. By age seven, he'd found himself forced to steal so he could eat. When the old whore died a few years later, he'd felt relieved, realizing he could keep more of what he stole for himself.

He'd vowed never to carry anyone else again, the only promise he'd ever kept.

Growing up poor had left him little time to worry over the identity of his father. As a small child, he'd asked his mother. On the rare occasion when she'd been sober, she usually greeted the question with stony silences or shrill demands that he never ask the question again. When she was drugging or drinking, she usually told him stories that as an adult he'd considered the ramblings of a woman gripped by insanity or stupidity.

She'd claimed she'd fallen in love with an Iranian who ran a small restaurant in the border town. He occasionally disappeared from Tijuana for days at a time and upon his return would refuse to explain his whereabouts to her. On one occasion, a pair of gun-wielding bandits had tried to rob his restaurant. Escobar's father had charged at them, putting himself between the criminals and Escobar's mother. He'd met their demands for money with violence, leaving one with a fractured arm and three broken ribs and the other with a smashed eye socket and a broken nose.

When she was three months' pregnant with Escobar, she'd walked into their apartment and found her lover stuffing clothes, cash and a small leather-bound diary into a battered suitcase. When she'd asked where he was going, he'd again refused to say, though he'd told her he worked for the government and he'd been called back to Tehran.

When she'd asked if he was a spy, he'd refused to answer. Instead he'd admonished her to forget all about him, to forget his name and face.

He had disappeared, leaving her pregnant and alone. As she'd often reminded Escobar, it was only after he was born that she'd turned to prostitution, and only to support him. If he'd ever had the capacity to feel guilt or gratitude about that, he couldn't remember such a time.

Escobar had spent his twenties building an arms-dealing empire. He'd started small, buying weapons stolen from the Mexican army and selling them to drug cartels and other criminals. As the cartels grew, they wanted better, more sophisticated weapons. That had forced him to take his operations global so he could tap into the flood of illicit weapons washing over hot spots in Africa, the Middle East and the former Soviet Union.

A trip to Argentina had turned everything upside down.

When the Colombian government had started spraying a drug lord's poppy crop, he'd decided he needed to acquire shoulder-launched missiles. Escobar had been able to procure several crates of SAMs through his connections in the Middle East and Africa. The drug czar had told Escobar he didn't want to meet in Bogota, but asked whether they could instead connect in Argentina.

For his part Escobar cared little so long as the man came with money.

He, along with a pair of his security guards, had met the man in a small apartment. The last thing Escobar remembered was something smashing against the back of his head and the explosion of white light behind his eyes at the moment of impact. After that everything had gone black.

HE AWOKE THREE days later in Ciudad del Este. His right arm was chained to the iron frame of a bed. His vision was fuzzy, his mouth dry. The ceiling above him was marbled with fine cracks and occasional brown rings from water damage. The cramped area was hot and smelled of mold. It took his mind a couple of minutes to wrap itself around his situation and he realized he had probably been drugged.

As he raised his head to look around, he saw a man sitting in a corner of a room. The guy had an olive complexion, thick black hair and a long beard of the same color.

"Where am I?" Escobar had demanded in Spanish.

The guard stared at him, but said nothing. Instead he pulled himself from the chair and left the room, with Escobar shouting after him.

Several minutes later the guard returned, following another man.

The new arrival walked to the side of the bed and stared down at Escobar for several seconds. A smile was fixed on the man's face, though Escobar saw no warmth there, only cold detachment as the man studied him.

"Bienvenidos, Señor Escobar," the man said. "I am Ahmed al-Jaballah."

"Where the hell am I?" Escobar demanded in Spanish.

"You needn't concern yourself with that right now," al-Jaballah said.

"Why am I here?"

"Ah, a much better question," he said. He turned to the guard and said something in a language Escobar didn't understand. Nodding, the guard reached into his pocket and approached Escobar, who tensed.

"It's okay," al-Jaballah said. "I'm going to have him take off the handcuffs. There's no need for them at this point."

"At this point?"

When the metal band sprang open, Escobar tried to pull his arm away, but it was numb and didn't respond immediately. He focused on trying to move his fingers, just to get some blood moving through his limbs while he waited for the guard to remove the cuff from his other hand.

"We brought you here to offer you a deal," al-Jaballah said.

"You could have called," Escobar replied bitterly.

The man snorted.

"Yes, I suppose we could have done that, but this is much easier to explain face to face."

Escobar's head was still fuzzy from whatever drugs they'd been feeding him to offer another sarcastic comment. Instead he just gave a curt nod to keep the other man talking.

"Would you like a bottle of water?" Another smile that seemed forced. "You've been under for a long time. The drugs can dehydrate you." The man turned to the guard and again said something in another language. Though Escobar couldn't understand it, his head had cleared enough for him to recognize a couple of the words as Persian, a language he'd encountered during his travels in the Middle East. The guard nodded and left the room.

"I really want to know why I am here."

"How much do you know about your father?"

Hardly considering the question, Escobar shrugged.

"Very little. He left before I was born."

"Left you and your mother alone. That must have been hard."

Escobar smirked. "My mother was a lazy hooker. My father apparently was a deadbeat who couldn't wait to get as far away from her once he'd gotten some ass off her. The only hard thing was stealing enough food to take care of my mother and me. Did you bring me here just to discuss my childhood?"

"Of course not, my friend. I brought you here to discuss your future. But the path to your future lies in your past."

That sounded like unicorns-and-crystals bullshit to Escobar, but he held his tongue, figuring the less he antagonized the other man, the better. "I'm not sure I understand," he said.

"Of course not. Not yet, anyway."

The guard returned carrying two bottles of water. Al-Jaballah took one and handed the other to Escobar, who snatched it from his grip. His throat felt dry and swollen from dehydration. The bottle of water was cold and wet and he figured it had been sitting in ice. Twisting off the cap, he brought the bottle to his lips and guzzled down half its contents before setting it down.

"Please drink up," the man said. "There's plenty more where that came from."

"Frankly, I'd prefer something stronger. And a cigarette."

"No alcohol," al-Jaballah said. "I do not drink. I'm a devout Muslim."

Fantastic, I've been nabbed by a band of Persian teetotalers. Escobar felt irritation begin to overtake him, smothering any fear and uncertainty he'd felt about his plight. Figuring he was in no position to raise hell—yet—he swallowed hard and nodded. "I didn't realize that."

"Of course you didn't." Al-Jaballah reached into his pants' pocket and pulled from it a pack of cigarettes and a lighter. He tossed both next to Escobar on the bed.

Escobar nodded in appreciation and gathered up the cigarette pack like a hungry dog with a bloody steak. He wasn't sure how long he'd been unconscious, but seeing the cigarettes made him keenly aware how much his body craved one.

"You know little of your father."

Escobar, who was focused on lighting his cigarette, shrugged his shoulders. "What's to know? He left when I was young. He ran a restaurant. He never married my mother. He came to Mexico in the 1970s and left in the 1980s. Not much of a story to tell."

By now he'd lit a cigarette. He took a deep drag from it and enjoyed the feel of the smoke filling his lungs. The hit of nicotine seemed to cause his vision to sharpen. He also realized he was damn hungry. Before he could say anything, though, al-Jaballah cut him off.

"Your mother told you nothing else?"

Escobar blew a line of smoke from the corner of his mouth and gave the other man a hard look.

"She said a lot of things. Most of it was bat-shit crazy. Loco. None of it was worth repeating."

"Try me."

"She said the old man was a spy, an Iranian spy."

"You didn't believe her."

The Mexican leveled his gaze at the other man. "Look, the woman did a lot of drugs, especially after my old man left. She was not in her right mind. He left her pregnant and alone. He took most of their money. That doesn't sound like a spy. It sounds like a damn deadbeat. But there you are. It's what happened. If believing he was a spy helped her sleep at night, fine. But I never believed it."

"She told you the truth. He was sent to America in the late 1970s after the revolution. He was part of a sleeper cell Iran set up in Mexico."

"To do what?"

Al-Jaballah shrugged.

"For the most part, nothing. Occasionally he'd cross the border and meet with a source, not that we had many in those days."

"We? So you're an Iranian spy, too."

"Something like that. We'll get to that in a minute. But your father was a highly trained operative. He and a dozen other men were sent to Mexico for a specific reason. When the Embassy was taken, the revolutionary government had no idea how the U.S. would react. Some thought America would wait it out. Others assumed they would attack Iran. If that happened, he and his counterparts were to cross the border and strike U.S. targets."

The revelation meant little to Escobar. If there ever had been a point where he'd cared about having a father, that part of him had died long ago. It really was only a matter of curiosity for him.

His body tensed. He'd moved close enough to the Iranian to try to lunge at him, take his weapon and knock him out. Just before he could act, though, the doorknob twisted and the guard returned. This time he carried a plate of food. Immediately the smells of the food reached Escobar. A pit seemed to open inside him and he remembered that it had been days since he'd eaten. He also knew he couldn't take two armed men at once, especially with him unarmed and weakened.

Instead he relaxed and kept pushing for more information.

"So what does this have to do with me?" he asked.

The other man smiled.

"An excellent question. Your father, before he died, was part of a small group of men who served the revolution, who agreed to martyr themselves if necessary to defend it."

"I still don't see..."

"Wait, I'm getting to that. He was a patriot. He was upholding something he believed in. Like my father who served with him, he hated the shah, hated the West and how they used our people and our resources for their own ends. He wanted to serve the revolution and he did."

"Okay, that's fine," Escobar countered. "I grew up in Mexico. I don't give a damn about you or your country."

The other man's smile widened though it didn't reach his eyes.

"I'd like to say I find your candor refreshing. I don't. I find it obnoxious. However, after the way we've..." He paused and seemed to be searching for the right word. "After the way we've inconvenienced you, you deserve an explanation.

"Your father and my father and other men like them served in a small group called the Circle. It's a unit of the IRG—the Iranian Revolutionary Guard."

"So what were they? Spies? Soldiers?"

"It's so much more than that," al-Jaballah said. "We are the firewall. We're what stand between the clerics, the civilian government and anyone who might try to take down our government. We go through the Guard. We find the people who aren't totally loyal to the cause or who may stop being loyal down the road. We eliminate them. We've taken out clerics. We've taken out members of the civilian government. Here's what this means for you… The world has changed a lot since the shah was driven from power. But in many ways it hasn't changed at all. What you have going for you is that you're at home in the Western world. You're well traveled. You can move with little or no obstruction. No one will link you to us."

"So you're recruiting me?"

"It's only recruitment when you have a choice."

Escobar bristled at that. He felt his neck and his cheeks flush as anger boiled up inside him. His muscles tensed as he became ready to uncoil from the bed and strike the Iranian. Instead he squelched his desire to attack. Clenching his fists hard, he stayed still. "So you're saying I have no choice in the matter."

"You don't."

"And you know this because…"

"If you say no, we'll destroy you and no one will know the difference."

"Why should I believe you?"

The other man shifted in his chair and stared at Escobar for several seconds.

"I notice you haven't asked about your entourage," he said. "That team of security people who were with you? The clerical assistant?"

The questions hit Escobar like a punch to the gut. It was only at that moment he realized he had no idea as to the whereabouts of his security team. He'd been so focused on his own plight that he'd forgotten about them. It wasn't that he was concerned about their welfare. No. But he knew their fates would likely forecast his own.

"What did you do to them?"

"They're all dead. It didn't happen quickly or painlessly. I took the liberty of filming their deaths. A few of the videos are a little long because we questioned them before killing them. Certainly makes the whole thing a little tedious. But you're welcome to watch the videos, if you'd like."

Escobar felt his stomach lurch. As terror seized him, he began to feel light-headed and a desire to vomit overtook him.

"What do you want from me?"

"Let me tell you."

Al-Jaballah's next words had blown Escobar's mind.

EVEN NOW THE whole experience seemed surreal to Escobar—a secret society within a secretive government.

In and of itself, Escobar cared little for geopolitics. He considered the bickering and posturing between countries foolish. But, as a businessman, he also wanted to know which countries were on the brink of a war, in a war or limping out of a war.

Escobar dropped a fresh ice cube into his glass, heard a satisfying clink. Tipping the whiskey bottle, he splashed more alcohol into the glass. When al-Jaballah laid out the Circle's plans for the Middle East, Escobar had considered him insane. He'd questioned not only the man's stated goals, but also the very existence of the group al-Jaballah was touting. As the years had worn on, though, he had witnessed the power the Circle wielded in Iran and the Middle East as a whole, all of it behind the scenes.

He still didn't give a damn about the group's goals per se. Or whether the story about his father was true or a convenient fiction aimed at clouding his judgment. None of that mattered to him.

What he cared about was money. He'd made a lot of it while selling guns and other weapons. He could make even more if he had unmanned aerial vehicles to sell. Anything else was a load of high-minded BS.

As long as al-Jaballah kept the money flowing, Escobar would be a good soldier. If that meant selling weapons to Alonzo Perez, fine; Escobar would do it. But if he thought Perez was here to cause trouble, he'd put the guy in the ground.

CHAPTER FOUR

Blancanales shrugged into the nylon shoulder rig. He then picked up the Beretta 92 from the top of the dresser and slid it into the holster before slipping on the jacket for his grey Armani suit. He buttoned the jacket and studied his reflection in the mirror to verify the pistol wasn't visible.

While Brognola supposedly had secured the cooperation of the Mexican government, Blancanales knew things were more complicated on the ground than they were in the office of a high-level bureaucrat. He was in a foreign country, traveling under a fake name but with a very real gun. And, if they ran his name and face through any of the myriad databases, they'd see he was an arms trafficker.

If the police picked him up, Lyons and Schwarz would have to vouch for his Justice Department ties. Or Brognola would have to rattle a few cages from Washington. All of that would take time. While getting picked up by the police might bolster his street cred, it also would cost him valuable time. And considering the rampant corruption in Mexican law enforcement, he knew any effort to spring him from jail could also result in blowing his and Ortega's cover.

He didn't want to risk an arrest. Not making it obvious he was carrying was one way to avoid attracting police attention—he hoped.

The door opened behind him. In the mirror, he saw Schwarz poking his face into the space between the door and jamb.

"Ortega's here."

Blancanales nodded. Turning, he exited his bedroom and followed his friend into the living room.

Ortega was perched on a barstool. A lit cigarette was pinched between the first two fingers of his right hand, which was resting on the bar. A glass holding a partially melted ice cube sat on the bar in front of him. He glanced at Blancanales when he entered the room and greeted him with a nod. Grabbing a bottle of Scotch by the neck, Ortega flipped it to a forty-five-degree angle and poured an inch or so into his glass.

"Go easy on that," Blancanales said.

The undercover agent shot him a sideways glance before downing the drink.

"I work better when I'm half lit," he said.

Blancanales marched over to the bar as Ortega was reaching out for the bottle of Scotch. The Able Team warrior grabbed it before the other man could get hold of it. Ortega swiveled around on his stool. His narrowed eyes locked on Blancanales and his body tensed, as if he was about to launch himself from the stool.

"Hey!" Ortega snapped.

"I said go easy. You want to drink yourself into a stupor, do it on your own time. We have work to do."

"I know we have work to do," Ortega said. "I was doing this shit long before you and your buddies breezed into town. Remember? Give me the bottle."

Blancanales handed the bottle to Schwarz, who carried it behind the bar.

Ortega, a scowl fixed on his face, followed Schwarz's movements until he'd packed the bottle away.

"I'm supposed to have a couple of belts in me," he said. "Escobar's people expect that of me. It's part of my cover. I always show up with a couple of drinks in me."

Blancanales shook his head.

"Not today."

"What? You don't drink?"

"I drink. More important, I don't give a shit whether you drink."

"Apparently you do."

"We're about to step into a hostile situation," Blancanales said. "You know the players. You know the vibe. If they're uncomfortable with me, you're going to sense it."

"And you think I won't sense it if I'm too liquored up. Bullshit. I know how to handle myself. I know how to handle a couple of drinks."

"Well, you're in luck because that's what you just had."

Ortega slid off his stool and, glaring at Blancanales, took a step toward him. The warrior kept his hands hanging loose at his sides, fingers open but ready to block anything the agent tried.

"Stand down," Blancanales said. "Now."

Ortega held his gaze for a few seconds. He cursed under his breath, turned and gathered his cigarettes and lighter from the bar. Pushing past Blancanales, he flung open a sliding-glass door, stepped onto the balcony and slammed it shut.

"Well played," Schwarz said. "You're making Ironman look like Dale Carnegie."

Blancanales shrugged.

"Needed to be done," he said.

"Because you despise the demon alcohol."

Blancanales flashed his friend a smile. "That's me. A card-carrying member of teetotalers anonymous." He glanced over his shoulder at Ortega, who stood on the balcony smoking a cigarette, before turning back to Schwarz. "I'm about to walk into a den of snakes with our friend as my primary backup. I want to see where this guy's head is at. If it was you or Carl, I wouldn't sweat this stuff."

"But it's not."

"Right, it's not. I'm going in with a guy who's spent years living a double life. He's got his own priorities and allegiances at this point."

"Leo Turrin does it," Schwarz said.

Blancanales jerked his head in Ortega's direction. "This guy isn't Leo Turrin."

"True."

"Add on top of that, that this clown wants to douse himself in Scotch before we meet Castillo. Suddenly, I am feeling nervous."

Schwarz crossed his arms over his chest and leveled his gaze at Blancanales.

"You don't think his head's on straight."

"As much as anything, me pushing him on the alcohol was a power play. I wanted to see how he reacted. I expected a little pushback. Someone who's able to do the undercover gig is probably going to have an independent streak. They won't take well to some outsider like me parachuting in and barking orders. And if the guy was a pushover, he wouldn't have lasted this long surrounded by Escobar's people."

"He looked more than a little irked, though."

"Yeah, I thought he might take a swing."

"That'd be awkward. Especially after you whipped his ass."

ORTEGA STOOD ON the balcony, puffed on his cigarette and seethed. Who did that SOB think he was, parachuting into Mexico City and telling him how to run an operation? Who the hell were any of them, for that matter? They thought they knew how to handle things.

Ortega knew better. He'd been swimming in this shit for what seemed like forever. And, yeah, maybe it had been getting to him recently. He'd had more than one night where his eyes had snapped open for no reason. A cold sweat filmed his skin. His heart slammed in his chest. Breath came in shallow gasps, when he could catch his breath at all.

But, hell, who could blame him?

He'd been consorting with scum his whole career. But Escobar was in a category all his own. The guy reminded him of a snake. Cold eyes that Ortega swore never blinked and an even colder smile, the sight of which usually heralded something awful for someone, somewhere.

After dealing with that, yeah, Ortega felt worn down, like a bundle of exposed nerves. And, yeah, it had made him sloppy and had caused him to cut a few corners.

He tossed the cigarette to the balcony and ground it under his heel, leaving a curved black streak on the floor. His throat suddenly felt dry and he wished he could have another drink. Not that he needed another one, he told himself. He just wanted one and he wanted it now, just to take the edge off before he had to deal with that prick Castillo. He hated that bastard almost as much as he hated Escobar. Almost. Escobar definitely was in a class of his own.

He dug around in his pants' pocket until he found his cigarettes and lighter. He lit another cigarette and dragged on it. If he couldn't have a drink, he'd damn sure treat himself to another smoke.

He didn't know what the angle was for these Washington pukes. His bosses hadn't told him shit.

"You have three high-level agents coming," his supervisor had told him during their weekly check-in call. "Give them whatever they need. Don't ask any questions. Just shut your damn mouth and do as you're told. Understood?"

Ortega didn't understand. He hadn't suffered quietly over it, either. He'd complained about it, of course. But he'd tried to keep it as subdued as possible. Not because he worried about pissing off his controller or being pegged as a guy with a bad attitude. Hell, pissing off some bureaucrat was the least of his damn worries, all things considered.

Still, he knew better than to gripe too loudly. He'd made some bad decisions in the past several months, and he guessed some of them would come back to haunt him. The last thing he needed was a trio of Boy Scouts from Washington jetting into his territory and job shadowing him. He'd racked up a laundry list of bad things while doing his job, none of which he'd reported.

And when he did something right, such as learning that Escobar had access to UAVs, he'd suddenly found himself up to his neck in unwanted help from Washington. He shook his head in disgust. Hard-won experience told him it was better to take his beating, to do all the team-player BS that was expected of him.

His cigarette burned down to the filter and winked out. Tossing the butt onto the balcony, he lit another smoke. He hadn't played it entirely straight with these guys or his bosses in the States. Over the past couple of months he'd gotten a bad feeling that Escobar was on to him. The Mexican could be as inscrutable as a snake and one hundred times more dangerous. Ortega had come to grips a while back that he only could make educated guesses when it came to Escobar's position on anything. Still, his gut told him the boss had misgivings.

Ortega rested his elbows on the balcony railing and stared at the skyline. Deep down, he knew he should have flagged his controller with the Justice Department, the technical team that was working with him here and now these other hotshots. Instead he'd kept his mouth shut. And he'd done it for no other reason than it was just easier.

His controller went home every night to a familiar home, a good meal, a wife and kids. Ortega spent every minute waiting on someone to see through his disguise, to slit his throat and bury his body in a landfill. Did he drink? Hell, yeah. Sometimes it was the only way he'd pass out at night, then he'd wake again in the morning, mind racing, fraught with worry, and he'd hunt for another bottle. None of these bastards understood that. So if he wanted to take the easy way out for once, not spill his guts to some bureaucrat who hadn't seen a real criminal in a decade or more, so be it.

Maybe his gut was right, that Escobar was on to him. More likely, though, it was his nerves. He wasn't going to have some useless bureaucrat yank him from the field, stick him behind a desk or put him on disability because they thought his nerves were shot. He'd put a bullet in his own head before he'd let that happen.

Grinding the cigarette on the top of the railing, he threw the butt over the side of the balcony. He turned and started across the balcony. He was the one in control, the professional, he told himself. There was no way Escobar questioned his loyalty; he was too valuable, too good at his job to slip up. He had nothing to worry about.

THE VAN'S INTERIOR was hot and stank of cigarette smoke.

It had been stripped clean of its factory-installed bench seats and outfitted with consoles stuffed with high-tech surveillance gear. Four low-back chairs were bolted to the floor. Two DOJ technicians were seated at the consoles. Their eyes bore into the computer monitors fixed to the walls and their hands moved over the controls with practiced ease.

Schwarz, an electronics whiz, had spent the past ten

minutes debating analog versus digital recording with Steve King, the older of the two technicians. King, a pale man whose hairline had receded enough to reveal a scalp dotted with dime-size liver spots, wore what was left of his hair in a long ponytail that dipped between his shoulder blades. A lit cigarette jutted from his mouth. A green plastic ashtray stood on the console, unused. When ashes fell from the cigarette, he brushed them onto the floor.

Lyons stared at the wall and fumed. Tapping his foot impatiently, he tried unsuccessfully to tune out the small talk. His Atchisson shotgun stood against the van's wall, canted at a forty-five-degree angle. Occasionally he let out an exasperated sigh.

Schwarz turned to his old friend.

"Something wrong, Agent Irons?" Schwarz asked, using Lyons's code name.

"Nothing!" Lyons snapped.

"Okay," Schwarz replied, his voice artifically brig ut. He spun back toward the consoles.

"Hell, yes, there's something wrong!" Lyons said.

"Let it out, big guy," Schwarz said, suppressing a smirk.

"We should be in there with him—that's what's wrong."

"Hard enough to get one newbie in there, let alone three," Schwarz replied. "This seemed like the best way."

"The best way," Lyons countered, "was to go in there, kill some of Castillo's guys and force him to talk."

King turned to the other two. "That's how you do things?"

"Turn around," Lyons growled. He didn't look at the guy. "Far as you're concerned, this conversation never happened."

King scowled but shook his head and turned back toward the monitor. "You're a prize, Irons," he muttered.

"We already agreed on this," Schwarz said. "We don't

want to hit them too hard or too fast yet. We need to know more. You said it yourself—we don't want to tip our hand too soon and cause these bastards to go to ground, especially if they are a global player. We needed someone we could trust to get us in there."

Lyons shook his head. "We're in there. Whether we can trust this guy is up for debate."

"Well, for once something smart came out of your fat mouth," King said.

Lyons pinned the technician with his gaze.

"What the hell are you yammering on about?"

King scowled. He looked at Lyons, then over at Schwarz. He pressed the heels of his palms against his eyes and moved them in a single, slow circle before pulling them away.

"Don't say it, King," the other technician warned.

King shot the guy a look like he was something on the bottom of his shoe.

"Shut it, twerp." He looked back at Schwarz. "We off the record?"

Schwarz nodded in agreement.

"I don't know how much you can trust Ortega. He's been underground so long, I'm not sure the guy knows what light looks like at this point."

"You think he's compromised?" Schwarz asked.

"I'm not sure," King said, shrugging. "It's just a feeling. Hell, I could be wrong. But…"

"Spit it out!" Lyons snapped.

"I get the feeling he's lost his way. He identifies way too much with these people. And there's another complication. Escobar's got this woman. Name's Nikki Vargas. She was a black swan. We never expected her to pop up. But here she is. And Escobar welcomed her with open arms. We're not sure what to make of her."

"Meaning what?"

"She's been on the scene for about two years. She seemed to have popped out of nowhere. She started doing little jobs for the guy. Next thing you know, he's brought her into his inner circle."

"He boning her?" Lyons asked.

King grinned. "What do you think? That's not the issue."

"So what is the issue?" Schwarz asked.

"Ortega's pretty taken with this lady."

"Aw, shit," Lyons muttered.

"Yeah, 'aw, shit.' And, unfortunately, I tried to sound the alarm in Washington. I told Ortega's supervisor about it. They blew me off."

"You think she's working Ortega? Maybe she knows what he's up to?"

"I wouldn't rule it out," King said. "If me and the kid—" he nodded at the other technician "—had our way, we would have been pulled out of here six months ago when all this started happening. Mark my words—she's bad news. She's bad news and now Ortega's up to his neck with her."

Schwarz let out a low whistle.

"And even if she wasn't going to betray Ortega," Schwarz said, "if Escobar finds out, he'll have Ortega's ass for it anyway."

King nodded. "Exactly. No matter what, the guy didn't just step off the reservation; he set it on fire, stole a car and drove six states away."

By now, Lyons's cheeks and neck were flushed red with rage. He slammed an open hand down onto one of the consoles, causing the monitors on the wall to shudder. He shot up from his chair, the top of his head just missing the van's ceiling.

"Damn it," he said. "And we have one of ours in there?

I knew this was a bad idea from the start. Never should have signed off on this."

"You couldn't have known."

"Really? Well, here's what I do know. If I get even the slightest inkling that Ortega's dirty, I'll deal with it myself."

King looked at him and scowled.

"Sounds ominous."

"It won't be pretty. Let's just say I'll solve the problem."

King turned away from the Able Team warriors and fixed his gaze on the computer monitors. "Yeah, I don't think I want to know any more about this. Look, we're trying to scoop up as much information as we can here. Our guys, they took their cell phones and put them in a sound-proof safe. Castillo's smart; he's vibrating the windows just to prevent us from snatching sound from the window-panes. We have to go by whatever Ortega and your buddy can wring out of the place."

"If they get out of there," Lyons said, scowling.

CHAPTER FIVE

Castillo lived in a penthouse overlooking downtown Mexico City.

Blancanales and Ortega arrived just before noon. A couple of Castillo's thugs greeted them at the door. Ortega entered first, nodding at both men and moving past them. One of the guys grabbed him by the arm and stopped him. He took a step back and held up his hands in a surrender motion.

"Hey, what's the problem?"

Blancanales watched as Ortega complied. A goon, his black hair pulled back in a tight ponytail, patted him down from head to toe, checking for weapons. A second gorilla, this one with a pockmarked face, ran a black wandlike device over him, probably checking for microphones or transmitters. When they finished, Mr. Ponytail turned to Castillo, who was seated at the bar and said, "He's clean."

Castillo nodded and gestured at Blancanales with his chin.

"Check that stupid bastard next," he said.

Blancanales raised his hands. "You are going to find a Beretta 92 on me, in a shoulder holster," he said. "But you aren't going to find any wires. Leave the gun where it is."

Ponytail grabbed him by the shoulder, spun him around and began patting him down. Before Blancanales knew it, the guy had slipped the Beretta from his shoulder holster. He heard metallic clicking behind him. He looked over his shoulder and saw the thug eject the magazine from the pistol. He then worked the slide and took the round from the chamber. With a couple more deft movements, Mr. Ponytail disconnected the slide and handed the gun to Blancanales in two pieces. The American took the pieces and looked down at them as they lay in his palm.

"There's your gun," he said, sneering as he pocketed the magazine.

Scowling, Blancanales put the slide in his right jacket pocket and the rest of the pistol in the left pocket.

"Thanks," Blancanales muttered.

"Our new friend is clean, too." The second thug had swept the Stony Man warrior for bugs even as the first guy had frisked him and relieved him of his pistol.

Castillo pushed himself from the stool and strode across the floor toward his visitors. The man was tall and slim, but with wide shoulders. He seemed to have more swagger in his movements than actual confidence. He wore black dress pants with a sharp crease down the front of each leg. His white button-down shirt gleamed under the artificial light. His shiny black wing tips clicked against the floor.

When he got close to his visitors, he held out his hand to Ortega, who took it. They shook hands. "It's good to see you," Castillo said. Despite the words, Blancanales detected no real warmth in the man's voice.

When they released hands, he turned and offered his hand to Blancanales.

"Any friend of Mr. Ortega's is a friend of mine," he said as they shook hands. "Sorry about the Beretta, Mr. Perez. You can't be too careful."

Blancanales forced a smile. "Of course."

Castillo took a couple of steps back and gestured at a pair of leather couches.

"Find a seat and we can talk some business."

Castillo turned and headed for the couches. The two Americans followed him and found seats. Blancanales ordered a Scotch, while Ortega ordered a double. The federal agent shot Blancanales a defiant look, and the Able Team warrior turned and stared out one of the big windows that overlooked Mexico City.

"I appreciate you seeing me on such short notice," he said. "I understand you run a very private enterprise. The last thing you want is a stranger coming to your door and trying to buy products from you."

"We don't usually do it this way. However, you come highly recommended. We figured we should at least hear you out."

The brute with the pockmarked face returned with a tray of drinks. He set the tray on the coffee table and left it there. Blancanales and Ortega leaned forward and picked up their cocktails. Ortega downed half of his in a single swallow and held the glass on his lap with both hands. Blancanales set his on the table and kept his attention focused on Castillo.

"So what exactly is it I can help you with?"

"I thought Ortega already filled you in."

"He did. I want you to say it. What are you after?"

"Fair enough. Maybe you know this, but I have customers in South America, good customers. They're people who need the kinds of products you have to offer. I'm talking everything from rifles and pistols to shoulder-fired rockets."

"If these are such good customers, you already had a pipeline, right? Why suddenly seek us out?"

Blancanales gave the guy a benign smile.

"It's not that," he said. "I had a supplier. A couple of days ago, someone hit his warehouse in Paraguay."

"Hit?"

"Blew it up." Blancanales leaned forward, plucked his drink off the table and sipped from it.

"Somebody planted a bomb in the warehouse?"

Blancanales shook his head. "No, I mean they blew it up. Somebody hit it with a missile from out of nowhere. The owner had paid off everyone in Paraguay so I don't think it was their government."

"Okay," Castillo said.

"A missile came out of nowhere, hit the place and burned it to the ground. Now it's gone. The man had some customers in the Middle East. I'm thinking the U.S. probably hit him with a drone strike."

"And he has no product left to sell after this? He had just one warehouse?"

"He's dead. He was on the premises when the missile hit."

"I see."

"And I have a customer in Colombia. A militia. The group has financial backing from a cocaine kingpin in the country. It has tons of money to spend. But I have no inventory, no access. And to top it all off, they're getting more exotic with their demands."

A smile tugged at the corners of Castillo's lips. "Exotic?"

"Crazy shit. A week ago they asked me to find them a drone. Apparently the leader of the militia has this grand plan to decapitate the Colombian government. Right now he doesn't even have a helicopter that actually will get off the ground. But he asked me to find him a UAV. Then I heard that maybe you guys might be into something like that."

"Like?"

"Drones."

"You've heard wrong."

A smile ghosted Blancanales's lips. "I don't think so."

"Trust me. You're wrong."

Blancanales shrugged. "Okay," he said. "But I have money."

"If you didn't have money," Castillo said, jerking his head at the door, "I'd never have let you in here."

"And if I thought all you had to sell was a few crates of AK-47s, I wouldn't be here. I could go to a bazaar in Afghanistan and buy that kind of shit."

Castillo gave him a cold look before he turned to Ortega.

"Did you know this?"

"He had no idea."

"I didn't ask you. Shut the hell up. Did you know this, Ortega?"

Ortega shook his head no.

"The guy seemed legit to me. I had no idea he wanted this kind of stuff…"

"Which we don't have," Castillo said, his voice emphatic.

"Of course," Ortega replied.

Blancanales slapped the tops of his thighs and stood.

"Well, gentlemen, it's been a pleasure meeting with you. But I need to find someone who actually has weapons to sell."

"We have weapons," Castillo said.

"Like I said, if I wanted to buy AK-47s, I'd go to a gun show. You two enjoy not selling anything."

Blancanales stepped past Ortega before the agent could uncoil from his seat. He'd made it halfway between the couch and the front door when Mr. Ponytail stepped into his path. The goon put his hand on Blancanales's chest to stop him.

BLANCANALES KNOCKED THE man's hand away. His left hand lashed out in a roundhouse punch that collided with the guy's jaw. The thug grunted but bulled forward, grabbing a handful of the Stony Man warrior's shirt and pulling back his fist. From the corner of his eye, Blancanales saw the second thug stepping forward.

Blancanales stomped hard on the arch of Mr. Ponytail's foot. The guy moaned and Blancanales buried a hard right in the man's stomach. His adversary fell to the ground, gagging.

The commando wheeled at the second thug, who apparently had less of an appetite for brawling. He'd produced a .45-caliber pistol and was aiming it at Blancanales.

Brilliant, Blancanales thought.

"What the hell is going on here?"

It was a woman's voice to Blancanales's right. Some of the certainty drained from the thug's eyes, but he didn't lower the gun.

Blancanales shot a quick glance in the woman's direction. Even with a brief look, he could tell she was beautiful. She was tall with a dark complexion and black, wavy hair. Her black jeans hugged the curves of her hips and accentuated the taper of her legs. Her fists were lodged on her hips, her legs spread slightly. Her red-painted lips were pursed and she was glaring.

"Put the gun down," she said.

"Lady…" the thug said.

"Gun. Down. Now."

The man shot a glance at Castillo, who wore a bemused expression on his face. Even with the violence exploding around him, he hadn't bothered to get up from the couch. Instead he'd sat there, slightly twisted at the waist, drink clasped in his hand, as though he were watching a fight on television. In response to the gun-wielding goon's unspoken question, he gave a curt nod.

Reluctantly the thug lowered his pistol and stowed it underneath his jacket, but didn't step back from Blancanales. During all of this, Blancanales noticed Ortega was spending more time looking at the woman than anyone else.

"It's all right, Pedro," the woman said.

A scowl spread over Pedro's scarred features, but he took a couple of steps back from the American.

Blancanales straightened his jacket. Already the adrenaline began to subside and pain registered in his knuckles. He glanced at his fist; saw that the knuckles were red but not split. He'd have to punch harder next time.

He turned to the woman. "Thank you, Miss…?"

"Nikki Vargas. But you can call me Nikki."

"Well, Nikki, thank you. Good to meet someone with some social skills. Now, if you'll excuse me…"

"You're not leaving, are you?"

"I'm afraid so. What I do have is a lot of money to spend. What I lack is patience to deal with this kind of horseshit."

"I'm sorry. Hector is one of Mr. Escobar's most trusted aides. But he sometimes lacks basic social graces."

"Hey!" Castillo snapped.

She ignored him and crossed the room, heading toward Blancanales. Widening her smile, she extended her hand to Blancanales, who took it. Up close, he got a real sense of her beauty. Her wavy hair framed an oval-shaped face. Her red lips were thick and her brown eyes wide. She raised a hand and brushed back some of her hair, tucking it behind her ear. The move exposed her slender neck.

"Please stay," she said. "I overheard part of your conversation and am sure Mr. Escobar would want to know more."

Blancanales looked past her at Castillo, who was fuming.

"Sure, I'll stay."

"Wonderful."

Blancanales returned to the couch and sat back down. He picked up his drink and saluted Castillo with it before swigging from the glass. "Thanks for having me, Hector."

Vargas sat on the couch opposite Blancanales. She crossed her legs and leaned slightly forward.

"So," she said, "you want to buy some drones."

He nodded. "Probably a drone," he said. "Maybe two. I know they're not cheap."

"Not in the least," she said. "We have a lot of costs wrapped up in them and Mr. Escobar needs to recoup as many of those costs as possible."

"Understood."

"And you heard about our drones how?"

Blancanales shook his head. "Suffice to say I found out. It's a trade secret. I can't say any more."

Castillo leaned forward and growled, "What if we want to know more?"

"I'd tell you to screw yourself with a tire iron," Blancanales replied. "But I wouldn't say that to Ms. Vargas." He smiled at her. "I'd just say no."

She returned the smile. "You are charming," she said.

"He's a jackass," Castillo said.

"He's a customer," Vargas countered.

"Just hear him out, Hector," Ortega said. "The guy's good for the money."

Still scowling, Castillo rose from the couch with his glass in his hand and went to the bar for a refill.

"Who are you representing in this deal?" she asked.

Blancanales shook his head again. "With all respect, I'm not ready to share that, other than to say it's a Colombian militia."

"And the money comes from a drug dealer?"

"Yes, does that bother you?"

"Yes. I have no qualms with how he got the money. But let's face facts, if he's rich enough to pay this much money, he's probably also under surveillance by the United States and other governments. Part of that surveillance would include tracking his finances."

"And you're worried his money will put more eyes on you."

"Yes."

"That's understandable. But, look, he's thoroughly scrubbed the money and stuffed it into accounts in the Cayman Islands. Then once I get it, I scrub it again before you get it."

"It's not foolproof."

"What is?"

"True."

"Wait a minute," Ortega interrupted. "You don't want to name the group?" He turned and looked at Vargas. "I didn't know about this before I came in, Nikki. I'm not sure Escobar would go for that. I'm not sure I'd go for it."

Blancanales let Ortega's protests roll off his back, figuring the guy wanted to deflect any suspicion that he was collaborating with Blancanales.

"Let me put it to you this way," Blancanales said. "Do you really want to know? What if these clowns do something awful with the stuff you sell them? Wouldn't you rather put some layers between your organization and theirs? The last thing you need is cops and spooks all over the world breathing down your neck."

"You raise a good point," she said. "But we'd rather know up front where our stuff goes, especially something like this. The last thing we want is a nasty surprise later down the road."

"A nasty surprise like?"

"There are all kinds," she said.

Blancanales pretended to mull their demands for a few seconds. "Okay," he said finally. "You want the customer's ID? I'll share it. But I'll share it with Escobar."

She leaned back. Her smile faltered.

"I'm sorry," she said, "but he doesn't usually do that."

"Well, tell him to think it over. It's a lot of money."

"I'll let him know," she said.

CHAPTER SIX

Blancanales slid into the driver's seat of the Mercedes sport coupe and slammed the door shut. The vehicle had been parked in a secure garage located underneath Castillo's building.

Ortega climbed into the passenger's seat, shut his own door and fished inside his jacket for a cigarette.

As Blancanales turned over the engine and backed the vehicle out, Ortega torched the end of a cigarette with his disposable lighter, took a long drag from it and blew twin plumes of smoke out his nose. Blancanales watched from the corner of his eye as the agent slid the hand clutching the lighter back inside his jacket and searched for something else. The warrior, adrenaline still coursing through his veins, felt his body tense.

Ortega's hand came back into view, this time holding a cell phone. He thumbed a number into the phone and brought it to his ear. Blancanales could hear the phone ring, followed by a voice answering on the other end of the line.

"We're clear," Ortega said. "See you in a few." He ended the call and slipped the phone back inside his jacket.

Blancanales guided the vehicle onto a ramp that led out of the underground garage and hesitated for a couple of seconds before pulling into traffic.

"So," he said, "what do you think? Do you think they bought it?"

"Guess it depends on how you define 'bought it,'" Ortega

replied. "I think they're willing to give you a second listen. But are they suspicious? Hell, yeah, they're suspicious. I would be, too, if I were in their shoes. You made a convincing case in there…"

"But they don't trust easily. I got it. Look, I just want to get close enough to Escobar that we can take them out. I'm not looking for a marriage proposal."

"That's good because I think Escobar's already taken."

"Speaking of taken…" Blancanales said. "What's the deal with Nikki Vargas?"

Ortega's lips tightened into a hard line. He leaned forward, stubbed out his smoke in the ashtray and glared at the Able Team fighter.

"What do you mean?"

"Which part of the question don't you understand? Look, I saw what happened when she came into the room. I thought your heart was going to jump out of your chest like some kind of a love-struck cartoon character. So what's the deal?"

"No deal. There's nothing there. I'd be dead meat if I even thought about it."

"Bullshit."

"Hey, she's Escobar's woman. Look, she's drop-dead gorgeous and I gawked. Everyone in the room looks when she comes in. What's your point?"

"Don't jerk me around."

"What? So now you're a human polygraph?"

"I'm just not an idiot. I haven't lived this long without learning a thing or two along the way. One of those things is to trust my gut. My gut tells me that there's something going on between you and this woman. If there is, and it's legit, fine. But I need to know about it. The last thing I need is to get blindsided because you can't control your dick."

Ortega's hands had clenched into fists, but he was staring through the Mercedes's windshield, avoiding Blancanales's gaze.

"Nothing's happening," he said through clenched teeth.

"Bullshit. Now, we can do this in the honest way or…"

"Or what?"

"Or I'm going to take you out of the picture. And by that I don't mean put you on a plane back to Wonderland. I may seem like a nice guy. But if you're putting my team or me at risk, I'll bury you."

"I can't believe you'd even suggest I'd compromise this mission. I've been doing this for a long time. I'm a professional."

"You're being defensive. That's strike one."

Blancanales saw an open stretch of curb. He jerked the wheel to the right, pulled the vehicle up to it and slammed the car into park. As his hand rose from the gear selector, he curled his fingers into a fist and snapped a quick back-fist into Ortega's nose. The guy cursed and his hands flew up protectively to cover his nose.

"Your focus getting better?" Blancanales demanded.

Several tense seconds passed as Ortega glared at him. Blood was seeping out from underneath his hands, and Blancanales wondered whether he'd broken his nose. Blancanales waited to see how the agent would respond. He'd obviously been walking a long leash for years and was used to being in charge. Would he take a swing? Pull his gun?

"I'm going to kill you," Ortega said.

"Not likely. Now, talk straight or I'm going to beat the truth out of you."

Ortega peeled away one hand from his face and reached around his back. Blancanales tensed. The guy's hand came back into view, clutching a handkerchief, which he pressed gingerly to his nose.

"You could've broken it," he said.

"There's always a next time."

Ortega turned away and, the handkerchief still pressed to his nose, angled his head downward.

"Okay," he said. "There's some interest there. There's been some talking. Maybe a little more."

"How much more?"

"Just a little. Not what you think."

"And you don't think your interest in this woman has compromised you?"

The agent shook his head.

"Like I said…"

"I know. You're a professional. It practically oozes from your pores. Now answer the question."

"I know what I'm doing. This hasn't clouded my judgment at all. You've got to believe me on that. She's just another way to get inside Escobar's head."

"Get in his head or her pants?"

"If you're not going to listen…"

"Go ahead."

"It was a good decision. I've got it under control. She's given me some great information. I can show you the reports. Great stuff."

"What do you know about her?"

Ortega shrugged. "Apparently she was a spook, technically, at least. From what she's described, she spent more time filing and organizing things than anything else. She had a low-level security clearance, which means she probably never saw anything important along the way. She got frustrated and left the organization she was working for and got picked up later by Escobar."

"You check all this out?"

Ortega scowled. "Yes."

"With?"

"My controller."

Blancanales nodded his head slowly, though his gut told him the guy was lying about that last part.

"If I asked your bosses, they'd confirm all of this?"

"Yes."

"You're an awful liar, Ortega," Blancanales said.

"Who the hell are you calling a liar?"

"Spare me the righteous indignation," Blancanales said. He turned in his seat, started the car and wondered what he'd stepped into.

CHAPTER SEVEN

Arlington, Virginia

Leo Turrin reached into the trunk of his red BMW and, with a grunt, pulled out his golf bag by its carrying strap. He set the bag on its end on the steaming hot asphalt of the parking lot of the Army Navy Country Club and slammed the two-seater's trunk closed.

He started to lift the bag onto his shoulder when his phone rang. Swearing under his breath, he glanced at the phone's display and realized he didn't recognize the number flashing there. He debated for a moment whether to answer the call or to drop the phone into his golf bag and proceed with eighteen holes.

Reluctantly, he decided to pick up. Though semi-retired now, he still was one of the U.S. government's high-level undercover guys in La Cosa Nostra. Sure, it could be someone trying to sell him vitamins through a multilevel marketing scam. Or it may be a matter of life and death.

If he didn't answer, he'd be testing his luck. And, considering his last few outings on the golf course, Lady Luck had turned her back on him a while ago. So he'd answer.

"Yeah?"

"This Leo Turrin?" asked a man with a heavy accent.

"Who wants to know?"

"I'm a friend of Michael Ortega."

Shit. Could be nothing. Could be bad.

"How is Mike?" Turrin asked, keeping his voice bright. "I haven't heard from him in a year, maybe more. He still working in Mexico?"

"Yes," the man said.

Turrin waited for the guy to say more.

After several seconds of dead silence, Turrin said, "Wow, you really know how to spin a tale."

"I need information."

"Bully for you," Turrin replied. "Give me your name and maybe I'll feel more talkative."

"Hector Castillo," the other man said. He let the words hang in the air, as though they should mean something. They did, though Turrin had to pretend otherwise.

"What can I do for you, Hector?" An edge was creeping into Turrin's voice. "Not that I don't love standing under the hot sun, listening to you breathe into the phone, my tee time kicks off in fifteen minutes. I don't want to be late. My kitchen pass expires quickly and I need to get home."

"Kitchen pass? What the hell? You work in a kitchen?"

Turrin rolled his eyes. "Never mind. Just ask your question."

"Michael has introduced us to a new client. His name is Alonzo Perez. Do you know him?"

"Sure," Turrin replied. "I know Alonzo."

"Tell me about him."

"Did Michael vouch for him?"

"Yes."

"Then why call me?"

"We like to be thorough."

Damn.

"Not much to tell," Turrin said. "A while back, a couple of our guys got nabbed by the Feds for importuning. Dumb shits. We eventually bought their way out of trouble. But it took time. The case drew lots of media coverage. The district attorney wanted to show off a little. We let him run a dog-and-pony show for a few months. Eventually he decided it was, um, in his best interest to pull the plug. Don't ask me why. I got nothing to say on that. Anyway, while all that worked itself out, we had a hole to fill. Mike was working for us at the time. He met Perez through a friend of a friend and convinced us to bring Perez on board."

"You trusted him?"

"Perez? I wouldn't let him skinny dip with my wife. But I trust him okay," Turrin said. He was trying to recall details from the legend Stony Man Farm had given him about Blancanales. "He had good skills. He still had the military discipline. Showed up on time and was polite to the boss. Worked hard."

"Why'd he leave?"

"He got frustrated. Some guys are happy to watch someone else make a lot of money. He was a good sport, but you could tell he wanted a piece of the action. I had to sit him down, explain he was an outsider and tell him he wasn't going anywhere."

"How'd he take it?"

"Like a champ. Nodded. Said, 'Yes, sir.' Went back to work. But when the time was right, he left."

"He was ambitious."

"He wasn't a knuckle dragger. Guy's smart and, yeah, ambitious. We've hired him since to do some, um, procurement for us."

"That work okay?"

"Never a problem. Hey, not to be an asshole, but the clock's ticking. You good?"

"I suppose."

"Good," Turrin said, and hung up.

The longer he stayed on the phone, the greater his chances of saying the wrong thing. Besides, he didn't want to oversell Blancanales and make Escobar's people suspicious. Best to cut it short. Later, he'd contact Stony Man Farm with an encrypted phone he kept at the house and let them know about the conversation. In the meantime, he gathered up his clubs and started across the parking lot. He silently wished his brothers in arms good luck as they again put their lives on the line for their country.

"WHAT DO YOU make of this guy Perez?" Escobar asked.

Nikki shrugged her shoulders. "I don't know," she replied. "He seems legitimate."

"Seems? That's not very reassuring."

"I know. But we checked out his references. I checked them. Castillo did, too. We found documents to back up every word he said."

"You're sure about that?"

"I wouldn't stake my life on it," she said, giving him a weak smile.

Escobar nodded slowly. "Interesting choice of words," he said. "Anyway, what do we know about him?"

Something in his voice made her body shudder and she immediately felt exposed.

"Jesus, Seif, turn down the air conditioner in here," she said, trying to cover. "It feels like a damn meat locker."

"I like the cold," he said. "Come to think of it, I like meat lockers, too."

Freak.

"Hey," he said, "answer the question."

"Sorry." Douche bag. Her throat suddenly felt tight. "He's an American. He spent time in the military, in the Army. He spent a lot of time in Central and South America while he was in the Army. When the U.S. supplied weapons to a country, he was one of the guys who went there to train the soldiers."

"He Special Forces?"

"Yes."

"What, you didn't think that was important to mention?"

"I was getting to it. What's wrong with you today?"

He gave her a cold smile and shook his head gently. "Nothing, babe. Why you so on edge? Keep going."

"He was in Colombia for a few years. Trained their anti-drug forces. Once he left the military, he decided to go for the real money. He started selling weapons. There's a list of customers in the file I prepared for you. It's not comprehensive, of course, just what I could piece together through various sources."

Escobar leaned back in his chair and stared at her for what seemed like an eternity. Didn't this SOB ever blink? Finally he said, "I read your report. It's good. You should be a spy."

"I was a spy," she replied. "You know that."

"Right. Was. He say why he wants to meet with me?"

"The usual thing. He's spending a lot of money. He wants to meet with the boss. I'm guessing he wants his ego stroked."

"Not going to get that from me."

"I know."

"He knows about the UAVs. That bothers me. It's been circulated among a few people, but we've controlled it pretty well."

"We have."

"So how does he know?"

"You told a few of our clients. Maybe one of them said something to him."

"Maybe," he muttered, sounding unconvinced.

"Okay, what's your theory?"

He leveled his gaze at her. "Someone inside the organization leaked the information."

"It's possible," she said.

"I don't see any other way."

"Who are you thinking?" she asked.

"The guy that brought him here, of course."

"Ortega? He told me the whole UAV thing was a surprise to him."

"And of course he's telling the truth."

"That's not my point. I'm just telling you what he told me."

He jerked his chin at the door. "I need to think. Get the hell out of here."

"Sure," she said.

By the time Nikki left Escobar's apartment, her breath was coming in shallow gasps, her heart raced and blood thundered in her ears. She replayed the conversation with him over and over in her head, trying to think of where she might have misspoken or drawn suspicion. He was a paranoid bastard, yeah, but rightfully so. Everyone really was out to get him—the law, the competition, even some of the families of those killed by his weapons.

Hell, even she was out to get him.

He thought she'd come out of nowhere, a rogue spy with a knack for organization and planning. She'd sold him on the idea that she was so fed up with her life that she'd willingly betray her country for money and excitement. She really was an agent with Israeli Mossad, part of a team that targeted gunrunners who sold firepower to terrorists.

She hadn't entered his inner circle immediately. Instead she'd been given such jobs as coordinating small arms shipments to a handful of Escobar's legal clients, militaries that purchased the arms from front companies without knowing the true source. Escobar even sold weapons to the Mexican military and some local police forces. Even though most government officials knew who and what he was, the kickbacks made doing business with him too lucrative to ignore. And he kept the deals in the country small enough that anticorruption investigators focused their energy elsewhere.

As she'd gained his trust, though, he'd brought her into his inner circle and eventually started sharing more information.

It had taken time.

The relationship had developed into more than professional, with them eventually sharing a bed. Unlike some spies, the sex never clouded her judgment or left her conflicted about whether to take him down. Escobar was the enemy; a stone-cold killer. She could feel it in his touch, which felt detached, almost clinical. The contact seemed to drain something from her. While she didn't consider herself a prude, the sex always left her feeling unclean and diminished somehow. Even the memory of his hands on her, his eyes regarding her like an object to be exploited, caused her to shudder.

Pull it together, she thought. Maybe Escobar knew she had a secret. Maybe he was just jerking her chain, trying to get a reaction from her. She knew from experience he was paranoid enough to administer occasional loyalty tests. And he was so opaque it was hard to tell why he did anything.

She couldn't blame him for being unsettled by Perez's request, though. She'd described how Perez had manhandled Castillo's hardmen without breathing hard. Other customers had demanded to see the main guy, but they usually were narcissistic ones, the guys with a hyper-inflated sense of importance. She hadn't sensed that with Perez, though. He struck her as confident, but not arrogant; a man who'd faced tough circumstances and come out on top. In some ways, Perez reminded her of Daniel Ben-Shahar. Ben-Shahar had been her father's oldest friend. And, though not related by blood, he'd been her favorite uncle and an influential figure in her life. She'd joined Mossad to honor him and follow in his footsteps.

All at once, she realized where her thoughts had drifted and her face flushed with embarrassment. Ben-Shahar was a decent man. Perez wasn't. He was a crook who ran a criminal enterprise. By his own admission, he was willing to broker the sale of drones to a bunch of terrorists to line his pocket. She'd charm and flirt with Perez. If he was feeding them a line of bullshit, she'd pretend to believe it.

But if Escobar decided it was good business to kill Perez, she'd make it happen, even if she had to pull the trigger herself.

CHAPTER EIGHT

The telephone on Blancanales's nightstand rang once. He rolled over, trapped it under his hand and brought it toward his ear. A glance at the screen told him the call was coming from Ortega.

"Yeah?" he growled.

"Hey, Sunshine, get your ass out of bed," Ortega said.

Blancanales heard a note of urgency in Ortega's voice. He threw aside his sheet and swung his legs over the side of the bed. The floor felt cool against the soles of his feet.

"What's going on?"

"You passed the first test," Ortega replied. "The man wants to meet with you."

"When?"

"Not for a couple of hours. He has a restaurant in town. Place is a freakin' dive. But it gives him a way to account for his extra cash, if you know what I mean."

Blancanales did. He was surprised at how freely the agent was speaking on the phone. Was the bastard drunk? It was early morning, but maybe the guy had stayed up all night drinking. It certainly wasn't unheard of.

"You need me to pick you up?"

"Negative," Ortega replied. "I'll drive myself if it's all the same to you."

"It's not."

"Tough shit. Last time I let you drive, I ended up with a

split lip and a bloody nose. I'd rather crawl over a mile of razor blades than lock myself in the car with you again."

"Sorry," Blancanales offered.

"No you're not. Look, you want the address for the restaurant or not?"

"Yeah," Blancanales said.

Ortega recited the address and Blancanales memorized it.

"We should go in together," Blancanales said.

"You're a big boy. You don't need an escort." The phone went dead and Blancanales swore under his breath. The idiot just seemed to be getting more reckless, as though he wanted to undercut the team.

Blancanales jumped from the bed, slipped on a pair of jeans, a polo shirt and a pair of moccasins and left the room to get the others. When he exited his bedroom, he found Schwarz seated on the living-room couch staring into the screen of a laptop poised on a coffee table in front of him. Schwarz greeted him with a nod.

"I couldn't sleep," Schwarz said.

"Carl asleep?"

"Yeah. Can't you hear him snoring? Sounds like someone using a chainsaw to cut through steel. What's up?

"Tell you in a minute." Blancanales moved to Lyons's door, rapped on it and called for Lyons to get up.

Five minutes later the three Able Team warriors had gathered in the living room. Blancanales quickly recounted his phone conversation with Ortega.

"This has 'trap' written all over it," Lyons said.

"I agree. But if it allows us to get close to Escobar, it's worth it. That's what we came for, right?"

"Yeah," Lyons said.

"So I have to meet with the guy."

"You do," Lyons replied. "But we're going to have a

plan. This thing stinks to high heaven and I think our lit-tle buddy Ortega will end up getting you killed, whether he means to or not."

Blancanales heaved a sigh. "You're right."

"Bet your ass I am. So, yeah, you're going to meet Es-cobar at that restaurant, but we're going to do this the right way."

"Meaning?"

"We take the direct approach. If we spook these bas-tards, then we'll deal with it."

"You can't go in with me."

"That's not what I mean," Lyons replied. "We don't have to go in with you. But we also don't have to sit five blocks away in some damn mobile home. We'll get in close so we can move quickly if you need us."

Blancanales nodded his agreement.

"So suit up," Lyons said. "It's time to wind this up. If we handle this right, we could take out Escobar and be back on our way to Virginia in a matter of hours."

BLANCANALES HIT THE Mercedes's accelerator and the car darted into traffic. His mind whirled as he weaved between cars, the sports car knifing its way to its destination. At the same time, his mind whirled with questions. Ortega had continued to ignore his phone calls. Was the guy really that unhinged? Had he been forced to call Blancanales? If that was the case, Escobar already knew the Able Team warrior wasn't really in the country to buy weapons, which meant he was hurtling right into a trap.

He glanced up into the rearview mirror and could see the top of the SUV carrying Lyons and Schwarz poking up over the tops of the cars between them. Their plan was simple: they'd follow him to the meeting, go EVA and surround the building. If everything was okay, Blancanales would turn off his phone. If something was wrong, he'd hit the emergency button and they'd blitz the building, guns blazing.

His phone trilled again. Blancanales hit the speaker button.

"Go," he said.

"I called the other members of Ortega's team," Schwarz said. "I got nothing but voice mail for any of them. No callbacks yet."

Blancanales swore under his breath. Schwarz continued, "Yeah. I dropped Hal a line so he can ring some alarms in Wonderland."

"Okay. Do we have addresses on these guys?"

"Yeah."

"We should call the locals," Blancanales said. A red light loomed ahead. He tapped the brake to begin slowing the car down. "Someone needs to check on those guys and see if they're okay."

Lyons interjected, "If the local police mobilize, there's a chance that would tip off Escobar. He probably has bought off more than a few locals."

"Understood," Blancanales said. "You have any ideas?"

"We have FBI and DEA agents in the city," Lyons replied. "We'll call Hal back, ask him to mobilize those guys. They can knock on some doors, do it discreetly, and free us up to do our thing. You hear any more from Ortega?"

"Negative. I called, but can't get through to him."

"Little prick," Lyons muttered. "He'd better not be dodging our phone calls."

"We should be so lucky," Blancanales said.

"You think they got to him?" Schwarz asked.

"Not sure," Blancanales said. By now the light had turned green and the car in front of Blancanales eased forward as traffic began to move. "The guy's a douche bag.

And he's plenty pissed at me. But I'm not sure he'd expect me to go into this blind."

"Don't be too sure," Lyons growled. "Guy's a walking disaster."

"Fair enough," Blancanales said. He eased down on the gas pedal. The Mercedes's power plant responded with a growl before it thrust the vehicle into the intersection. All but one of the line of cars between him and his comrades' SUV made it through the intersection before the light changed. He heard the squeal of brakes behind him and looked up into the rearview mirror again.

The car in front of Lyons and Schwarz had screeched to a stop, blocking them from going through the light. Another car was pulled up next to them. With Lyons at the wheel, Blancanales half expected to see the SUV jump the curb and dart through the light. Instead Lyons waited for the light to change.

Blancanales continued on. He glanced down at the briefcase that lay on the passenger's seat. It was outfitted with a GPS unit so his friends could track him even if they lost sight of him. And, if he was being watched, pulling to the side of the road to wait for the others to catch up would only arouse suspicion.

A couple of blocks later he turned the Mercedes right down a side street. His Beretta 92 rode in a shoulder rig. A small SIG-Sauer was strapped in an ankle holster, while his Gerber folding knife was stowed in his pants' pocket. It wasn't exactly full combat turnout gear, but it was enough.

The flat, feminine voice on the GPS unit directed him to make a left.

"Sure, sweetheart," he muttered, twisting the wheel. The street was nearly empty of pedestrians and only a few cars were parked along the curb. He rolled past the restaurant and noted that a sign in the window declared in Spanish that the place was closed.

His brow furrowed. What the hell?

His phone pinged, alerting him that he'd received a text message. He saw that it was from Ortega. He opened it.

Go around back. Door's unlocked.

Blancanales pulled the Mercedes to the curb and parked. He looked around at the cars assembled on the street, most of them older-model American imports with rusted bodies and scratched paint. No crew wagons or limousines were parked outside the restaurant. No guards milling around outside the building.

This only heightened his suspicions. If Escobar was inside the restaurant, he'd have his entourage with him. He wouldn't go out without a security detail. He wouldn't be cruising around the city in a shitty compact car.

Blancanales uncoiled from inside the sleek sports car. He slipped his sunglasses from his face, folded them and slipped them into the inside pocket of his sport coat, keeping his hand inside his jacket and within reach of the Beretta. He checked his watch. About five minutes had passed since he'd been separated from his comrades. They should have caught up with him by now. He pulled out his phone and thumbed in Lyons's number. It rang four times before sending him to voicemail.

A cold feather of fear brushed along the length of his spine. If he couldn't reach them, something was drastically wrong. Every instinct told him to climb back into the little black car, turn around and backtrack until he found the other two men. They'd already lost contact with nearly all of the Justice Department team. If Lyons and Schwarz were in trouble, they'd need his help.

He stowed the phone in his pocket, wheeled around and took a couple of steps toward the Mercedes. The growl of an engine sounded behind him. He spun around and saw a forest-green SUV barreling down the street at him.

A heartbeat later, tires squealed from the opposite direction, followed by the rumbling of another big-block engine. He threw a look over his shoulder and saw a black extended-cab pickup hurtling toward him.

He didn't hesitate. He yanked the Beretta free, spun a quarter turn and darted toward the mouth of a nearby alley. Out in the open he was vulnerable to multiple attacks from different angles. If he could get into the narrow passage, it at least would force his attackers to come at him in smaller numbers. He could hear the vehicles screeching to a halt behind him. When he reached the alley, he turned and saw a burly guy climbing from the backseat of the SUV, a shotgun cradled in his hands.

Blancanales raised the Beretta and squeezed off three quick shots. One of the Parabellum slugs lanced into the thug's right shoulder and jerked him around before a second round drilled into his chest. His finger pulled the trigger in a death reflex, and thunder pealed as a blast lashed out from the shotgun's muzzle. Another of Escobar's gunners was coming around the other side of the truck, pistol drawn. Blancanales fired off two more shots. Neither of the bullets hit their target but they did slam into the SUV's hide and caused the gunman to duck behind the vehicle's nose.

Blancanales darted a few yards into the alley. He heard the sound of rubber squealing against pavement and assumed even more of Escobar's people were coming for him.

At the back of his mind he wondered what had ignited all of this. Had Ortega given him up? If so, Escobar had probably already gone to ground. That'd make him all the harder for Blancanales and his comrades to find.

If he lived through the next few minutes.

Two more of Escobar's thugs lumbered forward, each with a weapon trained in Blancanales's direction.

He aimed the Beretta at the nearest gunner and squeezed the trigger. The second thug broke off his approach and ran for cover behind a rusty pickup.

Even as the man disappeared from view, Blancanales detected movement in the corner of his eye. He glanced left and spotted three ropes unfurling from the restaurant's roof. He looked up and saw three hardmen preparing to rappel down the side of the building.

LYONS SWORE THROUGH gritted teeth as the car in front of him slammed on its brakes. The force from the sudden stop pushed his body forward against the seat belt. From the corner of his eye, he saw Schwarz also being pushed forward.

"Damn it!" Lyons snapped. He smacked the heel of his palm against the steering wheel. He had wanted to keep close tabs on Blancanales, but now he was stuck at the light. He shot a glance at Schwarz, who was staring at a tablet computer that lay on his left thigh. The muscles of Schwarz's jaws bunched and released visibly as he worked his jaws. He had an app open on his tablet that allowed him to track the signal from the GPS unit in Blancanales's briefcase.

Lyons considered driving up onto the sidewalk and shooting through the intersection, but dismissed the idea. They'd only be stopped for a few seconds, more than enough time to catch up with Blancanales. He'd gain almost no time, but would attract lots of attention, including from any police that happened by. The last thing he or the other members of Able Team wanted was to end up going head to head with the local cops.

"He's still moving," Schwarz said.

Lyons acknowledged him with a nod but stayed silent.

When the light changed, the red sedan in front of them hesitated before it lumbered into the intersection. Another vehicle, a rusty pickup, was following on the left side of the SUV, with another car just behind it. Lyons was boxed in.

Lyons goosed the accelerator and rode on the other car's bumper. "C'mon, c'mon," he muttered.

In less than a minute the red sedan had gathered some speed and was starting to pull away from Lyons. After a couple of blocks, it was a few car lengths ahead.

The driver of a dark blue pickup gunned his engine and rolled the truck into the space behind them. A glance into the rearview mirror showed Lyons that, in addition to the driver, two other men were in the truck's cab. Instinct told him these guys weren't riding his tail because they were rushing out for a quart of milk or a six-pack of Dos Equis beer.

"I think we have a tail," Lyons said.

Schwarz glanced up from his tablet and shot Lyons a questioning look. Lyons nodded over his shoulder. "Blue pickup," he said.

Schwarz nodded. His hand disappeared under his jacket and came out gripping a Glock 18. The pistol, developed for an Austrian counter-terrorist force, had the ability to fire in semi-automatic or full-automatic mode. In full-auto mode, it fired around 1,200 rounds per minute. Schwarz had loaded the weapon with a 33-round clip.

Just as he brought out the Glock, his tablet beeped and he pointed at the intersection.

"Turn there," he said.

The lumbering red car turned ahead of them, prompting Lyons to swear under his breath.

Lyons fisted the Colt Python while he jerked the SUV's wheel right and threw the car into a sharp turn. The red car's brake lights suddenly flashed and it halted. The truck barreled around the corner in the same instant and slammed into the SUV's rear end, punching the vehicle hard and shoving it into the rear of the red car.

The force of the collision shoved Lyons and Schwarz forward hard against their seat belts. Schwarz's tablet sailed off his lap and struck the windshield. The sound of metal being twisted and bent filled the SUV for a second. The SUV's hood crumpled like paper; engine mounts broke off and the block crashed at an angle to the ground.

So much for avoiding any problems with the local police. Lyons whipped his head toward Schwarz. "You okay?" he asked.

Schwarz nodded and yanked on his door handle.

Lyons shoved open his door, stepped onto the pavement and brought the Python to shoulder height. Before he could take another step, the driver's door of the red sedan flew open and a hardman jumped from the vehicle's interior, a black handgun in his hand. The Python barked twice and a pair of holes opened on the guy's chest and neck. Blood spurted up from the wounds, and the force of the slugs spun the guy around as he crumpled to the ground.

Another shooter, blood streaming down his right temple, darted from the passenger's side of the car. The line of bullets chugging from the barrel of the hardman's submachine cut a deadly arc through the air just inches above Lyons's head. Before he could respond, though, the shooter suddenly went stiff as an onslaught of bullets from Schwarz's Glock ravaged his chest.

Lyons wheeled around and saw a rangy-looking dude in jeans and a dark blue T-shirt stalking around the front end of the pickup. The hardman held his pistol on its side and was lining up a shot at the Able Team leader. In better circumstances, Lyons would have called the guy a douche bag for shooting like a Hollywood action star, but time forced him to let the Colt do the talking as it spit a single Magnum slug. The bullet slapped into the man's forehead. Lyons glimpsed a red hole open in the shooter's skull before the force of the bullet shoved the corpse to the ground.

Lyons marched back a couple of steps to the SUV's rear driver's-side door while he continued to watch for other threats. As he flung open the door, he stowed the Colt inside his jacket. Reaching inside the vehicle, he snatched up an H&K MP-5 that lay on the floor.

Another of Escobar's men came around the front end of the truck, a shotgun held at waist level. Lyons threw himself forward, grunting as his elbows and knees absorbed the impact of the ground. The shotgun blast cleaved through the air where he'd stood an instant earlier. The guy was working the slide on the shotgun and readjusting his aim when the MP-5 came to life. A quick burst of slugs lashed out from the H&K's barrel, chewing into the man's legs and eliciting anguished cries.

His mind overwhelmed with pain, the gunner crashed to the ground, the shotgun barrel smacking against the pavement. A second burst from Lyons's SMG chewed into the other man's chest, killing him.

The commando hauled himself to standing and looked around for other adversaries. He barely noticed that his jacket was streaked with dirt. The cracked pavement had ripped one of the elbows of the jacket and also had torn open the skin on his left palm. Instead he looked for Schwarz.

He spotted him taking down another of Escobar's shotgun-wielding thugs with a burst of full-auto fire from Schwarz's Glock 18. From Lyons's vantage point, he also could see another of Escobar's thugs lining up a shot at Schwarz's back. Lyons swung the MP-5 in the hardman's direction and squeezed out a burst from the SMG. The hail of bullets lanced into Escobar's thug, whose finger squeezed the trigger in a death reflex. The pistol cracked once.

The sudden noise prompted Schwarz to spin around just in time to see the gunner collapse.

Schwarz gave his comrade a tight smile and a short nod, which Lyons returned.

"We're going to have to ditch the car," Lyons said. "Grab your gear and let's go find Pol."

CHAPTER NINE

Before Blancanales could react to the first men lowering themselves from the rooftop, a bald guy with massive shoulders and arms, thick legs and a paunch sprinted at the Able Team warrior. The guy had an AK-47, probably a knockoff of some kind, with a folding stock, held in both hands. The muzzle was swinging in Blancanales's direction, but he had no idea whether the thug actually planned to shoot him or just intimidate him into surrendering.

He had no time to figure it out. He raised the Beretta and squeezed off a couple of shots. The reports from the weapon echoed through the alleyway while the bullets lanced into the guy's torso. Before Blancanales could step out of the way, the massive corpse continued to bear down on him, like a car with a dead man at the steering wheel, and slammed into him.

Blancanales grunted and stumbled backward as his feet went out from under him. Though he willed himself to keep a tight hold on the Beretta, he still lost a moment as he pushed the dead hulk off him and tried to regain his bearings. Two of Escobar's thugs had scurried down the side of the building, and two more were running at him from the mouth of the alley. All of them were pointing guns at him and screaming in Spanish for him to drop his weapon and stop moving.

Even if Ortega was dead, Escobar probably had tried to quiz the undercover agent about this new arrival who'd appeared out of nowhere, trying to buy guns and other equipment. Blancanales had to assume Ortega had given him up; that Escobar knew Blancanales was a federal agent of some kind. He could try playing stupid and demand to know why they were attacking him, but he guessed it was too late for that routine.

Instead he let the Beretta fall from his hand and rolled away from it, flat on his stomach, the right side of his face pressed against the pavement.

He heard footsteps and looked up. Blue-jeans-clad legs were in front of him, the feet shod in snakeskin cowboy boots. The foot lashed out and kicked the pistol, sending it skittering across the ground. The creak of the boot leather registered with Blancanales, followed by fingers gathering a handful of his hair and jerking up. The Able Team commando scrambled first to his hands and knees, then just onto his knees, to lessen the pain.

He got a look at his antagonist. The thug didn't strike Blancanales as especially tall, though he was wide in the chest, shoulders and neck. The guy's free hand was clenched into a fist and it reminded Blancanales of a cinder block. His head was shaved clean, but a bushy black beard hung to the middle of his chest. A second person, shorter and slimmer, stepped around the big guy. When Blancanales's eyes drifted in that direction, the big guy rewarded him by releasing his hair and punching him in the jaw.

Blancanales's head whipped right and a white light flashed behind his eyes. The coppery taste of blood filled his mouth. He spit on the ground and swiveled his head back around.

Vargas stood over him, arms crossed over her chest. Her dark brown eyes, narrowed, studied him. A small pistol lay snug against the curve of her hip.

He thought of the Gerber folding knife in his pocket;

figured he could make one final play. The man mountain was close. He could launch himself from the ground, bury the blade in the guy's solar plexus, give it a twist, grab the woman, take her gun, use her to get Escobar's men to back down, at least to buy time until Lyons and Schwarz or the local police arrived.

Never work.

She'd put a bullet in him before he could surge up from the ground.

Best to let it play out.

"Where's Ortega?" he asked.

"I don't know."

Blancanales forced a smile.

"He wanted you to screw him," the commando said. "Sounds like you did."

"Take him," Vargas said through clenched teeth. Another brief explosion of pain erupted at the rear of Blancanales's skull and everything turned black.

CHAPTER TEN

Though he hated to admit it, the phone call had left Ortega with a hollow pit in his stomach.

Escobar had called and demanded a last-minute meeting with him. They had business to discuss, Escobar had said, before he would meet with Perez. Ortega had considered calling the guys with the Justice Department to clue them in. His instincts had told him to do just that, but he'd ignored them. Screw them, he decided. That bastard Perez wants to take a swing at me and question every move I make? To hell with him. This is my show. I've been running this op for years.

He arrived at the restaurant early. Stepping inside, he saw a couple of Escobar's thugs sitting at the bar, drinking and watching the door.

One of them slid off his stool, lumbered over to Ortega and greeted him with a curt nod.

"You're early," the thug said.

Ortega flashed a wide smile. "Hey, the big boss calls, you don't want to be late, right? If he asks you to jump, you jump. I figure I should be here as quickly as possible."

"Yeah, good idea. He seemed like he was in a rush to talk to you."

"Oh, yeah? What'd he say?"

The man ignored the question and jerked his head toward the back of the restaurant. "C'mon. He told me to escort you to one of the private party rooms. You want something to drink?"

"Hell, yeah, I want something to drink," Ortega replied, forcing another grin. "What do you think?"

Escorting him to the bar, the bodyguard said, "Wait here." The hardman walked around to the other side of the bar. Grabbing two glasses, he set them on top of the bar. With his other hand, he brought out a bottle of Scotch, which Ortega noticed was the most expensive the restaurant carried.

"Boss won't like it if you give a lowlife like me the best stuff in the house."

Escobar's thug shrugged his shoulders. "That's not what he told me. He said to give you the best stuff we had."

"Really?"

"Yeah."

That only made Ortega more nervous. Downing the whiskey, his thoughts began to whirl. Escobar was a cheap son of a bitch. He usually only served his people good booze if he planned to kill them. What had given him away? It had to be Perez. Damn it! Washington had promised they'd give the guy a bulletproof back-story. How could they screw up something so damned important?

Maybe he should run. The bodyguard was walking ahead of him. He could hit the guy in the back of the head, run out the restaurant's back door and escape in the car before Escobar became suspicious. And if he had to shoot his way out? Well, he was ready to do that, too.

He dismissed the idea almost immediately. What if he was overreacting? He'd blow his cover; one he'd spent most of his adult life building. Besides, he'd put Perez in danger, too. He didn't like the bastard or his entourage, especially that blond-haired, perpetually angry prick. But they were working for the same team and he couldn't imagine selling Perez or the others out. So, hell, he'd play it cool, stay right here and stick his head in the lion's mouth.

The thug opened the door to Escobar's private room and stepped aside.

Ortega plastered a smile on his face and peered inside.

He saw Escobar sitting at a large table, leaning back in his chair, arms crossed over his chest, his expression inscrutable.

Escobar gestured for Ortega to come inside. Against his better judgment, he did just that. A grim-faced Castillo was seated next to the head man. Castillo's eyes were narrowed and his lips were pressed together in a thin line. He looked as though he wanted to spring out of the chair at Ortega and was only barely restraining himself from doing so.

Even though the room was air-conditioned, Ortega suddenly felt hot, rivulets of sweat racing along his spine. Fear fluttered in his stomach and an almost overpowering urge to run welled up inside him. He knew he'd been made. Was it Vargas? Had she sold him out? No, he assured himself, she didn't know. It had to be the other agents. Not that they'd done it on purpose. But their sudden appearance had probably set off alarms and now they were going to take Ortega down, too.

If Escobar knew he was working undercover, Ortega needed to know that. More important, he needed to get out of this alive.

Vargas's absence only heightened his fear. She was always by Escobar's side. Well, almost always. Rumor was that when Escobar had to kill someone, he kept her away from it. That always mystified Ortega. Who the hell knew? Maybe it was the one chivalrous act of an utter psychopath. Even after all these years, Ortega couldn't pretend to understand the snake-eyed psycho who was staring at him.

"Sit," Escobar said, gesturing at a chair with his chin.

"Sure," Ortega replied, keeping his voice even. Moving to the table, he settled into one of the wing-backed chairs and unbuttoned his jacket. Resting his left elbow on the table, his forearm pointing straight up, he leaned forward and propped his chin on the notch between his first and second fingers. His right forearm rested on the table, the fingers of that hand hanging off the edge, putting them in reach of the Glock clipped to his belt.

A bottle of bourbon stood on the table near Escobar's elbow. He grabbed it by the neck and tipped it, splashing some into the bottom of a short glass. When he was finished, he slid the glass across the table to Ortega.

"Glad you could come," Escobar said. He nodded at the drink. "Help yourself. You're among friends."

Ortega forced a smile, lifted the drink and said, "Thanks." He drained about half of the contents, set the glass on the table and made a satisfied noise.

"You like that?"

"Hell, yeah," Ortega said.

"That's expensive shit. I don't hand it out to just anyone."

"You're very generous, sir."

"Here's the thing," Escobar said, "I grew up poor. You know that, right?"

"Yes, sir. I suppose I did."

"Dirt poor. No clean water. No clean clothes. My mother worked in alleys. She let strangers bang her brains out for money. Sometimes they didn't pay her. Sometimes they banged her, then hit her and took her money."

"That sounds terrible."

"Terrible? Maybe. Maybe it's just human nature. Hell, I don't know. You want another drink?"

Ortega nodded and Escobar slid the bottle across the table at him.

"Here's what I do know," Escobar said. "When someone

took her money, I didn't eat. So here I was, holes in the roof, holes in my clothes and some prick takes my momma's last peso after he bangs her."

"Terrible," Ortega repeated.

"No," Escobar said, rising from his seat, "predictable. At the end of the day, people are animals. They speak their peace, love and brotherhood crap all day long. But when it gets right down to it, they're a bunch of animals. They want to eat, screw and stay warm. That's all they care about. You agree?"

The agent shrugged. "Sounds pretty close to the truth."

"That's because it is the truth." Escobar shrugged his jacket from his shoulders, revealing a leather shoulder harness. "Take this, shithead," he said, tossing the jacket to Castillo, who snatched it from the air and busied himself folding it.

"Where was I? Oh, yeah. See, animals are hungry and you take their food, what do they do?"

Ortega shrugged.

Escobar unbuttoned the cuff of his left shirtsleeve and rolled it up once.

"You don't know what animals do?" he asked, voice incredulous. "Of course, you don't know. Or maybe you're just pretending. You're good at that."

"What? What the hell…"

"Shut up. I'm getting there."

"But…"

Escobar pinned Ortega with his stare. The latter man felt his stomach plummet and he moved his hand just slightly, putting it closer to his gun. Calm down, he told himself. You still can get control of this. Keep the guy talking so you can figure this out. Maybe he figured out Perez is a Fed and he'd just pissed at me for introducing them.

"Anyway," Escobar continued, "I watched this happen

maybe a half dozen times, these bastards hitting my mom, taking her money. I'm hungry and these bastards are taking our money. That means no food for me. You know what I did?"

Ortega shrugged again.

"Of course you don't know, you little pussy. You grew up in a nice suburb. What was it? Upstate New York? Daddy was a doctor?"

"I don't know—"

"Shut up." By now Escobar had rolled up his other sleeve. He crossed his arms over his chest and stared past Ortega, eyes fixed on a spot on the wall. "I'm trying to talk. Anyway, my mother comes home, crying, lip split open, eye swollen shut. She says she has no money. I'm a kid, but I'm furious, right?"

Ortega nodded, but was only half listening. He was running the numbers. If he shot Escobar, he had maybe a second to whip around and blast Castillo, who carried a nickel-plated Colt revolver in the small of his back, before Castillo shot him. Chances were Castillo would shoot him the second he put a bullet in Escobar. But at least Escobar would be dead. In some way, he would have accomplished his mission. He just needed to get his gun. That meant he needed Escobar to keep talking.

"Furious," he said.

"Furious. So I tell my mother… I say, 'Don't worry, Mama. I'll take care of this. Where did it happen? Who did this to you?' After a while, she told me. My father, he was gone. He'd disappeared before I was born. But he left us one thing. A .38 revolver. He knew Tijuana was a shithole and he was leaving his wife and kid there. Maybe giving her the gun made him feel better. Maybe he knew he'd never get through customs with it. Who the hell knows? I knew where it was, though. My mother had showed it to me a couple of times, told me if one of her 'friends'—that's what she called her tricks—came to the house, got rough with her, I should grab the gun and threaten to shoot him."

The corner of his lip twitched at the memory.

"Tell him what you did," Castillo said.

"The gun was in a shoe box under her bed, along with a box of shells and a switchblade. I took out the gun, loaded it. Then I grabbed the knife and went down to the bar where all this shit had happened. I was too young to go in, so I just waited outside for the son of a bitch to stagger out. When he did, I followed him home."

He still wasn't looking directly at Ortega. But the undercover agent felt as though Escobar could see his every move. He shifted a bit in his chair, moving his hand an inch or so closer to his gun, probably close enough for him to make a quick draw.

"Where's Perez?" Ortega asked.

Escobar flicked his eyes in Ortega's direction.

"You don't ask the questions here. I do." He turned his gaze away from Ortega and studied the nails of his left hand. "So I follow this guy home and while he's unlocking the door, I call his name. He turns around, all bug-eyed until he sees it's just a kid. Then he waves his arm and tells me to get off his property. Says he'll kill me if I don't leave.

"I just stood there and waited, said nothing. The drunk bastard started screaming at me, but I just stared at him. Finally he lost it and charged at me. I'd never shot a gun before, but it was easy. He was so close, I just emptied it into his chest. Six shots. Dead before he hit the ground. Then I went through his pockets and took what money I could and left."

Escobar fell silent for a couple of seconds. "See, here's the reason I tell you this. You know why I killed this bastard, huh? No? I didn't do it because he defiled my mama.

I didn't do it because he beat her up. None of that crap. No, I did it because he took money from my pocket. Someone does that to you once, they'll do it twice, maybe more. So I killed him. And I've killed one hundred like him since."

Ortega heard something change in the gunrunner's voice.

Escobar's hand stabbed for the pistol stowed under his arm. Ortega made a play for his own weapon, but he was too slow. The .38 was in Escobar's hand, flame stabbing out from the muzzle. The slug drilled into the undercover Fed's chest, the pistol's report echoing through the room. The gun barked again and a hole opened in Ortega's forehead as his skull jerked backward. His body suddenly went slack and he slumped in his chair.

ESCOBAR STARED AT the corpse. His dark brown eyes were fixed on the hole in Ortega's forehead, the crimson rivulet of blood rolling down his skin. The crime boss opened the .38's cylinder and pulled the spent shells from it. Taking a couple of bullets from his pants' pocket, he began reloading the weapon.

"Hijo de puta," he muttered.

"You did the right thing," Castillo said.

Escobar slammed the cylinder back into the pistol, whirled toward his lieutenant and aimed the weapon at his chest.

Castillo's eyes widened, flicking from the gun's muzzle to his boss's eyes and back to the muzzle.

"Do I look conflicted?" Escobar asked.

"No."

"Then shut the hell up. And get someone to get this pig's carcass out of here."

"Yes, sir." Castillo slowly rose from his chair, his eyes locked on Escobar's, and backed out of the room.

Escobar's phone rang. He picked it up from the table and brought it to his ear. *"Si?"*

"We have him," Vargas said.

"Alive?"

"Yes."

"You know what to do from here?"

"Of course."

"Then do it."

"Where's Ortega? He was supposed to be here for this."

"I put him on something else. Got an issue with that?"

She hesitated for a couple of beats. "No."

"Good," he said. "Just move Perez and I'll worry about Ortega."

He ended the call and set the phone on the table. He stared at Ortega's face, eyes locked open, blood carving trails down either side of his nose, past his mouth and off his chin, and realized he wasn't worried at all about the guy.

CHAPTER ELEVEN

Lyons rounded the corner in time to see the helicopter rising, the spinning blades scattering dirt and trash as the craft worked to gain some altitude. The chopper already was too high off the ground and too far away for him to try to grab hold of the landing skids, he decided. And even if he made it, what then? The pilot probably would shake him loose from the skids before he ever could gain entry to the helicopter.

Four of Escobar's men had stayed on the ground. They were facing Schwarz and Lyons, ready to keep the Able Team commandos from getting too close to the helicopter. Adrenaline-fueled rage pumped through Lyons's body, spurring him to move forward.

He wanted to know where Escobar was taking his colleague. The most immediate way of doing that was to grab one of these morons and beat the information out of him. It wasn't much of a plan, but considering how fast things were unfolding, it would have to suffice.

He surged forward, running in a zigzag pattern, at the assembled thugs. They responded in kind, unleashing withering waves of fire from the machine pistols they wielded.

Lyons's MP-5 rattled out short bursts that missed his opponents but caused them to scatter. Maneuvering the SMG in a horizontal line, he caught one of the men with a spray of lead that tore through the guy's legs. To his left, Schwarz was laying down his own barrage of autofire that cut down two more of the gunners. The fourth thug ripped off a quick burst from his Skorpion machine pistol even as he backed away from the Able Team fighters and maneuvered himself behind a parked car for protection.

By now the loudness of the sirens told Lyons they were about to have company.

The man with the Skorpion pistol popped up from behind the car, extending his arm over the roof and firing off quick bursts at the Americans.

Lyons and Schwarz in unison concentrated their fire on the car's windows. The storm of gunfire disintegrated the vehicle's safety glass, and bullets ripped into the man, killing him.

Lyons started toward the gunner who'd been shot in the legs. The guy was lying on the ground. He'd lost a lot of blood, but still was moving his head side to side and groaning.

Lyons had taken five steps when police cars careened around the corner, sirens blaring, tires screeching. He swore loudly and took another step. However he thought better of it as the first couple of cars stopped, the doors swung open and officers went EVA, their weapons drawn, shouting commands in Spanish.

The Able Team commandos had no choice but to put down their weapons and surrender. Lyons and Schwarz set their guns on the pavement and raised their hands.

Mexico City, Mexico

"This is bullshit," Lyons stormed.

"It is," Schwarz agreed. "But we can't do anything about it. At least not yet. We need to wait on Hal to get us out of here."

"If he knows we're in here. You know how it is. They

could keep us in here for two months without even telling the Embassy. For all Hal knows, we're in the middle of trying to infiltrate Escobar's organization."

Schwarz shook his head. "I doubt it," he said. "At this point, if Ortega's dead and his people are dead, they have to know that in Washington. If nobody checks in, they're going to start looking. They'll ask questions."

"But that's going to take time," Lyons countered. "We don't have time. We don't know what happened to Blancanales. For all we know, he could be dead right now."

Schwarz nodded his head slowly, estimating they'd already been in the cell for at least two hours. "Yeah," he said. "It's possible."

"And we're not going to figure a damn thing out if we have to stay in here."

Schwarz knew that Brognola pulled a lot of weight, not just in the United States, but with law enforcement and intelligence officials in other countries, too. With the U.S. working with Mexico to fight the drug trade, Schwarz guessed that when the big Fed spoke, Mexican officials would listen.

But what Lyons had said was right. They were losing time. The longer they spent cooling their heels in a jail cell, the more remote their chances of finding Blancanales and taking down Escobar.

They could only hope Brognola had gotten word that something had happened to Able Team and he could move fast enough to get them out of jail.

In the meantime all they could really do was sit and wait—not their specialty.

"This is bullshit," Lyons said.

"You just said that five times in the past hour," Schwarz replied. "We're stuck here. Get over it."

"No, not that. It's bullshit we're even in this situation."

"Meaning?"

"I knew this was a bad idea and I let Blancanales talk me into letting him go undercover."

"You can't blame yourself."

"The hell I can't. I'm supposed to be the commander. I'm the leader and I led you guys right into something awful. Now, here we are, stuck in jail and he's missing. I screwed the pooch on this one."

"This is no time for a crisis of confidence. We need to stay focused."

"Hell, I know we need to stay focused. I am focused. Part of what I'm focused on is figuring out why the hell I ever decided to lead us into this. What we should've done in the first place is come in and gone Scorched Earth on Escobar from the beginning."

"We didn't want to tip our hand. You know that. We didn't know what kind of repercussions there would be, not just here in Mexico, but globally. Obviously this guy is linked in with people overseas. If we had moved too aggressively…"

"Yeah, yeah. I know. If we'd gone too aggressively, they might all go to ground. Well, guess what. They've all gone to ground. And our asses are in a Mexican jail. I'm sure the trail's already being covered even as we speak. We accomplished nothing."

Schwarz struggled for a reply. He didn't question Lyons's skill as a leader.

The ex-cop was brash and mouthy. But he was a damn fine commander. But he was also right—they'd walked away with nothing. Schwarz remained silent.

A couple of seconds later Schwarz heard footsteps outside the cell, growing louder with each passing moment. He and Lyons turned their heads in unison toward the door. Schwarz heard keys jingle, followed a second later by the sound of a key being inserted into a lock and the thunk of a lock releasing.

The door came open. A pair of Mexican police officers stood outside the cell, one positioned in front of the other. The one closest to the door pointed at Lyons and then jerked a thumb over his shoulder.

"You," the officer said, "come on."

Lyons rose from the bed. He motioned at Schwarz. "What about him?" Lyons asked.

The officer shook his head. "He stays. You've got a phone call."

"Go," Schwarz said. "I'll be fine."

"Damn it," Lyons muttered. He walked through the door. He turned to say something to Schwarz, but one of the cops was already swinging the door closed.

The cop who'd spoken earlier grabbed hold of Lyons's bicep. Lyons jerked his arm away. "Do not touch me," he said. "I may be staying here, but it's only because I decided to come quietly."

Both officers glared at Lyons. The cop who'd grabbed Lyons's arm dropped a hand to his belt and started to reach for his collapsible police baton. The other police officer, who was younger, followed the first guy's lead, making a grab for his baton, too.

They hadn't tried to cuff him immediately, which meant they probably already had heard something from Washington. Or at least he hoped so. Lyons let his arms hang loose at his sides and stared at the officers.

"You do not want to take out that baton," Lyons said. "Chances are it will be used by me and not against me. If you thought I was a threat, I'd already be in handcuffs. You know I'm not a threat. Now, take me where we're going and do not touch me."

Five minutes later the pair of officers escorted Lyons up two flights of stairs and into a squad room.

A handful of uniformed cops milled around. A couple of men in civilian clothes were seated at desks. One was talking on the phone. The other had his eyes locked on the screen of his computer and was typing on a keyboard.

A third stood in front of a filing cabinet. He held open a folder and was studying one the papers stored in it.

In a weird way, Lyons suddenly felt at home. He'd spent more than his fair share of time in an LAPD squad room.

He turned to the cop who'd first tried to pull out his baton.

"Where am I going?"

The officer pointed across the room to a glassed-in office area. Lyons could tell it was the office of someone who held rank. Without waiting on the two cops, he moved to the office, twisted the doorknob, opened the door and stepped inside.

A man was sitting at a desk. A short stack of folders stood at the right edge of his desk blotter. Another file was spread open in front of him and he was leafing through its contents. With weary eyes, he looked at Lyons and scowled.

"You the gringo?" he asked.

"One of the gringos."

"Happy day. Can never have enough of you people here." He gestured at a chair. "Sit down."

Lyons's first instinct was to rebuff the offer, just because he was pissed. He checked himself and, with a nod, walked to the chair, dropped into it and leveled his gaze at the man.

"You're apparently well connected," the guy said. "I've had people from Washington lighting up my phone, the mayor's phone, everyone's damn telephone, telling us to let you go. My name is Juan Ruiz. I'm the shift sergeant. And you, my friend, have created a lot of problems here."

Lyons nodded once. "Yeah," he said. "I'd apologize for my transgressions, but I'm a hell of a lot more worried about finding my friend."

This didn't seem to faze the sergeant. "Yeah, you should be worried," he said. He shot a look over Lyons's shoulder at the two officers standing behind him. "Get out."

After some hesitation, the two officers nodded, exited the room and shut the door. Ruiz stared after them for a few seconds and waited until they'd put some distance between themselves and his office before he turned his attention back to Lyons.

"Look," Ruiz said, "Escobar has people in here. Those two who brought you here? I don't know about either one of them. I'm sure they're in somebody's pocket. Maybe it's Escobar's payroll. I'm not sure. But I wanted them out of here."

Lyons nodded his understanding.

"The best thing we can do is get you out of here," Ruiz said. "You and your friend both need to get out of here."

Lyons spread his hands. "I got no problem with that."

"But first you need to know where things stand. I mean, really stand."

A smile ghosted Lyons's lips. "Really? Well, please tell me, Sergeant Ruiz."

The sergeant backed his chair away from his desk, opened the lap drawer and reached inside. Lyons tensed. Was he reaching for a gun? His hand came out holding a stack of photos and Lyons relaxed a little. The sergeant dropped the photos on the desktop and shoved them over to Lyons.

The Stony Man warrior leaned forward and began picking through the stack. Immediately his stomach clenched. In one of the photos, Ortega was lying on the ground, his head turned to one side, the ground beneath it stained with blood. In another, Steve King, apparently in an apartment, hands bound, was hanging by his neck. In the third photo was the other DOJ technician. He was lying facedown on a bed, a small red hole in his back, just between his shoulder blades. The edges of a dark red blossom of blood had spread from beneath him across the surface of his mattress.

"So this is pretty much my week," Ruiz said. "I have three dead Americans in my city. I'm not even sure whether I have their real names. I have another guy who's missing. And two more who are running around with automatic weapons, shooting everything that moves."

"Sucks to be you."

"Tell me about it. But, hey, I'm thinking at least I have these two bastards in jail, right? You've filled up your share of body bags. I caught you. At least I can do something right." He paused and reached for the crumpled pack of cigarettes on his desk. "Except then the mayor gets a call from the president."

"Of the United States?"

"Smart ass. No, of Mexico. We have one of those down here, too, you know. It's a call from the president of Mexico saying, 'Hands off.' We need to let you guys go. So now I get to have a dozen or more unsolved homicides. I have to let two of the perpetrators go and pretend like I never met you."

"Harsh."

"But that's not the worst part."

"Okay."

"The worst part is, I have to do something nice for you. Okay? I'm going to give you a warning. You need to get out of Mexico City. Whatever you are into, whatever you've done, Escobar is on the warpath. He's killed at least three American federal agents and kidnapped a fourth in his own country. This is a guy who normally wouldn't get a traffic ticket in Mexico. You guys have put him over the edge. If he gets hold of you and your buddy, you two are dead men."

"I'm terrified," Lyons said, his voice even.

"I'm serious."

Lyons heaved a sigh. "I know you are," he said. "Listen, I appreciate the warning. But they have a friend of mine. The last thing I'm going to do is keep a low profile. And, if you asked my friend in the cell, he'd say the same thing. We're going after Escobar. We're not going to quit until we find him. End of story. *Comprende?*"

Ruiz stared at him for several seconds before he finally shook his head. "You are crazy, man. But, hey, it's your funeral. Go with God, you freaking lunatic."

CHAPTER TWELVE

Hours after Ortega's death, Castillo stepped from the charter jet's interior and immediately felt a wave of desert heat envelop him. A team of four gunners stood a few yards away, ready to escort him to his limousine.

The largest, a man named Lorenzo Lopez, stepped forward. The guy was a monster; his nearly seven-foot frame packed with muscle. From what Castillo understood, the guy was a brain, too. He'd used his size to earn a football scholarship at a university in California, where he'd studied physics or chemistry or something. A smart guy like Lopez probably could have risen through the ranks, maybe been one of Escobar's finance guys and helped him hide his millions in places where the pricks in the DEA, the FBI and Interpol couldn't find them.

From what Castillo understood, though, Lopez had a crazy streak in him. He liked busting heads more than he liked counting other people's money. Yet the combination of brawn and brains made him a good team leader for Castillo's security detail. He'd need someone good covering his ass if the Americans came for him.

Lopez extended a hand and offered to take Castillo's briefcase. Castillo waved him off. Aside from bundles of cash and a satellite phone, the case also contained a micro Uzi and a couple of extra magazines. A small-frame Glock rode on his hip, hidden beneath his sport coat. If things suddenly went bad, it was nice to have a security team, but even better to have your own guns. If bullets started to fly, Castillo considered Lopez and his trained dogs cannon fodder—living, breathing targets to take bullets for him while he escaped.

As Castillo moved away from the airplane, Lopez's team surrounded him in a diamond formation, one guard in front, one in back and one on each side.

When they reached the limousine, the guard walking point opened the rear door and gestured for Castillo to climb inside. He did. The door closed behind him and the cooler air enveloped him. A second later the front passenger door opened and Lopez squeezed himself into the front seat.

"You good, Mr. Castillo?" Lopez asked.

Castillo answered with a curt nod. Lopez told the driver to get the car moving, which the man did. Turning slightly at the waist, Castillo peered through the back window and saw the rest of Lopez's team climbing into a shiny black SUV. A matching SUV was idling in front of the limousine.

"We'll have you at the ranch in an hour," Lopez said over his shoulder.

"Fine," Castillo said. "How many guys you got here?"

"Here at the airport? Seven. In total, about a dozen."

"About a dozen or a dozen?"

"A dozen."

"Is that enough?"

"Depends on what you're expecting, sir."

"I expect a goddamn answer."

"They're some of the best we have. You should be fine."

Castillo nodded. He reached into his jacket and pulled out a silver flask. Unscrewing the cap, he brought it to his lips and took a big swallow of whiskey before replacing the cap and slipping the container back inside his coat. Staring out the window, he watched as the limo rolled off the tarmac, glided between a series of hangars and headed for the main gate.

The whiskey rolled into his stomach, which was balled up like a fist, and burned like the payload from a phosphorus grenade.

He'd left Mexico City in a rush. They'd suspected for some time that Ortega was a U.S. agent, or at least an informant. His behavior had become increasingly erratic. Most of the guys in Escobar's organization drank. Some did blow. It was no big deal. Escobar knew he wasn't running a damn convent. But Ortega had stepped over the edge. He'd drank too much. He'd wrecked a car and gotten into a couple of fights with a couple of Escobar's other guys. It was as though he'd wanted to call attention to himself.

Well, he'd gotten it.

Escobar was a paranoid SOB. Occasionally he drifted into crazy territory. But this time, damn if he hadn't been right. He'd suspected Ortega long before anyone else and had started digging into things. With all his drinking, Ortega had made himself an easy target, too. He'd accidentally made a couple of contacts to his Washington handlers using the phone Escobar had provided. When he'd met with his handlers, he'd made only cursory attempts to hide his tracks. He'd made it easy for Escobar to put a bullet in his head.

Fine, he'd played the game and lost. Castillo had no problem per se with Escobar killing the undercover Fed. He'd always considered the guy an insufferable prick. But Escobar had taken a step further and killed his entire team. He'd nabbed another guy who might also be an American agent.

Along the way, Escobar had ranted something about sending a message. Well, mission accomplished. He'd sent a message that probably had red alerts blaring all over

Washington. This was the kind of thing Escobar didn't need. Sure, they'd already attracted attention; otherwise the U.S. never would have infiltrated the operation. Maybe if Escobar had handled the killing right, they could have made it work. They could have made it look like Ortega'd been killed in an accident, or by a rival gang—something to deflect the attention away from their organization. Escobar had decided against it.

Castillo heaved a sigh and stared out the window. The anger roiled in his gut, causing it to squeeze harder. He knew why his boss had thrown caution to the wind and had done something so damn dangerous.

It was the woman. Aside from drinking himself into a stupor and crashing cars, Ortega also had started spending time with Vargas. Castillo guessed the dumb bastard thought he was getting away with something. Maybe he'd really deluded himself into thinking she'd wanted to sleep with him. All he'd really accomplished was the signing of his own death warrant.

She'd been pumping Ortega for information and taking it back to Escobar. Surprisingly, Ortega never had been stupid enough to tell Vargas he really was a Fed. Escobar never had clued her in on that little fact, either. She was a smart woman and it was conceivable she knew. But Ortega also had been a good undercover agent who'd fooled a lot of people over the years.

In recent months Escobar had heard rumblings about Ortega from former employers, little things like him accidentally taking critical documents home or disappearing for a day or more with no explanation. Taken individually, the incidents hadn't seemed like much and most of his former bosses had thought nothing of it until after he was gone. Castillo had dismissed it, but Escobar had heard it enough from different sources that it had spurred him to investigate. While he'd never quite found the proverbial smoking gun, he'd seen enough to convince him something was wrong and he'd killed Ortega without hesitation.

Even though Castillo had been with him for years, Escobar's cool detachment and swift hand when it came to dealing death still unnerved Castillo. If Escobar could kill with such cold brutality, Castillo reasoned, how could he be safe working for the guy? When was he going to do the one thing that made Escobar classify him as a liability rather than an asset?

He tried not to think about it. And when he did think about it, he downed some whiskey from his silver flask, rolled up his sleeves and tried to make Escobar more money. He produced the flask and swigged from it again.

Maybe money couldn't buy happiness, he thought, licking traces of whiskey from his lips, but in Escobar's organization it could buy another day on earth, maybe two.

For the moment Castillo needed to get off the grid until the storm passed or until Escobar called for help. Kidnapping one Fed and killing the others would bring his boss trouble, Castillo knew. From what he'd gathered, several of Escobar's men had lost their lives grabbing Perez. The Americans would be pissed. They'd turn every possible agent, satellite and drone on Escobar and his crew. For Castillo, that meant more time spent looking over his shoulder, waiting on the hammer to fall.

He threw a glance at Lopez. The man-mountain was on his mobile phone, riding some poor bastard back at Castillo's ranch about last-minute security details. Good. If the Americans came for Castillo, he wanted them to hit something immovable; he wanted to draw blood.

Stony Man Farm, Virginia

BROGNOLA STOOD IN the center of the War Room. Acid bubbled in his stomach. His mouth turned down in a scowl, arms crossed over his chest, he stared at his team as they worked furiously at their computers.

Barbara Price was pacing in another part of the room while speaking into a headset microphone. The big Fed guessed she was either trying to pry information from one of her old NSA cronies or arranging for some other type of support.

When he caught snatches of her conversation, her voice sounded cool and professional, though he still could hear an edge of tension, too. Having one or two of their commandoes end up in a local jail was just another day at the office for Price, Brognola and the others. Same went for cleaning up the messes the teams occasionally made in the field. Price handled these situations with a cool detac. ment and efficiency that never failed to impress. But when one of their people got hurt or went missing, a few hairline cracks in her composure started to show.

Brognola was no different. Word that Blancanales had been snatched even as a team of federal agents had been killed was like a gut punch for the big Fed. On days like this, he wondered why he'd ever quit smoking.

"The Escobar file is sealed?" Price was saying. "Maybe you should unseal it. What? Yes, I said unseal it—as in open it and tell me what it says. We have a man missing in Mexico City. Taken by armed criminals. Mortal danger. Unsealing that file yet?" She paused. "No? Are you waiting for a letter opener?"

She glanced at Brognola and made a frustrated gesture with her hand. He gave her a tight smile. She forced one of her own before turning her back to him and continuing her phone conversation.

Screw this, Brognola thought. It was time for him to call Washington, Fort Meade and Langley, and start lighting fires under a few butts. Wheeling around, he took a step toward the door but froze when he heard Kurtzman call his name. He spun toward the cyber wizard.

"You got something?" Brognola asked.

"Maybe," Kurtzman said.

Brognola rushed over to Kurtzman's workstation and stared over his shoulder at the computer screen.

With his index finger, Kurtzman pointed at a spot on the chart displayed on his monitor. "See this?" he asked. "That's a tail number. It belongs to an export company based in Mexico City."

"Okay," Brognola said, hoping he hadn't missed the punch line.

"The company belongs to Escobar," Kurtzman continued. "It's what we in the crime-fighting business like to call a front company."

"What a coup," Brognola said. "Maybe Lyons can beat the plane with a rubber hose until it gives up Rosario's location."

Kurtzman sighed. "Fine," he said. "The tail number isn't exciting. I stole that information from a restricted ATF database. But here's the point—a pilot filed a flight plan."

"So Escobar's on the move," Brognola said.

"Escobar or one of his people."

"Does the flight plan give a destination?"

"It does."

"Snag it and send it to Lyons."

CHAPTER THIRTEEN

A pair of Polaris MV850 ATVs rumbled along the desert floor, bouncing and jerking as they rolled over rocks, bushes and other vegetation. The vehicles, driven by Lyons and Schwarz, were carving a path toward Castillo's sprawling ranch.

Both men were decked out in camouflage fatigues, boots, ballistic helmets and sunglasses. Lyons's Colt Python was holstered on his right thigh.

Apparently, Escobar had put out a contract on one of the detectives in charge of the property room at the jail. When the cop heard that Lyons and Schwarz were planning to wax Escobar, he'd been only too happy to pull some strings and recover Lyons's prized sidearm, as well as some of their other gear.

When the cop had handed the pistol to Lyons, his expression had been grim. "You probably won't live long enough to use it, but here's your pistol," he'd said. *"Buenas suerte."*

"Bullshit," Lyons had replied, snatching it from the detective's grip. "I don't need luck. I'll mail you that bastard's head in a box."

Shrugging, the cop had turned and walked away. *"Vaya con Dios,"* he'd muttered. "Put some dry ice in the box, too."

In addition to the Python, Lyons had picked up a Glock 21, chambered in .45 ACP, along with several 13-round magazines. Strapped on his back was an M-4 outfitted with a cut-down Remington 870 shotgun fixed underneath the assault weapon's barrel, similar to a grenade launcher. The shotgun was loaded with three 12-gauge breaching rounds.

Lyons glanced to his right at Schwarz, who acknowledged him with a brief wave of his gloved hand. Schwarz had equipped himself with an M-4 A-1 CQBR, a cut-down version of the assault rifle geared toward close-quarters combat. The M-4 was capable of firing up to 950 rounds per minute and boasted a muzzle velocity of 2,600 feet per second. Additionally, Schwarz had picked up a 15-round Glock 22 for his main sidearm, as well as a subcompact 9 mm Glock 26 as backup.

Both Lyons and Schwarz also carried grenades, garrotes and knives in the pockets of their fatigues.

Castillo's spread was another half mile or so away, according to the coordinates received from the Farm. Kurtzman had also forwarded satellite photos of the property, though he'd noted most were dated because Castillo seldom used the place. Given the urgency, Brognola had made calls to the Pentagon and the CIA, asking them to divert a drone to the ranch to secure additional, updated footage.

Though the Pentagon had dispatched its closest drone, it was hours away, and Lyons guessed it would be too late. Despite his cynicism about damn near everything, he believed the military wanted to help them find Blancanales. The real question was whether they could put a bird over the site in time.

He guessed not.

But, if he had his way, the drone would capture great footage of the place burning to the ground.

He blamed himself for Blancanales's predicament. All along, his gut had told him sending Blancanales in undercover was too risky. He'd ignored his judgment and now a team member was missing. In one respect, though, he'd been lucky. Finding Blancanales fit well with Able Team's goal of taking out Escobar. Good thing. If it had come down to either finding and killing Escobar or tracking down his old friend, Lyons would have faced an awful choice. A stroke of luck.

As it stood, all they had to do was find their teammate, who was God knew where, and do it before Blancanales ended up with a bullet in his head, and get through maybe a couple dozen well-armed thugs to do it.

No sweat.

TEN MINUTES LATER the pair stopped their vehicles a couple hundred yards from Castillo's ranch. The ATVs stood on a stretch of golden poppies, hidden behind a copse of cacti, some of which stretched forty feet or more toward the sky.

Lyons had slipped off his sunglasses and, with a pair of binoculars pressed to his eyes, was studying the land that lay between them and the ranch. Though rough, he judged the terrain was nothing the four-wheeled ATVs couldn't handle.

Thanks to Kurtzman and the cyber team, they already knew a chain-link fence topped by razor wire surrounded the property. There was also a guard shack at the main gate. From what they knew, Castillo liked to tell people he owned a ranch, but he kept no cattle or other livestock there. In addition to the big house, which had a stucco exterior and a red-tiled roof, there was also a barn and a large stable on the property. Rumor had it Castillo had won the ranch in a poker game in Mexico City.

Other details such as the number of guards, their background, the security team's command structure and the types of weapons they carried were scarce. That didn't worry Lyons, and he guessed it mattered little to Schwarz.

They were used to walking into deadly situations with little or no information; used to making it up as they went.

He focused on the guard shack for a minute or so. As best he could tell, there was one guard in the shack. An air conditioner jutted from one of the windows. Condensation dripped from the bottom of the AC unit, the water falling into a dark water stain on the concrete. A cobalt-blue SUV, the sunlight glinting off the dark tinted windows, was parked next to the shack. Lyons looked at a tailpipe poking out from beneath the SUV, but saw no signs of heat or exhaust belching from the vehicle.

Another slow sweep of the binoculars revealed at least two more rifle-toting hardmen walking around the grounds.

"What do you think?" Schwarz asked.

Lyons lowered the binoculars a few inches and glanced at his partner.

"If it's only three guards," the Able Team leader said, "this should be easy."

"Our track record for walking into easy situations isn't too hot," Schwarz replied.

"Castillo is Escobar's lieutenant. But Castillo is sitting in the middle of nowhere with three guards?" Lyons shook his head. "Doesn't play."

"He knows someone will come after him," Schwarz replied. "He just doesn't know how or when. If anything, he's taken some steps to protect himself."

"Meaning?"

Schwarz gestured at the big house. "He probably has more gunners in the house with him. He knows why we're here."

Lyons nodded in agreement. "Be my guess. Once we start the buzz saw, he may send a few of them out of the house to intercept us. But pushing our way through the house will probably be the worst part. Be a hell of a lot easier if we didn't have to keep Castillo alive."

"At least until we can interrogate him," Schwarz corrected. "After that, all bets are off."

"Yeah," Lyons growled.

Schwarz brought around his own binoculars and trained them on the ranch, studying the property for a minute or so.

"Any ideas on how to get in?"

Lyons's lips quirked into a half smile. "Front door, baby."

SCHWARZ CROUCHED BEHIND one of the towering cacti located thirty or so yards from the security fence. He peered around the big plant and scanned the ranch. The same two guards, each armed with a submachine gun, continued to patrol inside the fence, one buzzing around the property on a three-wheel ATV, the other moving around on foot. The latter guard occasionally would stop and stare out at the acres of scrub brush, rocks and cacti that populated the desert, before readjusting the rifle strapped on his shoulder and moving again. Whether he actually sensed Schwarz watching him or the guy was just breaking up the monotony, Schwarz never would know. After all his years as a soldier, Schwarz and the other Stony Man warriors had developed a keen sense for danger. It stood to reason that Castillo's gunners also could sense danger. It came with the territory.

Schwarz pulled back behind the trunk of the cactus. Bringing around the M-4, he broke open the grenade launcher, slipped in an HE round and snapped the launcher closed. His goal was simple; he wanted to make a lot of noise and snag the attention of Castillo's thugs. Though it was late in the day, the sun still beat down on his back. He could feel heat and sweat collecting beneath his ballistic vest and his kneepads. He'd ditched the ATV a few dozen yards back. Even with the specially adapted mufflers, the ATV wasn't silent and the people inside the fence were sure to hear the engine's growl if he'd brought the vehicle much closer.

Once things started, Schwarz guessed the hit would move quickly. That was fine with him. Like Lyons, he wanted to locate Blancanales before it was too late.

Castillo was their best chance for getting the information they needed, which meant they'd burn down every one of Castillo's thugs to talk with him.

Lyons's voice buzzed in Schwarz's earpiece. "You in position?"

"Roger that," Schwarz said. "Just waiting for the official okey-dokey."

"Do it."

Schwarz eased his body out from behind the cactus, brought the M-4 to his shoulder and pulled the launcher's trigger. The round arced up and over the fence before it fell back to earth, thudding against the ground next to a dark green SUV. An explosion rent the air. Orange-yellow flames lashed out at the vehicle's underside, igniting a second explosion. Fire tore through the SUV's interior even as the vehicle was thrust into the air, where it seemed to hover for a heartbeat before it crashed down again, its grille shattering, its steel hood crumpling against the concrete. The nearest guard sprinted away from the blast, putting a couple of yards between him and the mayhem before the concussive force from the explosion hit him in the back and shoved him to the ground.

At the same time Schwarz was tracking the guard on the ATV. The guard threw the vehicle into a sharp turn until he was facing the burning wreckage. His mouth gaping open, he slid his fingers into his jacket, probably looking for some hardware or a two-way radio. Having already lined up a shot, Schwarz squeezed the M-4's trigger, unleashing a punishing burst from the compact rifle. A ragged line of bullets tore across the guy's chest. He jerked in place under the withering fire for a stretched second before falling from the ATV's seat.

Schwarz heard the growl of an engine to his left. He turned his head toward the sound and spotted Lyons's ATV rumbling toward the gate.

A hardman burst from the guard shack. The SMG he clutched was rattling out a sustained burst. Bullets slammed into the gravel driveway leading up to the gate, kicking up a half dozen geysers of dirt and stone fragments.

Navigating his vehicle with one hand, Lyons fired his M-4 with the other. The weapon was spewing a storm of 5.56 mm slugs that tore into the torso of Lyons's opponent. The guard's SMG suddenly fell silent and he stumbled backward until he bumped against the shack.

As he climbed to his feet, Schwarz watched as Lyons continued to guide the ATV toward the gate. Schwarz moved from his cover and, running in a crouch, moved toward the gate. He could see Lyons climbing off the ATV. Schwarz guessed his comrade was going to search the dead thug for a key card or some other way to unlock the gate. If nothing else, they could climb into the parked SUV and slam it into the gate, Schwarz thought.

By the time he reached the gate, Schwarz saw Lyons swipe a card through a reader. With a jerk, the barrier began to roll open. Lyons went through it while Schwarz covered him.

From their current position, they were diagonal to the house, maybe one hundred yards or so away. Four more hardmen had exited the house. Two of the men were walking several yards apart from one another, each cradling a submachine gun. Jagged flames spit from the muzzles of the weapons as the gunners tried to take Lyons down with an unrelenting onslaught of autofire

The other two hardmen were hanging back. One of the thugs had crouched alongside an exterior wall of the house and was snapping off a couple of quick bursts from an M-16-style assault rifle. From what Schwarz could guess, he was trying to provide cover fire for the other two guards who were making their way toward Lyons. The fourth gunner, an MP-5 held against his hip, was sweeping the weapon's muzzle in the direction of where Schwarz had been crouched moments ago.

Schwarz had loaded a fragmentation round into the launcher. He aimed the weapon at the guy wielding the H&K and fired. The round pounded into the ground a couple of yards from the advancing gunner and exploded with a sharp crack. The sudden swarm of wire shrapnel chewed into the thug, ripping through clothes and flesh, sending him crashing to the ground in a blood-soaked heap. Schwarz broke open the M-203, thumbed another HE shell into it and snapped it closed.

From the corner of his eye, he saw Lyons hosing down the two gunners who'd been marching toward him. As they folded to the ground, Lyons started moving again. Another shooter emerged from behind the house carrying a rocket-propelled grenade launcher. Raising the launcher, he set it on his shoulder and was preparing to fire it. Lyons's M-4 rattled out a sustained burst that cut the man down just before he could fire the RPG's deadly payload.

As they closed in on the front of the house, they heard glass shatter. A hand clutching a pistol poked through one of the first-floor windows and the owner began firing it. Schwarz doused the window with a concentrated volley of 5.56 mm rippers. The bullets shattered what was left of the windowpanes and frame, shredded curtains and chewed into the house's exterior. The arm hung limp from the window, fingers curled; the pistol lay on the front porch.

Lyons moved up to the door. He aimed the KAC-870 Masterkey at the door lock and squeezed the trigger. The cut-down version of the Remington 870 roared and a breaching round punched through the lock. The door swung inward and Lyons went through it.

Lyons tried to size the place up as he moved inside. A large area furnished with a big dining table and hutches with glass doors was located to his left. A wide staircase rose up in front of him. To his right, he caught movement and turned in that direction. He spotted a guy pointing a MAC-10 with a sound suppressor at Lyons. The MAC coughed and a swarm of bullets sliced past his right ear. The former cop's M-4 churned out a short burst that caught the guy in the face and neck, causing most of his skull and neck to disappear in a red mist.

Ejecting the magazine, Lyons grabbed another from his web gear and started to slide it loose from the pouch. A pistol cracked behind him and he felt a bullet tug at his sleeve, tearing through the fabric. With fluid movements, he rammed a fresh magazine into the M-4 and wheeled around to see a muscular guy, head covered with a do-rag, moving down the stairs, a smoking gun clutched in his hand.

Lyons swung his rifle's muzzle toward his enemy and squeezed the trigger, stitching the man across the chest. Bullets punched through flesh and bone, causing half a dozen red geysers to spring up from his battered body. He wobbled on his feet for a moment before gravity took hold and dragged the big man over the stairway railing. He crashed headfirst into the hardwood floor.

The Able Team commander moved through the rest of the first floor, but found no other people. He activated his throat mike.

"Sitrep," he said.

"Took down two more chuckleheads outside," Schwarz said. "I'm coming through the front door."

"Sure, now that the hard work's over."

Schwarz came through the door and gave Lyons a thumbs-up signal.

"There's no basement," Lyons said. He nodded at the stairs. "There's only one way left to go."

"Right."

Lyons moved up the stairs first, with Schwarz right behind him. When they reached the top of the stairs, a corridor stretched out ahead of them, with doors on either side. Lyons used hand signals to tell Schwarz he was going to clear the rooms on the right, while Schwarz should check the rooms on the left.

Lyons checked two rooms without finding anything. When he reached the third door, he stood off to one side and listened for a few heartbeats. He heard a floorboard creak on the other side of the door.

WHAT THE HELL had happened? Castillo wondered. Holed up in his upstairs office, he heard the crackle of gunfire outside the house and could tell it was coming closer. Crossing the room, he stood to one side of the window and chanced a look outside. Two of his guards lay sprawled in the dirt, arms and legs twisted at unnatural angles, the dirt beneath them stained with their blood.

He moved away from the window and with his thumb speed-dialed Lopez. It rang four times and with each successive ring he felt his throat constrict a little more with fear. If he was gone, Castillo wasn't sure who he'd called. He didn't even know the names of his guards, let alone cell numbers or other information, including the one guard stationed in his office with him. They were interchangeable parts as far as he was concerned.

On the fifth ring, someone answered.

"Yeah?" Lopez said.

"What the hell is happening out there?" Castillo asked. The panic in his voice surprised him.

"They sent commandos after us," Lopez replied. "They're chewing through us like a buzz saw. It's insane."

"Kill them," Castillo yelled. "Quit whining and kill them!"

"But—"

Castillo ended the call and stuffed the phone in his pocket. Stripping away his jacket, he tossed it onto the floor and took out his Glock. A shotgun blast from below startled him and prompted him to wheel in the direction of the door. More gunfire rattled inside the house on the first floor.

"They've breached the house, Mr. Castillo," the guard said.

"No shit, idiot."

The guard jerked his head at the window. "We have a rope ladder," he said. "We could lower you to the ground, make a run for the limo."

"Run for the limo? That's your advice? Why don't you just kill me here, moron? It's at least two hundred yards to the garage. They'd shoot us in the back before we covered half of that."

"Sorry, sir, I didn't think…"

"Focus on the door. If the doorknob moves, shoot the door. If someone opens the door, shoot him. If it's one of our guys, too bad."

"Sure, Mr. Castillo."

The shooting downstairs stopped. Castillo gestured for the guard to move closer to the door even as Castillo himself backed away from it. A few seconds later a small red light on the wall blinked. Castillo's already rapid heartbeat kicked into overdrive. Someone had activated a pressure plate on the stairs.

His guard shot him a questioning look, making sure he'd seen the light. He acknowledged the guy with a nod.

Castillo circled behind his desk. Crouching, he used the top to steady his hand as he aimed the Glock at the door.

A loud boom sounded from the other side of the door and sent it swinging inward. Grey-white gun smoke hung in the air and a bulky shape surged through the doorway.

LYONS SLIPPED ANOTHER breaching round into the 870 and aimed the weapon at the doorknob. He probably could kick the door in. But he knew the thunder and smoke that accompanied the breaching round would have a psychological effect on whoever was inside the room, maybe buy him a second before they could regain their wits and start shooting.

With the M-4 in one hand, he drew the Colt Python from his thigh holster and went through the door.

CHAPTER FOURTEEN

Lyons bulled his way into Castillo's office, a vision of hell, bristling with weapons, face covered with a film of trail dust streaked by sweat. The Python was poised in front of him as his eyes swept the room for a target. Instinct told him to clear the doorway. He threw himself forward, the sound of a gunshot echoing in his ears as he struck the floor.

He rolled onto his side and brought up the Python. A thug, pistol extended in a two-handed grip, was lining up another shot at Lyons. The American's Colt barked twice and bullets drilled into the hardman's chest. The impact from the .357 slugs shoved the gunman backward into a wall before his limp body collapsed to the floor.

The Able Team leader brought himself to sitting before hauling himself to his feet. He found Castillo had stepped out of hiding, a Glock clutched in his fist, arm extended at shoulder level. He swung the pistol in Lyons's direction.

"I'll shoot," Castillo said.

Lyons squeezed the Python's trigger. A slug from the big revolver drilled into Castillo's shoulder and jerked him around 180 degrees. An anguished cry erupted from his lips and he let the Glock slip from his fingers.

"Me, too," Lyons said.

The Colt aimed at Castillo, Lyons crossed the floor and kicked the Glock across the room.

The Mexican was on his knees, jaws clenched, eyes

squeezed tight with pain. He'd slapped a hand over the shoulder wound. Blood slipped through his fingers and wound down the contours of the back of his hand.

"Bastard!" he hissed through clenched teeth.

Looping the M-4's strap over his shoulders, Lyons reached down. His now-empty hand lashed out and he grabbed a handful of Castillo's shirt. Yanking him to his feet, he spun him ninety degrees and with a hard shove sent him sprawling into a nearby couch.

"Get comfortable," Lyons said. "It's time for us to talk."

AL-JABALLAH HAMMERED the heel of his fist against the top of the table. The impact caused his teacup to rattle in the saucer and the round plastic ashtray to jump. The Browning Hi-Power that lay on the table stayed still.

He leaned forward, positioning his face less than a foot from the screen of his laptop. Escobar's face stared back at him through an encrypted transmission. His black eyes looked dull, unconcerned.

"You lost how many people?" al-Jaballah asked, the disbelief evident in his voice.

"More than a dozen," Escobar replied.

"How many more than a dozen?"

"Don't know. We're still counting."

"Still counting? This is unacceptable!"

He saw Escobar's lip curl up in a sneer, and the impulse to throw a punch at the computer screen welled up inside him.

"I've lost maybe a couple dozen men in the past twenty-four hours," the Mexican said. "Quit your crying, you old woman. I'm the one taking the beating here."

"Bastard! Pull it together or…"

"Or what? You'll work me over? Maybe make me the target of an elite commando team? Apparently, I'm already there, amigo. It's going to take me months, if not years, to rebuild."

"If this falls apart," al-Jaballah said, "you won't get your money. Tell me… How will you rebuild with no money?"

Escobar's lips pressed into a bloodless line. Al-Jaballah thought he saw uncertainty flicker in the other man's eyes, just for a moment, before his gaze hardened again and another sneer formed on his lips.

"Don't even think about screwing me over," Escobar warned. "It will not turn out well for you."

Al-Jaballah laughed and leaned back in his chair. Taking a crumpled pack of cigarettes from his shirt pocket, he shook one into his palm and stuck it between his lips. He patted his pants' pockets for his lighter.

"What will you do, my friend?" al-Jaballah said. "You said it yourself. Your organization is broken. I have many resources to draw from. I'd prefer to pour them into the job at hand. But, if you want to threaten and undermine me…" He shrugged and focused on lighting his cigarette.

"Fine," Escobar said, his voice cold. "What's our next move?"

"My next move," al-Jaballah replied, "is to decide whether I can trust you. To do anything."

Leaning forward, he slammed the laptop's lid shut and smiled. Chew on that, he thought.

He rose from his chair and moved away from the table. The small sense of victory was almost immediately extinguished by worry. The events in Mexico were more than an inconvenience; they put everything—the years of careful planning, the huge investment of money, the hundreds of hours of training—at risk. Failure could very well put al-Jaballah's whole operation at risk. While he had supporters, not everyone in the Iranian government supported al-Jaballah or the Circle. For some in the Revolutionary Guard and Hezbollah, his operation was a competitor for money, resources and attention.

The handful of moderates who knew about the group considered it the equivalent of a live grenade, pin pulled and ready to explode. They feared the Circle. They feared him, in particular, almost as much as they feared the mullahs running the country. His organization undertook high-risk missions, the kind that—if discovered—could ignite wars. Inside the country, he kept files on anyone who showed the slightest qualms about the government. In some cases, such as with Revolutionary Guard and Hezbollah commanders, he'd fabricated entire dossiers, pictures, films, anything to put their balls in a vise. He'd destroyed dozens of men, many by his own hand, others from a distance.

If he failed in this latest venture, there'd be no shortage of his countrymen waiting to tear him apart, put him in the grave.

So he couldn't fail. Escobar remained useful for the moment. But if he became a liability? He'd end up dead. The same went for the American commandos. His phone buzzed, letting him know he'd received a text message.

Crushing his cigarette in a nearby ashtray, he wheeled around, headed back to his desk and picked up his phone. He read the message once and then reread it. He shook his head in disbelief.

He read it once more.

Ran the picture. She's Mossad.

He called and had another conversation with Escobar, this one even more unpleasant than the last.

SCHWARZ WAS APPLYING a field dressing to the shoulder wound of Castillo, who was still seated on the couch. He'd cut away most of Castillo's shirt, which had been soaked with blood, and taped a dressing over the wound to staunch the blood. With his index finger, he pushed down the last strip of tape against Castillo's skin before standing and taking a step back.

He stared down at Escobar's lieutenant and scowled.

"Seems a waste," Schwarz said, "to patch this son of a bitch up when we're just going to put more holes in him."

Castillo's eyes darted to Schwarz, then to Lyons and back to Schwarz, as though gauging whether the Americans were kidding.

"You won't kill me," he said.

"Thanks for the heads-up on that," Lyons said. "I'm guessing your guards would offer another opinion—if they weren't sprawled on the ground, drawing flies."

"They drew on you first. You had to kill them. I'm not armed. Hell, I'm wearing handcuffs. If you kill me, it's cold-blooded murder."

"Or justice," Schwarz said. "Depends on your perspective."

"Besides," Lyons said, "if we killed you, who the hell would know? It's not like your buddies are going to tell anyone anything."

Castillo licked his lips and shuddered. Lyons guessed the guy would go into shock pretty soon.

Schwarz, who was applying another dressing to the exit wound on Castillo's back, chuckled. "You're lucky," he said to Lyons. "The bullet went clean through. Didn't hit bone. Even has a small exit wound."

Lyons scowled. "Next time, I'm breaking out the hollowpoint bullets. No sense shooting someone with a .357 if it's not going to make a big hole."

"True," Schwarz said. "Maybe it's the bullets. Maybe you're just losing your touch. Ten years ago, you'd have knocked his entire shoulder out. The shock and the blood loss would've killed him. I would've been screaming at you for killing him before we could get any information. But now he's alive."

"For the moment," Lyons growled.

Castillo swallowed hard. "You're insane," he said.

He leaned into the back of the couch, but immediately groaned in pain and sat forward to ease the pressure on his wounds.

"You're wasting your time," Castillo said. "Your friend is dead. He has to be."

Lyons's neck and cheeks turned bright scarlet with rage. He took a step forward and Castillo flinched before Lyons checked himself.

"Where the hell is he?"

"I told you—"

"You didn't tell us dick," Lyons replied. "Where is he?"

Castillo shifted on the couch and his face screwed up in pain. "I want something for this," he said. "You have to give me something for the pain."

Lyons nodded slowly. "You'll get something," he said. "First, though, you have to tell us where our friend is. Then we can help you."

"You're lying. You're not going to help."

"That your final answer?" Lyons asked. "If it is, you're screwed. We could just leave you to bleed out."

"Bullshit. I have information. You need it."

Lyons shrugged. "Maybe," he said. "Maybe we can get it somewhere else."

Looking away from Castillo, he ran his eyes over the large room's interior. "We take your computers, your cell phones, have our people go through them. In no time at all, we'll figure out where he is."

"In the meantime," Schwarz added, "we leave your body out there for the vultures and the foxes to gnaw on. My friend and I like to travel light."

"Son of a bitch!"

"Where is he?"

The Mexican squeezed his eyes shut and, after a few seconds, licked his lips.

"Escobar's in Paraguay. That means your friend went to Paraguay, too."

"What the hell's there?"

"Training camp."

"For?"

Castillo's eyelids looked heavy and Lyons guessed the guy was going into shock.

"Coordinates," Lyons barked. "Where's the camp?"

Castillo muttered the numbers and Lyons committed them to memory. He guessed Schwarz had done likewise.

Lyons asked, "What's the training camp for?"

"Hezbollah. Some other Shiite groups."

"Wait," Schwarz interjected, "Escobar's running a summer camp for Hezbollah?"

"It's a training camp."

"Why does he have it?" Lyons asked. "And why does he give a crap about the Shiites?"

"He doesn't give a crap about them," Castillo countered.

"So it's a money thing?" Schwarz asked.

"No," Castillo said.

"Then why the camp?"

Castillo shook his head.

"Not sure," he said. "Not completely, anyway. Not many people know this, but he's only half Mexican. His father was Iranian."

"So he's trying to help the Iranians?" Lyons asked.

Castillo snorted. "He doesn't help anyone." Castillo fell silent. The creases in his forehead deepened. He opened his mouth to speak once, twice. "What the hell? You guys are going to toss me in a hole somewhere, right?"

Neither of the Able Team warriors said anything.

"I guess Escobar knew nothing about his father growing up. Maybe he knew the guy was from Iran or something, I don't know. But that was it. A few years ago this guy, Ahmed al-Jaballah, an Iranian, grabbed him in Argentina. Told him all these wild stories about his padre. How he'd been a spy. How he'd been part of an ultra-secret paramilitary unit for the Muslim government. I don't remember all the crazy stuff. Escobar told me bits and pieces. I dismissed most of it as crap until…"

"Until?" Schwarz asked.

"He bought some property in Paraguay, a coffee plantation. Dumped lots of cash into it. Not his own money. The Iranians and Hezbollah coughed up most of it. If they hadn't, he wouldn't have built the place. He doesn't care about their politics. I just think he's scared of the Iranians and wanted to give them what they wanted."

"What about al-Jaballah?" Schwarz asked. "What do you know about him?"

"Nothing. I met him a couple of times. Coordinated some weapons shipments for him. Otherwise, I stayed out of it. This whole thing was just a distraction, far as I'm concerned."

Lyons and Schwarz asked a few more questions about the facility, but Castillo knew little else about it. "He kept most of it from me, and I didn't want to know. I have enough to worry about. We move weapons all over the globe. Escobar has a fleet of airplanes that need to be maintained. That stuff doesn't just take care of itself. You know what I mean?"

"Not easy being a high roller," Schwarz said.

He turned to look at Lyons when something caught his eye. A glass cabinet stood against a wall, several feet behind Castillo's couch, and the door leading into the room was reflected in the glass. The silhouette of a man filled the doorway.

Schwarz reacted quickly. He tackled Lyons, hitting the bigger man in the torso and knocking him off his feet. They fell to the ground; Lyons landing on his back, Schwarz landing on top of him. Gunshots rang out. Schwarz rolled off Lyons and came up in a crouch, the muzzle of his compact M-4 searching for a target.

The man in the doorway swung the smoking barrel of his Beretta toward the Americans. Schwarz's M-4 churned out a fast burst and a ragged line opened up along his opponent's chest, killing him.

At the same time, the roar of another gunshot filled the room. Schwarz whipped his head in the direction of Castillo in time to see a geyser of blood sprouting up from the guy's chest, his body tumbling backward, rolling to the floor in a dead heap.

Schwarz looked at Lyons, who was sitting on the floor, the Python extended forward in a two-handed grip. Smoke curled from the Colt's muzzle. Lyons hauled himself to his feet and holstered the Colt.

"I guess it's Paraguay or bust," Schwarz said.

CHAPTER FIFTEEN

Blancanales wasn't sure how long he had been unconscious when he finally came to.

A faint musty smell registered with him and even through the fabric of his trousers, the floor felt hard and cold against his legs and buttocks. He also caught traces of cologne and cigarette smoke in the air. The smells were too weak to be current. Had someone watched him while he'd been unconscious? Probably.

His skull throbbed from the hit he'd taken. His mouth was dry and he could still taste blood. He must have been restrained at some point; he could see the marks where handcuffs had bit into his wrists, and his hands felt heavy, numb.

Where the hell was he? He strained his ears. He could hear voices. The words were muffled, as though coming through a wall or a door, which seemed likely. But they also were gaining in volume and he guessed the speakers were heading for his cell.

He heard the door lock release and the door swing open. His breath caught in his throat and the muscles of his shoulders tensed as he steeled himself for whatever was next. One guard, a grim-faced SOB, filled the doorway and glared at Blancanales. He raised his left hand and Blancanales saw a pair of handcuffs dangling from the guy's curled index finger.

A second guard stood behind the first, positioned in the hallway, an AK-74 held in his hands.

"Get up," the SOB in the doorway ordered.

Blancanales hesitated for a couple of heartbeats. His warrior's mind automatically began to run the numbers. The guy with the handcuffs had a pistol holstered on his waist and his hand rested heavily on its grip. Maybe ten feet lay between Blancanales and the guard. Blancanales's head still hurt like hell, and his muscles were stiff from spending an untold amount of time unconscious and inactive. Then there was the second guard who was glowering at him, looking more than happy to put a bullet in Blancanales's head.

Yeah, Blancanales could try to make a stand. But he'd end up dead. Not that he was afraid to die; he'd had too many close scrapes in his career to sweat death. But his gut told him now wasn't his time. Maybe he still could pull this out.

He hauled himself to his feet, took a step forward, but let his hands dangle at his sides.

The hardman tossed the handcuffs at Blancanales, who snagged them in midair.

"Put them on," the SOB said. "Escobar wants to see you."

Blancanales slapped a ring around his left wrist and then cinched the remaining ring around his other wrist. He let his hands hang in front, fingers curled into fists.

The guard led him from the cell. The one who'd been standing in the hallway walked behind Blancanales, occasionally nudging him in the back with the muzzle of his AK-74. The other hardman walked next to the Stony Man warrior. They probably figured he wasn't about to run. And, for the moment at least, they were right.

As he walked Blancanales felt the stiffness in his legs begin to ease.

"How long have I been here?" he asked.

Neither guard answered him.

They led him into an elevator. The guy with the assault rifle went in first, followed by Blancanales and the other thug. The guard who'd handed over the cuffs jabbed the first-floor button on the elevator's control panel. Blancanales glanced up at the number bar over the door and saw that he was being kept on the third floor of the building.

When the elevator doors parted, Blancanales stepped for the door to see how the others would react. Neither man made a move to stop him, which told him they were confident he wasn't going to escape. He exited the elevator and found himself in a cavernous room with smooth concrete floors, the overhead steel beams exposed.

Along one wall stood several bunk beds; lockers lined another wall. The room almost reminded him of a military barracks. Unlike his cell and the corridors on the upper floors, the air in this room was hot, still and thick, reminding him of a jungle climate. A door along the wall with the lockers was open and the sunlight coming through it and the windows provided the only illumination.

From somewhere outside the building, he could hear the rhythmic slapping of feet against the ground, accompanied by an occasional shout by someone in command.

What he saw on a third wall caused a cold sensation to race down his back, and he had to suppress a shudder. A yellow flag was draped over it. In the center was the green silhouette of a hand clutching an AK-47 rifle.

It was the Hezbollah flag.

THE GUARD with the rifle jabbed Blancanales in the spine with the barrel. Blancanales turned his head and glared at the guy, who gave him a nasty smile.

"You recognize that?" the guard asked.

"What? You don't?" Blancanales replied.

The thug's smile evaporated. He raised his rifle, the barrel sliding over his shoulder and the rifle butt slowly arcing in Blancanales's direction.

The Stony Man fighter thought he might try to hit him in the back of the head with the rifle. The warrior tensed, ready to dart to one side and let the guy hit air if he tried to strike him. Instead the other guard pushed Mr. Kalashnikov to one side and gestured with his chin at the door.

Saying nothing, Blancanales turned and headed for the door. As he neared it, he could hear someone yelling in a tone that reminded him of a drill sergeant, even if the words were in Arabic. Why would Escobar, a Mexican national, be mixed up with Hezbollah? The latter was a Lebanon-based terrorist group; one with ties to Iran. Was Escobar providing weapons to them? And, if so, was that his only link to al-Jaballah?

He stepped through the door and found himself squinting against the sun for a few seconds as his eyes adjusted to the sudden onslaught of natural light. As his eyes got used to the sunlight, he swept his gaze over his surroundings. He was standing on a pad of concrete that extended out from the building maybe twenty feet before it gave way to a wide expanse of bare earth that stretched the distance of two football fields. A high fence topped with razor wire surrounded the property.

He saw a group of maybe two dozen men, all dressed in desert camouflage uniforms, running in formation around the big property. A cluster of people stood at the edge of the concrete, watching the fighters as they ran. Blancanales immediately recognized Vargas, who cast a sidelong glance at him before turning her eyes away. He also recognized Escobar and realized after a couple of seconds that Castillo was nowhere to be seen, which struck him as significant.

Where the hell was Escobar's second in command, especially if they were in the middle of a crisis?

One of the guards gave Blancanales a hard shove in the back. He stumbled forward a couple of steps before he could regain his footing.

"Go," the hardman ordered.

Blancanales whipped around and saw the guard with the pistol sneering at him.

"Hope you enjoyed that," the warrior said. "It's going to cost you."

The guy jerked his chin at the cluster of people. "Escobar's over there," he said.

Blancanales turned back around and walked toward the group.

Escobar broke away from the others and rolled up to Blancanales, who stopped a few yards away from the gunrunner.

"You're awake? Good." Escobar nodded over his shoulder at the group. "Nikki over there…she was worried maybe we'd dosed you too heavily. I wasn't, though. You're a big man. I'm sure you can take it."

Blancanales held the other man's stare, but said nothing.

"Quiet, huh? Understandable after all you've been through. I'm sure you're heartsick about what happened in Mexico City, losing your friend, Ortega."

"No friend of mine," Blancanales said. He nodded in the direction of Vargas, who was walking toward them. "Your girlfriend on the other hand was fairly close to him."

One corner of Escobar's lips curled up into a slight smile. He shook his head.

"There was nothing there," he said. "I knew they were talking."

Blancanales decided to twist the knife. Get into Escobar's head. He guessed the weapons broker didn't "love" the woman at his side. But he sure as hell wouldn't want to share her, either, especially with someone like Ortega, who he probably considered somehow below him.

The Stony Man warrior smirked.

"Talking? Is that Spanish for 'screwing'?"

Escobar, his eyes narrowing into slits, took a step forward, cocked back his fist and rocketed it forward at Blancanales's head. He'd telegraphed it enough that Blancanales was able to thrust his head back and roll with the punch. Even so, the force of the blow threw his head to one side.

The taste of blood filled his mouth. He gathered up a glob of saliva and blood and spit it on Escobar's shoes.

"Hijo de puta," the crime lord said.

Blancanales raised his handcuffed wrists, gave them a slight shake so the chain rattled.

"Slip these off, hero, and we can have a real discussion."

Escobar hesitated and seemed to consider the challenge. Blancanales wasn't surprised. By now, the Hezbollah thugs had clustered together several yards away. A couple of men, both neatly dressed, with olive complexions and black hair, had moved in closer to stand next to Vargas. A few of Escobar's hardmen had formed a half circle behind him, eyes alternating between the two men facing one another.

It was the oldest trick in the book. Blancanales had put the bastard on the spot. A guy—a prisoner in handcuffs, no less—was challenging him. Escobar needed to act. His hand slipped inside his linen jacket and, judging by the murderous look in his eyes, the Able Team warrior guessed he wasn't looking for the keys to the handcuffs.

Blancanales at this point really didn't care how the guy responded. He was just trying to buy time, enough that maybe Lyons and Schwarz would ride in to the rescue. Or enough that he could get some information about Escobar's plans.

The Mexican crime lord was bringing his hand from beneath his jacket.

Vargas stepped between them and rested a hand on Escobar's forearm.

"You're forgetting your guests," she said, her voice soft.

Escobar whipped his head in her direction, eyes beaming pure rage. He jerked his arm away from her, but when his hand came into view from beneath his jacket, it was empty.

An instant later his expression went flat again, as though the rage had just evaporated. He grabbed his lapels, straightened his jacket and gave her a curt nod.

"I should check on our guests," he said.

He fixed his eyes back on Blancanales.

"Take him back to his cell. I'll deal with him later."

CHAPTER SIXTEEN

Blancanales stood in the middle of his cell, massaging his right wrist, where the cuffs had bit into the skin, with the fingers of his left hand. The last of the guards backed out through the cell door and slammed it shut.

This time the SOB had put some distance between himself and Blancanales. He'd tossed him the keys, directed him to unlock the cuffs and toss back the keys. The other guy had kept his assault rifle locked on Blancanales, which seemed like overkill since he was unarmed. But apparently they weren't used to someone, especially a prisoner, busting Escobar's balls. That made him a little more dangerous and them a little more uneasy.

Mission accomplished.

I'll deal with him later.

Escobar's words—and the menace behind them—echoed through Blancanales's mind. His brief encounter with Escobar had left him with more questions than answers. Why the hell was Escobar training Hezbollah fighters in the middle of a South American jungle? Did he have links with Hezbollah itself or with Iran? How deep did the ties go?

All good questions, Blancanales told himself. Unfortunately, under the current circumstances, solving mysteries was a luxury he couldn't afford. His first priority was to stay alive. If he uncovered information along the way, so much the better. But first he needed to survive.

"EXCUSE ME FOR a moment, gentlemen," Escobar said to his two guests.

Before either man could answer, Escobar turned, grabbed Vargas by the upper arm and squeezed hard. She winced and he felt a small sense of satisfaction spread through him. He guided her away from his visitors and his hired muscle.

Escobar's two guests were high-ranking members of the Iranian Revolutionary Guard. One was a general, with a pipeline directly to the mullahs who pulled the strings in Iran. The other was a colonel who, in spite of his military rank, spent much of his time running the IRG's private ventures, such as trading in counterfeit electronics and cigarettes, as well as some construction ventures in South America and Africa. In other words, he generated the money paying for this training facility.

Once they'd put some distance between themselves and the Iranians, Vargas jerked her arm away from Escobar.

"You son of a bitch," she snapped. "What's wrong with you?"

"I want more information from Perez."

Escobar's sudden change in direction seemed to surprise the woman.

"Information?"

"Information. Who the hell is he? Who does he work for? What was his connection to Ortega?"

"You manhandled me just to tell me that?"

"Get me some answers."

"Didn't you say Ortega worked for the Justice Department? Can't you just check with your sources there?"

He shook his head. "We already checked and came up with nothing. We sent photos and physical descriptions to our people in Washington. They found no pictures, no nothing in any of the files."

"Maybe he really was trying to buy weapons for the Colombians. Just because Ortega was working undercover doesn't mean this guy is lying."

"Maybe that's what you want to believe."

"What?"

"You heard me."

"I can run his picture again."

Escobar shook his head. "We've already tried that. No, we need to push him a little harder."

He saw something flicker in her eyes before they went flat again. She gave a small shrug. "I can do that," she said.

"I don't want you to do that."

"Then what? You're talking in circles."

"Get Javier. Tell him to bring his tools. He can work on this son of a bitch."

She stiffened at the mention of Javier's name. She hoped Escobar didn't notice.

"Javier might kill him in the process."

"I have no issue with that. I just want answers. He's just one more dead *federale* to me. And he probably won't be the last. Now, go, deal with it."

She opened her mouth to say something else. Before she could utter a word, Escobar wheeled around and walked away, rejoining the IRG commanders.

A SHUDDER PASSED through Vargas as she stared after him. He knew. She'd betrayed him and he knew it. That meant only one thing: if he had his way, she was going to die. Maybe today. Maybe tomorrow. But it was going to happen.

She had to do something. Maybe run. Maybe try to kill Escobar. Whatever. But she had to act or she'd be dead.

Turning on a heel, she headed back into Escobar's stronghold. She would call Javier. Not calling him would only compound Escobar's suspicions. Though she'd called

Javier on Escobar's behalf before, she'd never met him.
What she did know was downright chilling. From everything she'd heard, he was at least as soulless as Escobar; little more than a bag of meat, a working body, with no heart.
At one point he'd been a special forces soldier in the Mexican army, but had proved too unstable for the work. So the
cartels had picked him up as an enforcer. He was good as
hired muscle, but even better as a torturer and interrogator.

If Javier was turned loose on Perez, the guy was as
good as dead.

So what? If Perez was a gunrunner, a man willing to
arm terrorists, maybe she should let Javier tear him apart.
It'd buy her some time to flee and also guarantee that at
least one last bad guy died.

But what if Perez wasn't another criminal? What if he
was working against Escobar? If she left him to die, she
could claim plausible deniability to her superiors. They
might suspect she'd offered him up as a sacrifice—if they
even knew about Perez, which was unlikely.

It didn't matter, she told herself. She'd know that maybe
she'd left an innocent man to die. She'd never be able to
live with herself.

She returned to her makeshift office on the building's
second floor, unlocked her desk and pulled out a secure
satellite phone, the one Escobar had provided, not her own.
She dialed Javier's number and waited for him to answer.

CHAPTER SEVENTEEN

Seated on the cot in his cell, Blancanales closed his eyes, tilted his head back and rested it against the cool brick wall at his back. The image of the Hezbollah flag flashed in his imagination and his eyes snapped open again. Though he had no clock, Blancanales was certain it'd been a couple of hours since his encounter with Escobar, and Hezbollah's presence still puzzled him.

He probably shouldn't be surprised, he told himself. Even though Escobar was Mexican, he had links to the Iranians, who were in bed with Hezbollah. Escobar would be an obvious choice to sell weapons to Hezbollah, especially to its operatives in South America, but to run a training camp? Blancanales wasn't sure he saw the connection. Pretty soon it might not matter. If he didn't figure out a way to escape, he was good as dead himself.

The sound of the security bolt being pulled back jerked him from his thoughts. Setting his gaze on the door, he pushed himself to the edge of the cot. The door swung inward and Blancanales saw another stranger standing in the doorway. He pegged the guy at maybe five feet, eight inches tall, with a slight build and a disproportionately large head that made him look like an alien. The guy wore a blue Oxford-cloth shirt, khakis, black wing tips, and carried a briefcase in his left hand.

He stepped through the door, three of Escobar's heavies flanking him, and moved up on Blancanales. His hair had receded, exposing his wide forehead. He regarded Blancanales quietly, tilting his head to one side and sucking at his teeth as he did. Probably a minute passed in near silence before one corner of the guy's mouth twitched.

"You'll break," he said.

A FOURTH GUARD stepped through the door, this one carrying a wooden chair. When he set the chair on the ground, the alien-looking guy stepped aside and the guards closed in on Blancanales. The room was small, which forced the guards to move in a small knot. Blancanales sprang to his feet and threw a fist into the nearest face. A nose caved under his knuckles and spurted blood. Fingers wrapped around him. He wheeled a quarter of a turn and his foot came up in a vicious arc, the top of his ankle smacking into another thug's balls. The guy groaned and staggered back.

From his peripheral vision, he caught something hurtling at his face.

Before he could react, a fist caught him in the side of the face. The force of the blow spun him around and staggered him. He saw the guard, a scowling gorilla with his fist cocked back, moving in. As the guy launched a second punch at the Able Team warrior, Blancanales threw up a forearm to block the punch and put all his weight behind a counterpunch that he buried in his opponent's gut. The guy's jaw fell open, he belched out the contents of his lungs and staggered back a couple of steps before he lost his footing and fell on his ass.

Blancanales sensed Mr. Bighead moving in at him from his left and he wheeled in the guy's direction. Suddenly he felt a stinging sensation as something sharp buried itself in his chest, followed by twin talons of fire digging into his flesh. His body collapsed to the floor and he could hear himself screaming in pain. Just as the fire in his chest subsided, his eyes opened and he struggled to catch his breath. He opened his eyes in time to catch sight of a black blur hurtling at him. An instant of sharp pain erupted in his temple before he slipped into a black abyss.

SOMETHING FRIGID SMACKED into Blancanales, stung his skin and jerked him from the blackness. His eyes snapped open. Water and light seeped into them even before he could take in his surroundings. He tried to bring his hands up to shield his face, but found they wouldn't move.

The sensation of steel cutting into his wrists told him his hands were cuffed. As the water rolled down the contours of his face and onto his neck and chest, he tried to suppress a shiver, but failed. He saw Mr. Bighead standing in front of him. The slender man had donned a leather apron that reached down to his knees. Dark stains that Blancanales assumed were blood occasionally interrupted its smooth brown surface.

The little man had rolled up his sleeves to the elbow and sheathed his hands in leather gloves. His arms were crossed over his narrow chest and his eyes were fixed on Blancanales with cold detachment. The Able Team fighter glanced to his right and saw that a small metal table had been moved in. It was topped with several electric surgical saws, a few scalpels and a plastic face shield that he could use to keep his face from getting splattered with blood.

Blancanales felt his mouth turn dry and his heart rate began to accelerate as he took things in. Judging by the little psycho's tools, Blancanales only could imagine what he was about to face.

One of Escobar's hardmen—a muscular guy with three teardrops tattooed under his right eye—leaned against the wall, arms crossed over his chest, his expression neutral. A Kalashnikov rifle was slung over his left shoulder.

"Welcome back, Mr. Perez. My name is Javier," the little man said, his voice flat.

He took a step forward. He paused at the table and picked through the selection of scalpels before picking one up. He held it in front of his face and studied the blade for a few seconds before continuing toward the American.

"I have some questions," he said.

"If it's 'do you need a shrink?'" Blancanales said, "the answer is yes."

Javier smiled serenely. "You think I'm crazy?"

"People who like to cut on other people usually are."

The other man shook his head.

"It's just business."

By now he was right next to Blancanales. He stood there, very still, and Blancanales felt his own breath hang in his throat. The guy obviously was a pro; one who knew the anticipation of pain could be just as bad as the pain itself. Blancanales heard the soles of the man's black wing tips scuff against the concrete and his stomach plummeted. A second later Javier appeared on the opposite side. He leaned forward.

"Who are you?"

"My name is Perez. I already told Escobar and Ortega."

"Who are you really?"

"Perez."

"Bullshit."

"Suit yourself."

Javier straightened and looked at the guard.

"Soften him up a little."

The guard scowled, as though holding up the wall was more important. He slipped the AK-74's strap from his shoulder, bent down, leaned the weapon against the wall, crossed the room and stood in front of Blancanales. Bringing his right hand up, he brought it down in a blur. The knuckles smacked into Blancanales's cheek and whipped his head sideways. The hardman hit him twice more in the same fashion before Javier said, "That's enough."

The guard shrugged, turned, returned to his spot on the wall and studied the back of his hand.

Blancanales's cheek stung and blood was filling his mouth. His left eye was tearing up and already beginning to swell.

Javier stood in front of him again, spindly arms crossed over his chest, his black eyes studying Blancanales's injured face, like a scientist studying a tumor on a lab rat.

"Did that hurt?" Javier asked.

The soldier gathered up a mouthful of blood and saliva and spit it on the floor just in front of Javier. If the guy had been close enough, Blancanales could kick him, shatter his kneecap. But the guy was just out of range, probably to prevent that from happening. Blancanales guessed the psycho was better at dealing pain than enduring it.

"I asked you a question," Javier said. "Did that hurt?"

"You're a weird one," Blancanales replied. "You know that?"

Something flickered in Javier's eyes. Blancanales knew he'd hit a nerve. Now that he'd opened a wound, he decided to jam a thumb into it, see if he could make the guy howl. Maybe he could shake the guy's concentration. Or maybe he'd just piss the little psycho off enough that he'd kill him quickly instead of skinning and gutting him like a river carp.

Blancanales smirked. "Weird. Weird. Weird."

Javier stared at the warrior for several seconds, but said nothing.

"You have a weird uncle? You know, some freak who yanked on your junk?"

The tattooed muscleman, still staring at the floor, snickered. Javier whipped around and shot him a dirty look. The thug replied with a bored look and flipped his middle finger at Mr. Bighead.

"Don't look at him, freak," Blancanales said. "I'm talking to you."

Javier spun back around, fingers wrapped around the scalpel's handle, the blade jutting forward. Rage flashing in his eyes, he stalked toward Blancanales, the scalpel's blade gleaming. He walked a wide circle around Blancanales, still aware enough to keep out of range of Blancanales's feet, and moved to the Able Team warrior's side. He grabbed a handful of the American's hair, yanked his head back, exposing his throat, and pulled back the hand clutching the scalpel, ready to bury it in Blancanales's throat.

Send For
2 FREE BOOKS
Today!

I accept your offer!

Please send me two free
novels and a mystery gift (gift
worth about $5). I understand
that these books are completely
free—even the shipping and
handling will be paid—and
I am under no obligation
to purchase anything, ever, as
explained on the back of this card.

166/366 ADL F495

Please Print

FIRST NAME

LAST NAME

ADDRESS

APT.#   CITY

STATE/PROV.   ZIP/POSTAL CODE

Visit us online at
www.ReaderService.com

▶ Detach card and mail today. No stamp needed. ▶ GE-O2D/13-GF-13

NO POSTAGE
NECESSARY
IF MAILED
IN THE
UNITED STATES

BUSINESS REPLY MAIL

FIRST-CLASS MAIL   PERMIT NO. 717   BUFFALO, NY

POSTAGE WILL BE PAID BY ADDRESSEE

HARLEQUIN READER SERVICE

PO BOX 1867

BUFFALO NY 14240-9952

CHAPTER EIGHTEEN

When Vargas reached the security door leading into the bedroom she shared with Escobar, she reached up to punch in the security code. She hesitated, hand poised over the keypad.

The short hairs on the back of her neck rose and she threw a glance over her shoulder to see whether someone had followed her, whether she was being watched. It was a reflexive move, one driven by emotion instead of logic. Security cameras were poised at either end of the long corridor and, since it was Escobar's floor, someone, somewhere probably was watching. Fortunately, Escobar didn't have security cameras in their room.

She quickly punched in the code. The control emitted a small beep, the lock clicked open and she pushed open the door and moved inside.

The room was large, but sparsely furnished—a large bed, a pair of dressers and a small makeup table for her. She scanned the interior and felt a jolt of fear pass through her when she didn't immediately see her suitcase. Crossing the room, she threw open the closet doors, saw her suitcase standing inside the cramped space and felt herself relax at least a little.

She yanked the suitcase from inside the closet, carried it to the bed and heaved it on its side onto the mattress. Pulling a small key from her pants' pocket, she unlocked the suitcase, pulled open the top and, using her fingertips, gathered some of the fabric in the lower right corner. She peeled back a small corner of the fabric, revealing part of a sheet of Kevlar that made up a false bottom for the suitcase.

She ripped the fabric from inside the case, unlocked the false panel and pulled it from the suitcase, revealing several molded plastic compartments. Picking up the 9 mm Glock and a magazine, she loaded a magazine into the grip and jacked a round into the chamber. Pulling a custom-made sound suppressor from the case, she threaded it into the Glock's muzzle. She set the weapon on the mattress and pulled a leather shoulder holster from inside the case and slipped it on. With the suppressor, she couldn't fit the Glock in the holster, though the rig did contain three additional clips in a pouch. A Gerber folding knife went into her pocket. Finally she pulled out a shoulder bag stuffed with a satellite phone, U.S. currency and a fake passport, and set it aside.

With everything going to hell in the past twenty-four hours, she'd failed to check in with her Mossad handler. Now, as far as he was concerned, she'd disappeared, which likely had set off alarms back in Tel Aviv. Add to that Ortega's death and the other bloodletting in Mexico City and she guessed her people were sweating.

She needed to contact them, yeah. But first she needed to get away from Escobar. She knew without him saying a word that her cover was blown. Given enough time, he'd kill her. She didn't plan on giving him that much time.

She needed to get out of here. Fast.

Before that could happen, though, she had to help Perez.

As THE ELEVATOR carried her to the first floor, Vargas felt sweat gathering on her palm. She tightened her grip on the Glock. Before leaving their quarters, she had donned a light jacket to cover the shoulder holster she wore. She had slid the Glock into her shoulder bag so she could hide it from the surveillance cameras. Once the shooting began, she knew she'd have a minute or two before Escobar's men realized what was happening and came for them.

Two minutes. Not much time. But she'd have to make it work.

The elevator door slid open. She eased through the opening and swept her gaze over the main lobby of the building, looking for threats. Through a set of glass doors, she could see a pair of guards standing outside. One was smoking a cigarette, the other was staring at the screen of a smartphone.

Vargas crossed the lobby and moved to a black security door on the back wall. She punched a code into the keypad to unlock the door and passed through it into a short hallway.

She slid the Glock from her bag and glided along the wall. The smell of cigarette smoke registered with her and she heard a man cough. A few yards ahead, a second corridor would branch off from this one. That was where she'd find Perez.

Pausing at the edge of the doorway, she glanced around the corner and saw one of Escobar's guards, his back to her, staring at a wall and puffing a cigarette. She'd met him earlier in the day. His name was Enrique, and he'd boasted that he would be chief of security in six months.

Maybe not.

She went around the corner, leveled the Glock at his back and squeezed the trigger. A pair of 9 mm slugs drilled into the guy's back, severing his spine and tearing through his heart. Blood burst from his chest and splattered on the wall. He wobbled for a stretched second before his knees buckled and he crashed to the ground.

It'd been years since she'd killed someone. The last time,

it had been a kill-or-be-killed situation, where a Hezbollah operative had drawn down on her and she'd taken him out with a bullet to the forehead. This time she'd shot a man in the back, and she knew it'd bother her. For the moment, though, she forced herself to ignore the crumpled form on the floor, the gleaming crimson sunburst covering the wall, and instead head for the cell door.

She hesitated. She'd have to enter a security code to unlock this door, too. That meant Javier and anyone else in the room would hear the electronic beeps as she punched in the numbers. They'd be expecting someone to enter—just not her.

She hoped.

She entered the code, unlocked the door and shoved it inward.

Javier stood next to Perez, clutching a handful of his hair, waving a scalpel in his face.

A guard—a muscle-bound man she'd seen earlier—was leaning against the wall, arms crossed over his chest, head turned toward the door. For whatever reason, when he saw it was her, he started to smile. Even though Javier was threatening Perez, the guard had a gun, making him the bigger threat. He needed to be neutralized first.

She raised the Glock and his smile faltered. The pistol coughed once and a 9 mm slug pounded into his forehead, snapping his skull back hard.

From the corner of her eye, she could see Javier let go of Perez's head and sprint for something.

Nikki didn't wait to see whether he was dead. She swiveled ninety degrees, locked Javier in her sights and fired twice.

One of the bullets lanced into his chest and released a geyser of blood before it tore through his torso and punched a grapefruit-size hole in his back when it exited.

When she turned her attention to Perez. He eyed her warily.

"I'm here to help," she said.

He nodded once. "Okay," he said.

"Where are the keys to your handcuffs?"

He shook his head. "Not sure. I was unconscious when they put these things on."

Cursing under her breath, she moved to the table and quickly picked through the surgical tools, scalpels and other implements lying there. Finally she found a set of keys under a saw and unlocked his cuffs.

Blancanales hauled himself from the chair and headed for the downed guard. Kneeling next to the corpse, he grabbed the AK-74 that had slid from the dead guy's shoulder and onto the floor.

Vargas watched as his hands moved expertly over the rifle, working the bolt to make sure a round was in the chamber. He unhooked a web belt bristling with ammo pouches and a combat knife, slipped it from the dead guard's waist, cinched it around his own and uncoiled from the floor.

Something had changed in him. Gone was the confident, too slick gunrunner who'd tried to curry favor with Escobar. Instead his eyes looked flinty, his mouth set in a grim line. This man wasn't a criminal. He was a warrior. He looked ready to spill blood.

He took a couple of steps toward her and she tensed, unsure what was coming.

"We need to get out of here," she said.

He shook his head.

"First, you answer questions."

"What? There's no time for that."

"Make time."

She looked over his shoulder at the open cell door.

"They're going to come for us. What if they see the dead guard on security cameras?"

He shrugged.

"Lady, you were part of the crew that snatched me from Mexico City, brought me to this hellhole, crawling with Hezbollah. Now I'm supposed to believe you suddenly want to help me? Sorry. I need something to go on."

"You're going to get us killed!"

Blancanales swung the AK-74's barrel up and locked the muzzle on her stomach.

"Start talking or Escobar's the least of your worries," he said, his voice steady and sure.

She studied him, searching his eyes for signs of a bluff, but saw only determination.

"You'd kill me? After I saved you?"

"All out of gratitude," he said. "Now, talk. Who are you?"

"My name is Abaigael Katz. I'm an Israeli."

"And you're hanging with Escobar because…? You have a fetish for Latino men? Or are you Mossad?"

Damn! "Mossad," she muttered.

"And Mossad's interested in Escobar…why?"

She scowled. "Israel's not exactly on good terms with Hezbollah," she said. "In case you haven't noticed, this place is crawling with them. You saw the flag, didn't you?"

He nodded. "Fair enough," he said. "So you got close to Escobar to keep tabs on Hezbollah?"

"Something like that."

"And you were cozying up to Ortega…why? You thought he was Hezbollah?"

"I thought he was part of Escobar's organization. I had no idea until today he was an American agent. If I had known…" Her voice trailed off. "I thought he was a criminal until today."

"And when you learned otherwise?"

She cursed under her breath and a sudden urge to avoid his stare overtook her. She looked down at her shoes.

"When I learned otherwise," she said, "it was too late. Okay? He was gone and all I could do was help you. Now, I'm starting to wonder what the hell I was thinking."

She could feel him looking at her. She raised her eyes and met his stare.

"Doesn't help that Escobar's going to kill you, does it?"

She inhaled sharply. "You're a bastard," she said.

"I saw it in his eyes. One way or the other, he knows you betrayed him. You think he knows you're Mossad."

She shrugged. "Anything's possible," she said. "But I doubt it. I've been under a long time. It's been ten years since I've even been to the Middle East."

"He made Ortega."

"Ortega was a fool. Now, do you have enough information? Can we get out of here?"

He shook his head no.

"You go, if you'd like. In fact, it's probably for the best."

"What are you going to do?"

"I'm going to kill Escobar."

"There's no way," she said. "Those Hezbollah troopers you saw upstairs? There are ten more somewhere on the property. And Escobar has fifteen guards in his personal entourage. Some of them are damn good. Former Mexican military, some of them were trained by U.S. Special Forces to fight the drug wars."

"What's his end game?"

She shook her head.

"I'm not sure," she said. "But it's much bigger than what we're seeing here. These thugs here? That's just a small part. Even Escobar's just a small piece of something much bigger. I haven't been able to wrap my arms around it. He plays it all so close to the vest. But, knowing him, knowing the people involved, it's something awful."

She fell silent. The American stared at her for a couple of seconds. Finally he jerked his head at the door.

"Let's get you out of here."

"I don't need your protection," she snapped. "I rescued you, remember?"

"Not protection," he said, shaking his head. "You can take care of yourself. But if the information you have is that important, we need to make sure you don't end up dying here."

"I'm not going to die here."

The American smiled. "Keep telling yourself that," he said. "You might actually get out of here alive. What's the best way out?"

She thought about it.

"Helicopter," she said. "There's a helipad on the northern edge of the estate. There's a helicopter waiting there to take the Iranians back to the airport."

"Is it guarded?"

She shook her head.

"The pilot hangs close by in case Escobar gets the urge to fly out of here at a moment's notice. A couple of mechanics, too. Nothing too heavy."

"You could force the pilot to take the helicopter and fly out of here?"

She nodded once. "I could." She gave him a hard look. "What about you?"

"We can't just walk out to the helicopter and ask for a ride. Someone has to stay behind and keep these bastards busy. Otherwise, neither one of us would make it to the helicopter. You have the information, so it only makes sense that you get the first shot at leaving this place."

She pressed her lips into a thin line and considered this for several seconds.

"You're right," she said. "I'll go. If I can make it to the chopper."

BLANCANALES TRAILED THE woman as she retraced her steps out of the basement, where his cell had been located. She stayed close to the walls. Her movements were economical and confident. Blancanales guessed it wasn't just because she knew her surroundings. She obviously was a professional warrior. She'd just taken down three men and if it bothered her, she gave no outward signs of it.

When they reached a pair of double doors, she gestured for him to stop and he did. She took a couple of steps forward and pressed an ear to the door as he looked on.

Raising her pistol so the barrel pointed skyward, she pressed her other hand on the release bar and pushed gently against it, easing the door open. Blancanales felt himself tense as the door swung wide. He pointed the AK-74 at hip level and moved up on the door as it came open.

She pointed at the doorway and held up two fingers. Blancanales took that to mean there were two guards waiting in the lobby. Acknowledging her with a nod, he stepped up to the door, peered through it and saw two guards positioned there. One sat on a folding chair, right ankle crossed over his left knee, and smoked a cigarette. The other was talking on a two-way radio.

"Heard from them?" the guard was saying. "No, I haven't heard from them. The little freak is torturing someone. You think they're going to come up here and give me a progress report?" The guard paused and Blancanales assumed he was listening to the person on the other end of the line. "Go down and check on them? ¡Dios mio! The further I stay away from that little creep, the better."

Another pause. "What? Escobar said to check? No way, man. Okay, I can do it. I'll call back."

He took the radio down from his ear and muttered a curse.

The smoker looked up from his cigarette. "What?"

"Gotta do a prisoner check," the guard replied.

"Prisoner check? That guy's not going anywhere."

The other guard shook his head.

"They aren't worried he'll escape. They're worried Javier might kill Perez. Guess he loves his work a little too much, if you know what I mean."

The other man snorted. "Freak, that's what he is, a damn freak."

"No kidding. I guess Escobar brought him in to interrogate someone a few months back. He ended up killing the bastard. Escobar was livid. He doesn't want a repeat of that fiasco."

"Go ahead," the other guard said.

The guard who was standing made a disgusted noise, turned and took a step in Blancanales's direction just as the Stony Man warrior came through the door. The guy clawed under his jacket for some hidden hardware. Blancanales stroked the trigger of the Kalashnikov and a quick burst of autofire lashed from the weapon's barrel. The volley chewed into the man's torso and caused him to jerk to a halt in midstride, stumble and crumple to the ground.

The second guard's mouth gaped open and his cigarette fell from it. A Glock autoloader lay on the table in front of him. He made a desperate grab for the weapon, slapping his open palm down on top of it. A small black hole appeared in his forehead, just above the bridge of his nose, before it tunneled through his skull. His now-limp body slammed down hard onto the tabletop.

Blancanales glanced left and saw Vargas standing there,

her Glock gripped in both hands, smoke curling from the sound suppressor. Blancanales gave her a nod. He scooped up a discarded radio and slipped a jack into his right ear so he could eavesdrop on any radio traffic between Escobar's shooters.

She stared at him and he knew she was struggling over the decision to leave him behind.

"I'll let them know you're here."

He almost told her not to bother. Barring a miracle, he doubted he'd live through the next hour. The odds were not on his side.

"Thank you," he said.

She nodded and dashed toward the nearest exit. Blancanales stared after her. Had he made the right decision? He hoped so. He'd seen the look Escobar had given her. There was no doubt in the Able Team warrior's mind that Escobar planned to kill the woman the first chance he got.

Blancanales owed it to her to make sure she had a shot at escaping. He knew he was at least partially to blame, having jabbed Escobar about her relationship with Ortega. And she had saved his life when she should have been running as far as possible from Escobar's estate.

In the meantime he'd try to buy her some time and, hopefully, kill Escobar in the process.

CHAPTER NINETEEN

Lyons trudged through the dense jungle, occasionally swinging a machete to clear cable-like vines and other growth blocking his way. Schwarz walked a parallel path about ten yards to his right, maintaining distance so they weren't too bunched up if someone started shooting at them. A military helicopter had dropped Lyons and Schwarz about two miles from Escobar's stronghold. Togged in jungle fatigues, their faces striped with green, brown and black combat paint, the pair had already trudged most of that distance. A glance at his GPS unit told Lyons they were about two-tenths of a mile from Escobar's place.

Within minutes of killing Castillo, Lyons had called Stony Man Farm and asked for intel about the stronghold. Other than some satellite photos, there'd been little data to mine. The training camp was in the middle of nowhere. Obviously whoever had built it hadn't filed architectural plans with local city authorities. Any sewage, water and electrical infrastructure had been paid for by the owner and built privately. The only paperwork the cyber team had found was a deed from when Escobar apparently had purchased the property through a front company ten or so years ago.

In other words, Lyons and Schwarz had no idea what they were wading into. More guards, more guns, at least one hostage. After that, it was a big question mark.

Schwarz's voice sounded in Lyons's earpiece. "Almost there," he said.

"Yeah," Lyons replied. "Keep your eyes peeled. I have to think Escobar's expecting us or someone like us to hit. He has to have sentries working outside the fence."

"If he has the manpower."

"Assume he does," Lyons growled. "And stay hydrated. It's stinking hot out here."

"Yes, mom," Schwarz replied.

Lyons could feel sweat gathering on the back of his neck, his shirt sticking to his back and chest, sweat darted down the length of his thighs and along his calves before being absorbed into his socks. He guessed it was ninety-plus degrees with humidity levels off the chart. The canopy of trees overhead kept the sun off them, but also trapped the heat and humidity like a greenhouse.

Since they'd chartered a plane from Mexico to Paraguay, the Stony Man warriors had kept most of their weapons from the hit on Castillo's ranch. Playing a hunch, Lyons had switched out the Masterkey on his M-4 and replaced it with a grenade launcher, which was loaded with a fragmentation round at the moment. He'd also added a .357 Desert Eagle as a backup gun.

They'd walked another two minutes when Lyons heard something up ahead; the sharp snap of someone stepping on a branch. He stopped. A glance at Schwarz showed he'd done likewise.

"Stay put," Lyons said. "I'll check it out."

"Roger."

Lyons pressed ahead. As they closed in on Escobar's place, the brush seemed to thin out some. He started to see real signs of life: a cigarette pack crumpled and discarded, footprints pressed into the dirt, brass shell casings, probably from when a bored guard decided to fire off a couple of rounds at a bird.

Then a scent reached him and he froze. It was the smell

of men's cologne or soap. Someone either was close by or had been close by just recently.

"Someone's out here," he whispered into his throat mike.

A minute or so later he reached the edge of the jungle. Ahead, he could see man dressed in camouflage pants and a black T-shirt, head tilted down and tightly focused on his hands as they rolled something. Lyons stared for another few seconds and realized the guard was rolling a joint or a cigarette.

"Got a guard out here, rolling a joint," he whispered.

"Toss a ham sandwich at him," Schwarz replied. "He'll forget all about us."

Lyons suppressed a grin. Reaching down to the ground, he picked up a rock about the size of a baked potato and threw it to his left. Leaves rustled as it flew through the air and bounced off a tree. The guard whipped his head toward the sound and stared for thirty seconds or so. Finally he muttered something under his breath and slipped the ingredients for his joint into a clear plastic sandwich bag, which he then pocketed.

Bringing around his AK-47, the guard moved into the woods a few yards from Lyons and began walking toward where he'd heard the noise. Lyons slipped a knife from his belt and crept up behind the guy, trying to bridge the gap between them while making as little noise as possible. Within seconds, he struck. His arm snaked out and he wrapped it around the guard's neck and jerked him hard off his feet, robbing him of leverage he'd need to fight back. Lyons stabbed the blade's tip into the side of the guard's neck and sliced outward, tearing a wide gash in his throat.

Once the guy stopped struggling, Lyons let him fall to the ground.

As he turned, he saw that another of Escobar's people

had come up behind him. The guard had his Kalashnikov held snug against his waist and he was preparing to shoot.

Lyons had no time to think. He threw the knife. It sliced through the air and buried itself in the guy's throat. He stiffened and his finger tightened on the trigger. A burst of 7.62 mm shredders lashed out from the rifle and punched through the air to Schwarz's right before the guard's body finally realized it was dead and collapsed.

"What the hell?" Schwarz asked.

Lyons keyed his mike. "Almost got shot, but I'm okay. Took the guy out."

"We have to assume they heard that."

"Right. Proceed as planned."

"We'd planned on a silent entry."

"All right, improvise."

Lyons moved out from the dense vegetation, rolled up on the fence and began snipping through the links with a hand cutter. They were at the northwest end of the property, which left some distance between them and the main building.

Schwarz emerged from the jungle a dozen or so yards away, brandishing his M-4 and scanning for threats. He moved close to Lyons, covering him while he worked on the fence.

Once Lyons finished with the fence, he slipped through it, brought around his M-4 and returned the favor to Schwarz by covering him.

Schwarz had just made it through the hole in the fence when a pair of men came into view, jogging toward the Able Team warriors, their assault rifles blazing. Lyons fired the grenade launcher into the air. The round flew up, arced and crashed back to earth, blowing up just behind the running men. Countless bits of razor-sharp metal shredded the gunners' backs, legs and skulls. Both were dead before they reached the ground. Lyons broke open the launcher and thumbed another fragmentation round into it as he rose to his feet and caught up with Schwarz, who already was making a beeline for the main building.

After studying the satellite photos, the pair had decided it was most likely Blancanales was inside that building. They'd start there and, if they couldn't find him, they'd tear the rest of the camp apart. Escobar was about to see Scorched Earth tactics in action.

As THEY NEARED the building, Schwarz heard the buzzing sound of an engine to his right. He whipped his head in that direction and spotted a pair of ATVs shooting out from behind a nearby building. The twin vehicles launched into wide turns and bore down on the Stony Man warriors. Each vehicle carried two people, a driver and a guy wielding a gun. The shooters were unloading their pistols, though the rounds flew wide of their targets because they were being jostled as the ATVs rolled over bumps and holes in the ground.

Schwarz fired his M-4 in a wide horizontal arc. The initial swath cut through the ATV nearest the Stony Man warriors, bullets ripping a ragged line across the driver's chest. The guy's fingers uncurled from the handlebars and his dead form began to slump sideways. A microsecond later the front wheel struck a rock, which caused the ATV to launch into a hard right turn. The vehicle overturned and rolled. The dead driver was thrown in one direction, arms spinning like windmills as he sailed through the air, before flesh and bone collided against hard-packed earth.

The shooter, blood streaming from beneath his hairline and into his face, pushed himself up from the ground with one hand and squeezed off a couple of shots from his pistol.

The Stony Man warrior stitched the guy from right groin to left shoulder with another volley.

The second ATV spun around and knifed a path toward them. The shooter on the back of the vehicle apparently had emptied his pistol and was scrambling to reload his depleted weapon.

Lyons's M-4 cut loose with a sustained barrage of auto-fire. The bullets sparked against the handlebars and head-lights and savaged the driver's torso, but didn't change the vehicle's trajectory. Lyons gave Schwarz a hard shove in the left biceps that sent him stumbling backward. Lyons dived to the left, where he pounded into the ground. The Able Team leader rolled and brought himself up in a sitting position, spraying the guy on the back of the ATV with a storm of bullets as the vehicle passed, killing him.

Lyons grimaced as he rose. His elbows and knees stung from striking the ground, though elbow- and knee-pads had absorbed much of the impact.

Schwarz hauled himself to standing and brushed dirt from the front of his shirt. He looked at Lyons and grinned.

"Sore, old man?" he asked.

"This old man just saved your ass."

"Hey, thanks. Prune juice cocktails for everyone."

"Damn kids," Lyons muttered.

"Should we hit 'em again?"

"Hell, yeah."

WHEN HE HEARD the first pops of gunfire coming from outside the building, Escobar looked at a couple of his gunners and gestured at a pair of double doors leading from the gymnasium. "Check it," he snapped.

The men nodded and ran for the exit.

Escobar turned to Boudri, one of the senior Iranians. At least outwardly he seemed unfazed by the gunfire.

"We go this way," Escobar said, jerking his head to the far end of the gymnasium. Boudri and his entourage of half a dozen high-ranking Iranians nodded their agreement and fell in beside their host.

It galled Escobar to turn away from the gunfire. It wasn't that he hated to leave his men behind; he just didn't want to run from a fight. He wasn't a coward, he assured himself. His every instinct called on him to run toward the shooting. But he knew he had to wait. His first priority was to evacuate Boudri and his people from the building and get them to the helipad. Normally he would have held off on evacuating them. After the past several days, however, he knew he at least needed to be even more cautious than usual, especially with a captured American agent under his roof. He'd escort them to the helipad and have the pilot warm up the engines, just in case.

When they reached a single steel door on the far wall, Escobar punched a code into a keypad on the wall. The lock released and he yanked open the door. He gestured for the men to pass through. Boudri nodded for one of his men to go through first. The guy did and then a few seconds later, Boudri followed, the rest of his entourage filing in behind him like baby ducklings trailing their mother.

Escobar was last through the door. He shut and locked it. They were gathered on the landing when he turned. He pointed to a set of stairs to his right that led down into the ground.

"It's two flights," he said. "Follow them and you'll end up at a tunnel. It leads to another set of stairs. Climb those and you'll end up inside the hangar. The pilot will escort you to the helipad and fly you out of here."

Boudri eyed him with suspicion. "You're not going with us?"

"No," Escobar said, shaking his head. "I'll catch up with you later. I have things to deal with here."

Boudri regarded him for a few more seconds. Finally he shook his head in agreement, brushed past Escobar and descended the stairs with the others following him.

Escobar stared after them briefly before turning and heading back into the gymnasium. Pulling the .38 from inside his jacket, he crossed the large area, weaving between a couple of boxing rings, weight machines and other equipment.

Questions tumbled through his mind as he moved. Who was doing the shooting? Was it Vargas? He couldn't picture it. While he knew she was tough and she had ample motivation to go on the offensive, he couldn't see her being dumb enough to take on a camp full of armed people by herself unless she was desperate. That would be suicide.

Perez? The guy had the combat chops to launch a counterstrike and probably the balls to try it. By now, though, he shouldn't be in any shape to walk, let alone fight. Escobar had seen Javier's work before. If he'd been able to ply his talents, there was no way Perez was even vertical.

If Javier had started to work on him…

Escobar produced his cell phone and speed-dialed one of the security guards assigned to Perez. The phone rang a half dozen times, his jaw clenching a little tighter with each tone.

He ended the call and dialed two more of the guards assigned to Perez, neither of whom answered. He swore under his breath and started for the stairwell leading into the basement. As he moved, he called Vidal, a former Mexican army captain and one of his security team bosses.

Vidal answered on the second ring. Escobar could hear automatic weapons fire in the background.

"Yeah, boss?"

"The guys watching Perez—you heard from them?"

"No."

"That seem strange to you?"

Vidal hesitated, as though surprised by the question.

"Hell, yeah, it seems weird."

"Which is why you have no one looking into it, right?" Escobar killed the connection and dropped the phone into his hip pocket. Creeping through the basement door, he moved slowly down the steps, the .38 pointed in front of him. No sound emanated from the basement. By the time he reached the last couple of steps, the basement hallway came into view. One of his guards lay facedown on the floor, blood pooling beneath his body. The door leading into Perez's cell hung open and light spilled from inside.

Exiting the steps, he moved past the fallen guard and slipped into the holding room, where more carnage awaited him. He found Javier and the remaining guards, their bodies ripped apart by bullets, the walls splattered red with blood. As he looked the room over, something else caught his eye. On a white island of tile, between two rivers of red, something glinted at him. Scowling, he crossed the room and, careful to not touch the blood, bent at the knees until he could reach the object. Though he recognized it instantly as a woman's earring, a corner of his mind still denied what he was seeing until he picked it up between his left thumb and forefinger and brought it in for a closer look. He recognized the curve of the white-gold setting, the shape of the diamond, and it stoked rage in him.

Six months ago he'd given a pair of earrings to Vargas during a weekend sailing trip to Acapulco.

She'd been in this room. She'd helped Perez.

He knew in his gut she'd been working against him, had known it for a couple of months, even if he hadn't known specifically who she worked for.

He'd put off dealing with it and it'd bit him in the ass.

Well, he'd deal with it now. He'd hunt her down and shoot her like a dog.

Then he'd do the same thing to Perez.

Wheeling around, he headed for the stairs. Escobar still believed she was too damn smart to willingly throw herself up against a small army of his men. For whatever reason, she'd helped Perez and they were together, he thought. But they had to be running for the helicopter, not making a last stand.

Escobar mapped it all out in his mind. He'd travel back through the gym, slip through the underground tunnel and show up on the other side of the compound, where he could get the drop on them.

LYONS AND SCHWARZ searched a couple of the smaller buildings on the property. One contained two more ATVs, a workbench and a couple of tool chests. The other was packed full of riding lawnmowers, hand tools, burlap bags filled with seeds and other landscaping gear.

When those searches yielded nothing, they moved to the large building situated in the northeast corner of the property. While they'd searched the other buildings, a pair of Escobar's thugs had stepped outside, but stayed close to the front door.

The Able Team warriors were crouched behind the repair facility, sizing up the sentries. A waist-high concrete barrier provided partial cover for the hardmen.

"Give me ten seconds," Schwarz said. "Then start shooting."

Lyons nodded his understanding. Schwarz turned and walked away from Lyons, edging along the shed's exterior. When he reached the end of the building, he turned the corner and disappeared from view.

When Lyons finished his count, he wrapped himself around the side of the building, aimed the M-4 and fired off a couple of bursts at the guards. A round bit into the upper arm of one of the guards and caused him to yelp in pain, while the other rounds flew wide.

The other guard cut loose with his own SMG, spraying the contents of its magazine in a wide arc. The rounds hammered into the building protecting Lyons and chewed through the wood planks making up its exterior. Once the guy emptied his weapon, he dropped down behind the barrier with his injured comrade.

Lyons came around the edge of the building and cut loose with another firestorm from the M-4. In the midst of the assault rifle's chatter, he heard a popping sound and he ducked back behind the building, knowing what was about to happen. A heartbeat later he heard a loud explosion in the direction of the hardmen he'd been exchanging shots with. He peered around the corner and saw smoke rising from behind the barrier.

Hauling himself to his full height, he broke from his cover and met up with Schwarz, who was kneeling and thumbing a fresh round into his grenade launcher.

When they reached the main building, they stepped over the remains of the two gunners, moved to the door and went inside. The first room they encountered was large with high ceilings, almost like a lobby. Lyons gestured at a pair of corpses sprawled on the ground. He shot Schwarz a look.

"Blancanales?" he asked.

"Unless they've become a suicide cult," Schwarz said.

"We should be so lucky."

As they continued into the building, a corridor opened to their right. Lyons entered it first, followed by Schwarz. They found a half dozen or so rooms filled with rows of desks and white boards fixed to the walls.

"Classrooms," Lyons muttered.

In an adjoining hallway, they found several small offices filled with desks, computers and papers, but no people.

"Probably a gold mine of information in here," Schwarz said.

"I'm more focused on the gold mine of targets," Lyons said.

"If Pol left any," Schwarz said. "I think these morons have a tiger by the tail."

They followed another corridor that led into the gymnasium. Lyons went through the door first and spotted three guards standing around a steel door on the far wall. When they saw him, they raised their weapons and began firing. Lyons darted to the left, spraying autofire at the thugs as he moved. One of the shooters got caught in his spray-and-pray barrage.

Schwarz, in the meantime, hosed down the other two with a relentless volley that punched into their torsos and legs, causing them to jerk wildly under the storm of gunfire.

When the last one fell, the Stony Man warriors cautiously crossed the room and looked at the steel door, now nicked in several places by bullets. Schwarz grabbed the handle, pulled at it, but it didn't budge.

"Looked like they were guarding this," he said.

"What is it?" Lyons asked.

"Door."

"I know it's a door. Where does it go?"

Schwarz jerked his chin at the dead guards. "Ask them."

Lyons glared at him then turned his attention first to the door, then to the keypad next to it.

"We need a code to open it," he said.

"Yeah, we do."

"Which means we keep searching the building," he said.

"Right."

CHAPTER TWENTY

Abaigael Katz darted across the manicured lawn toward the helipad, her feet thudding against the trimmed grass. A black Sikorsky 76 helicopter stood on the helipad, waiting, the sunlight gleaming on the craft's windshield. Nearby was the large hangar that housed Escobar's planes and helicopters when they needed maintenance.

The bay door was pulled shut and the Mossad agent guessed the mechanics were holed up inside the air-conditioned office. She looked around for the pilot, but didn't see him. The realization caused panic to well up inside her. Her chest grew tight and she had to force herself to pull in deep breaths. She couldn't fly the helicopter. And, without the pilot, she couldn't leave.

Her grip tightened on the pistol.

As Katz moved closer to the craft, she slowed her approach. Her eyes darted around, looking for some clue about the pilot's whereabouts.

He's not here. She stopped and stared at the helicopter, as though she could will him to appear. Katz threw a glance to her left at the hangar. It was her only chance to find him, and even then there was no guarantee it would do any good. With every passing second, the chance that Escobar would come looking for her increased.

She had to do something.

The sensation of something white-hot tunneling into the back of her calf, just below her right knee, registered with her, accompanied by the sharp crack of a pistol. Her breath hissed through clenched teeth. She tried to whip around, but her right leg faltered under her, causing her to crash to the ground.

Jaw clenched, she rolled onto her back. The hand clutching the Glock swung around in an arc at the same instant she saw him standing there.

Escobar was positioned maybe twenty yards away, right arm extended forward, hand filled with that damn Colt of his. The gun cracked again and a hot sensation drilled through her shoulder, elicited a cry of pain.

The Glock slipped from her fingers. Furiously she shoved her left palm into the earth and tried to push herself up from the ground. A second dose of white-hot pain lanced through her body.

Escobar was standing next to her, the Colt's barrel pointed at her face, its snout locked on her forehead. His eyes stared down at her. She saw no traces of pity or compassion, no signs of rage or betrayal in his eyes. Just that same damn dead-eyed stare of his.

"Nikki?" he said.

She said nothing.

After a few seconds he continued. "I'm disappointed."

"Good," she said, the effort causing her to wince.

"Are you disappointed? I mean, here you are, stuck in a jungle, and yet you know so much. You could do so much to help your homeland. Yet here you lay, bleeding in the grass, sweating like a cheap hooker. You're going to die and for what?"

Her vision blurred and a shudder seized her. The cold meant shock was setting in.

"You almost made it to the helicopter. Do you feel like you've won?" he asked.

She didn't, but she also wasn't going to admit it. Had

Perez made it out? She thought she heard the pop of gun-fire in the distance, but she couldn't tell for sure; every-thing she heard sounded like it was coming to her through a long tunnel.

"I knew you'd come to the helipad," he said. "You al-ways were predictable."

She heard voices and felt hope surge through her. Perez? Was he coming to help? Her eyes drifted past Escobar and she could see two figures moving toward them.

Following her gaze, the crime lord looked over his shoul-der before he turned his eyes back on her and shook his head.

"Mine," he said.

"You've met Mr. Boudri already," Escobar said. "The others are his associates."

Her tongue felt dry and swollen, the flesh of her throat felt dry, tight, as though it could crack. She wanted to say something to him. Do you think this will work? Do you think al-Jaballah will let you in his inner circle? She wanted to say all these things. But when she spoke she could only emit a pitiful-sounding croak. Her gun had fallen out of reach and he had kicked it away from her.

Even through the veil of pain, she could see his black eyes held no warmth for her. An Iranian walked between them, throwing her a glance before continuing on. An-other of the men, Hezbollah or IRG, she couldn't really tell, stopped, stared down at her and grinned before moving on.

"I considered taking you with us," he said, "but decided not to. Even if we tortured you, you'd never tell us anything. Besides, the real problem isn't what we know about you, but what you know of us. That's the real danger. It can be fixed easily."

Bastard!

She forced herself to speak.

"Fix it," she said. Her voice was cold and resolute.

The pistol cracked once and she was gone.

Escobar stared down at the woman, his expression flat. He'd lost his capacity to feel anything, save for rage, decades ago. He felt no attachment to her, certainly no guilt for slaying her. She'd been little more than a sack of meat to him while alive. Now, sprawled on the ground, her life fluids all but drained from her, she was even less.

He kicked some dirt on her face, whirled around and started back to the main building.

The men who'd attacked his compound had taken so much from him, nearly everything as a matter of fact.

He'd allowed the Hezbollah operatives to flee, so they could follow their mission in Baghdad. He'd stayed behind on purpose—he wanted to finish this.

But first he had a stop to make.

He walked to the hangar, found the side door and slipped inside. At the far corner of the building stood a small office. He made his way to it, tried the knob and found it was locked. He drove the point of his elbow into the glass. When it broke, it made a sharp snapping noise, like a branch breaking. The shards rained onto the floor, most shattering when they struck the concrete.

Reaching through the glass, he unlocked the door and stepped inside the office. On the other side of the room stood a large gun safe. Crossing the floor, he punched a code into the keypad and listened for the lock to release. When it did, he pushed the lid up and sorted through the contents of the rectangular cabinet, which in some ways reminded him of a refrigerator lying on its side.

He found an FN P-90 submachine gun chambered in 28 mm ammo. With its bullpup design, the weapon had a rate of fire of 900 rounds per minute. He loaded a magazine into the P-90 and strapped on web gear that enabled him to carry four more magazines. In addition, he grabbed a pair of M-67 grenades.

Leaving the hangar behind, he moved back in the direction of the main building and training center. The Americans had stripped away or destroyed everything that mattered to him, that he'd built. A lot of those things he'd have to rebuild or buy back. It would take time to accomplish this. One thing he could do right now, though, was to get revenge on the bastards who'd done this.

BLANCANALES SPRINTED ACROSS the lawn. He could hear the thrumming of the helicopter blades and knew he needed to act. He already had seen Escobar and the Iranians duck out, leaving their foot soldiers to fight the battle. Katz had mentioned there was a helipad on the compound. And, while he had no idea where it was, he'd assumed that was their destination.

Now that he was outside, he could hear the helicopter's engine and the whipping of the propeller blades. He headed for the sound. He'd put maybe one hundred yards between himself and Escobar's stronghold when he heard the whine of the engines climb in pitch. He swore. An instant later the whirling propeller came into view, followed by the body of the craft.

Sunlight glinted off the craft's exterior and suddenly the crackle of gunshots intermingled with the helicopter's rhythmic beating. Yellow muzzle-flashes winked at Blancanales, and the deadly storm of bullets drilled into the ground around the Stony Man warrior.

He dropped into a crouch, angled the Kalashnikov up at the helicopter and squeezed the trigger. Bullets struck the Sikorsky, sparked against its hide and whizzed away. When a couple of steel-jacketed slugs pierced the windshield, someone in the craft apparently decided to declare victory and run. The helicopter turned ninety degrees and skimmed off over the treetops.

With a pause in the shooting, Blancanales hoofed it in the direction of the helipad. He could now see that the ground sloped upward a few dozen yards before leveling off again. He ran up the short hill and when the ground leveled off again, he could see the helipad and a building that appeared to be a hangar or maintenance structure.

He saw something else that caused his blood to run cold.

A crumpled form lay on the ground; one leg bent slightly and the other jutted straight out. Her arms were twisted at awkward angles.

Damn. He ran for the fallen woman.

BLANCANALES LOWERED HIMSELF to one knee beside Katz's corpse and surveyed the body.

The killer had put a single round into her heart, the fabric around the hole burned black by the muzzle-flash. Blood drenched the front of her shirt. Her head lolled to the right, her unseeing eyes open, lips slightly parted. The Able Team fighter reached out and closed her eyelids. Gently he wrapped his fingers around her right wrist and moved her arm so it lay parallel to her ribs. He did the same thing with the other arm before straightening her bent leg.

They hadn't been allies for long, each mistaking the other as an enemy even as they fought for similar causes. But without her last-minute help, Blancanales figured he would have been dead or would have suffered vicious treatment at Javier's hands. He'd seen other torture victims as he'd fought on the world's killing fields and knew death would have been the preferable alternative.

Distant gunshots grabbed his attention. He uncoiled from the ground and turned his head in the direction of the gunfire. Recognizing Lyons's trademark spray-and-pray barrage, he turned his attention to the compound's main building.

He knew he needed to head in that direction and help his teammates as they mopped up Escobar's men—and the man himself.

Blancanales jogged toward the main building, at first unaware someone was watching him.

STILL INSIDE THE hangar, Escobar stood at a window and watched as Perez rose from beside the dead woman. The agent's efforts to somehow make the dead woman more comfortable amused Escobar.

Obviously this guy was weak. No doubt he was deadly. But at his core he was weak.

He'd die easily.

Escobar watched Perez turn and head back toward the barracks and training center. For a couple of seconds the Mexican considered moving in the opposite direction. If he ran two hundred yards in any direction, he'd find himself in jungle. As cautious as he was, he'd buried sealed plastic tubs filled with a couple days' provisions, satellite phones, knives and Beretta 9 mm handguns at a various points in the surrounding wilderness.

He could bolt from his property, dig up one of the phones, call for help and wait out the Americans who were tearing through his property.

Forget it, he told himself.

He'd rather die here than run.

Glancing out the window again, he saw Perez crest a short hill and, without pausing on the top, start down the other side and quickly disappear from view.

Exiting the hangar, he picked up the other man's trail, slowly ascending the hill. He didn't want to move too fast.

He wanted Perez to stay just far enough ahead of him that Perez wouldn't realize he was being followed.

The way Escobar figured it, the closer the American got to the larger fight that lay ahead of him, the more focused he'd be on it and the less tuned in he'd be to his rear flank. That would make him an easy target for Escobar. Then he could deal with the other two, if his security team hadn't already done so.

With long, steady strides he rolled up the side of the hill, slowing his approach as he neared the top. If the American had realized he was being followed, he could be lying in wait, Escobar thought. Dropping into a crouch, he moved over the rise and could see Perez had already returned to level ground and was heading for the main building.

He had him.

CHAPTER TWENTY-ONE

The cluster of buildings that comprised the heart of Escobar's complex lay a hundred or so yards from Blancanales. Only sparse cover stood between the buildings and him: three black Hummers parked on a large concrete pad and a small wooden utility shed.

Before he'd covered a dozen or so yards, his combat senses began calling for his attention, warning him of danger.

An instant later a man armed with an MP-5 surged from behind one of the Hummers. Jagged flames and bullets lashed out from the H&K's barrel. Slugs chewed a line in the ground just a few feet ahead of Blancanales.

The AK-74 in his hands chattered, letting loose with a maelstrom. The barrage lanced into the hardman's chest, killing him. Propelled by momentum, the corpse hurtled forward another couple of feet before the legs gave out and it smacked facedown on the earth.

Even as the hardman fell, a second popped up from behind the Hummer nearest Blancanales. Laying his SMG on the hood of the big vehicle, the gunman fired off two quick bursts that cleaved through the air just to Blancanales's right.

He threw himself down, putting him out of the shooter's sights, and rolled to his left and unfolded from the ground in a kneeling position.

Bringing the AK tight against his shoulder, he locked

his sights on the vehicle the shooter had been hiding behind. From his line of sight, he couldn't see the guy. He moved in a wide circle, hoping to outflank the shooter. He stepped onto the concrete pad where the Hummers were parked and moved a couple yards forward.

More autofire rang out to his right. Blancanales whipped his head in that direction and spotted Escobar, a submachine gun tucked against his side, approaching him. Bullets ripped up chunks of concrete near the Stony Man commando's feet. He squeezed off a fast burst in Escobar's direction to disrupt his approach and bolted.

In the same moment the other shooter came into view and was lining up a shot at Blancanales, who hosed him down with a murderous barrage from the AK.

Blancanales ejected the AK's magazine, tossed it aside and fed a new one into the rifle.

Escobar had followed him. The guy came around the back end of one of the Hummers and unloaded more fiery death at Blancanales. The Stony Man warrior wheeled around and fired the Kalashnikov, moving it in a figure-eight pattern.

The 7.62 mm slugs stitched half a dozen holes across Escobar's chest. The onslaught spun him halfway around. His finger in a death spasm squeezed the trigger and the rifle fired through part of its magazine, the bullets spraying into the sky. Blancanales ran to the fallen man. The PN-90 had slipped from the guy's grip. He stared up at Blancanales, his breath coming in ragged gasps, a trickle of blood trailing from the left corner of his mouth.

Escobar turned his head. *"Hijo de puta,"* he rasped.

The soldier switched the rifle to single-shot mode and put a round into the crime lord's forehead.

Escobar's body went still.

INSIDE ESCOBAR'S HOUSE, Blancanales found carnage but little else.

The gunfire had ceased. He walked through the first floor, checking room by room for Lyons and Schwarz. He heard no voices, either, and for a chilling moment wondered whether his two friends had been injured or even killed.

In several rooms he found Escobar's men, dead, sprawled on the floor, draped over furniture like a discarded jacket. One body floated facedown in an indoor pool in the building's gymnasium, the water turned red by blood.

Riding the elevator into the basement, he stepped back into the corridor that led to the room where he'd been held captive. Immediately images and physical sensations from his time as a captive began to replay through his mind and body. Before he got too lost in that line of thinking, he heard the murmur of voices up ahead.

With the AK held tightly at his side, he moved through the hallway, the voices growing louder the closer he moved to the sources. Finally he could make out Lyons's voice and a smile ghosted his lips.

"Hey, Ironman," he shouted, "is that you?"

A brief pause followed by, "None other. You okay?"

"I'm alone, if that's what you're asking."

"Good."

"And I'm okay."

"Even better."

In less than a minute the three men were face to face.

"You're a sight for sore eyes," Lyons said. He extended a hand and Blancanales shook it.

"Can I have a hug?" Blancanales quipped.

"I'm going to stick my foot up your ass and break it off," Lyons said.

"That's a no," Schwarz said, grinning. "And don't even bother to ask me."

"Fair enough," Blancanales said, grinning. With the adrenaline beginning to subside, he was starting to feel tired.

"You see Escobar?" Schwarz asked.

Blancanales nodded.

"Dead. I killed the bastard."

"Score one for the good guys," Schwarz said. "We've got a helicopter about a mile west of here. You okay to walk?"

"Yeah," he said. "Hey, Escobar's girlfriend, Nikki Vargas, is dead. She was Mossad. She's the reason I'm alive."

Lyons nodded. "The Farm found out a couple of hours ago she had connections to Israel," he said. "Worked out good for you. Helps to have a friend on the inside."

"Not so good for her."

"Yeah," Lyons said, "not so good for her. Hey, she'd probably be dead anyway. I'm guessing Escobar would've figured it out sooner or later. At least she died on her terms, right?"

"And we got Escobar for her," Schwarz said.

"Even so…" Blancanales responded, thinking of the sacrifice the Mossad agent had made to save his life.

CHAPTER TWENTY-TWO

Kinshasa, Democratic Republic of Congo

David McCarter was the last member of Phoenix Force to enter the secure conference room in the basement of the U.S. Embassy. A cold can of Coke gripped in his right hand, he moved to one of the leather chairs surrounding the large circular table and dropped into the seat. Stifling a yawn, the tall, fox-faced Briton opened the soft drink can, took a long pull from it, set it on the table and swept his gaze over the occupants of the cramped, stuffy room.

His fellow Phoenix Force warriors—Calvin James, Gary Manning, T. J. Hawkins and Rafael Encizo—were all seated around the same table. Stony Man Farm's ace pilot Jack Grimaldi was on his feet, his lanky form propped against a wall, the bill of his baseball cap pulled low over his eyes, which were closed.

McCarter's muscles felt stiff and his brain fuzzy from lack of sleep. The group had spent the past two days breaking up a weapons-smuggling ring in Yemen that had been sending rocket-propelled grenades and other ordnance to al-Shabab terrorists in Somalia. Once they'd wrapped up that mission, McCarter had planned to jet to London for some R&R.

But just as they'd finished loading their weapons and their fatigued bodies onto the plane, they'd been summoned to Kinshasa. From the airport they'd been transported to the Embassy in a caravan of limousines and led to the secure briefing room.

There'd barely been time for McCarter to nick a can of Coke before the meeting. Even on his best day, the former British Special Air Service soldier was fueled by caffeine. Coming straight off a mission, though, he felt like he could use a cooler filled with the stuff. McCarter was a product of London's East End who, during his career, had become an ace pilot, a small arms expert and an Olympic-level pistol shooter.

The one Embassy staffer in the room was Richard Austin. Austin was of average height, slim, with a thick head of neatly trimmed salt-and-pepper hair and a disarming grin that he flashed frequently. The grin never reached his eyes, though, and he seemed to be sizing up his new guests with the cautious gaze of an experienced spy. He was listed as a mid-level bureaucrat for the State Department, but actually was the CIA station chief.

"Welcome to paradise, gentlemen," Austin said. "Hope you enjoy your stay here in Kinshasa."

"Loving it already," Grimaldi muttered. His eyes were closed and he was resting his chin on his chest.

Austin checked his watch, swore under his breath, darted to the table and stepped in between Hawkins and Encizo. Punching a couple of keys on a laptop, he gestured at a white screen that hung from the ceiling.

An image of the State Department symbol set against a blue background emerged, filling the screen.

"Boring," McCarter muttered.

The image faded and was replaced by a close-up shot of Barbara Price, her honey-blond hair pulled back in a ponytail, a black headset fitted on her head.

"Much better," McCarter said.

"Excuse me?" the former model asked.

"Good to see you," the Briton said, flashing a lopsided grin. "Where's the old guy?"

"Catching a power nap," Price said. "In a few hours, he has a private briefing with the Man. We have Able Team in the field and the Man wants to be brought up to speed on that. He'll also want an update on your mission to Somalia."

"We made friends and influenced people," McCarter quipped.

"Don't you always?" Price replied. "By the way, your host, Mr. Austin, is an old friend and cleared to hear what we're talking about. He's always happy to cooperate with NSA paramilitary forces such as yourselves."

"Always glad to help the NSA," Austin said, either not knowing or not caring that he was being lied to.

"We appreciate that," McCarter replied before swallowing some more Coke.

McCarter guessed Price was pegging them as NSA employees to deflect further questions. A sweeping glance around the room told him that none of his comrades reacted to the reference, either. His team was used to moving in the shadows.

Encizo stifled a yawn. A native of Cuba, Encizo as a younger man had participated in covert attempts to unseat the government. A physical fitness enthusiast, Encizo had spent time as a scuba instructor and participated in diving operations off the coasts of Jamaica and Puerto Rico, searching for treasure from sunken Spanish and British ships. Though he'd contracted at various times with the CIA and DEA, he'd refused to join either agency. A few strands of gray running through his jet-black hair were the only hints he might be older than forty. He'd also worked as a professional bodyguard and an insurance investigator at various points in his career.

"So we're here to discuss Hal's sleeping habits?" Encizo asked.

Price smiled. "I wish it was something that mundane. It's not. We need you to move on something before it gets out of control."

In spite of his fatigue, McCarter felt his heart kick up a notch at the prospect of some action. He guessed his fellow soldiers were feeling the same thing.

Price asked, "You heard about Blake Pearson, the ambassador who was killed, right?"

Price didn't wait on them to nod their heads, but instead continued speaking. "The killers used an IED to blow up his limousine. The motorcade was outfitted with all kinds of jamming and detection equipment, but somehow they still were able to get them. It was a very professional hit."

"It was the Lord's Resistance Army, right?" Manning asked.

Price nodded. "An offshoot group of the LRA, actually. The killer team was led by Jules Nmosu. He used to be a mid-level commander in the LRA before he and a couple others jumped ship and started their own group. According to our files, he had some decent military credentials to his name, but nothing to indicate he could pull off something of this sophistication. They apparently knew Pearson's route, faked an auto accident to divert him from it, trapped the motorcade and attacked. From what the forensic teams could tell, some of the parts used to make the IEDs were shipped through an export company owned by Seif Escobar."

"So he's our target?" Encizo asked.

Price shook her head no. "The other guys are handling him right now. We need you to take care of something else. Like I said, we find this Nmosu's involvement in this troubling. We've given the LRA some hell over the years.

And, according to the intelligence we have, he's narcissistic enough to try something like this. Once you set the obvious stuff aside, though, it doesn't pass the smell test."

"Explain," said Manning. The Canadian only spoke when he had something important to say. A perfectionist and a workaholic, he was considered one of the world's foremost experts on explosives and demolition. These skills had helped him succeed in the construction and mining industries as well as in combat. In addition, he was an excellent marksman and had helped form a counter-terrorism unit within the Royal Canadian Mounted Police.

Price acknowledged Manning with a nod. "Well, for starters, the alleged mastermind of this hit— Mr. Nmosu? The local authorities found him at the scene, dead."

"Killed by one of his own?"

"That's the theory. The authorities swear they didn't do it. And we have no trouble believing that. It took them a couple of minutes to get to the scene, especially with the main roads clogged by an accident and emergency crews already tied up on a call. And, frankly, I'm not sure why they would lie about it."

Scowling, Manning rubbed his chin with his thumb and index finger. "I'm not sure a betrayal scenario makes sense, though," he said. "If they were going to do that, you'd think they'd do it before the murder."

"Because someone thought it was a dangerous move," Encizo offered.

"Right," Manning said.

"You raise a good point," Price said. "Unfortunately him getting killed by one of his friends is the best theory we have at this point. Unless someone just happened by just after the explosions and—for reasons I don't understand— decided to take him out and disappear."

"You're right," McCarter said. "That theory's daft."

"Thank you," Price said. "In addition, he has some ties to some shady characters."

"Duh," Grimaldi muttered.

"I know. I know. I mean, high-level shady characters. The other team's in the field right now investigating his links to a Mexican weapons smuggler, Seif Escobar. We believe Escobar provided him the components used in the IEDs. It's possible he even provided the training and had his own people construct the IEDs."

"Which goes back to the question of motivation," Manning said. "If this Escobar guy knew what the weapons would be used for, why would he build and sell them? Even a greedy sociopath would know better than to piss off the United States over small change."

"Right," James said. "All he's done is draw unwanted attention to himself."

Born on Chicago's South Side, James was one of Phoenix Force's two native-born American members. As a younger man, he'd joined the U.S. Navy, eventually becoming a SEAL. After he left the Navy, he moved to California, where he began studying medicine and chemistry. His academic pursuits were cut short when criminals killed his mother and sister. That event spurred him to join the San Francisco Police Department, where eventually he joined the department's SWAT team.

"Right, his motive is murky to us," Price said. "We have theories, but no answers at this point. Of course, we found out about his shipping the IED parts through one of the undercover agents placed in his organization. Escobar wasn't brazen about it. The Feds just had a person in the right place at the right time. Otherwise we might still be in the dark."

"Fair enough," McCarter said. "So if we're not hunting Mr. Escobar, what's our role in all this? Or are we just chatting?"

Price showed a weary smile.

"Hardly," she said. "Word came down from the Man. He wants Nmosu's organization dismantled. Part of it's retribution for what they did, obviously. But the links between Nmosu and Escobar are troubling. And…Escobar's been talking with someone in Iran, which only heightens the mystery. It may be nothing. It may be something."

"Any ideas on where to start?" McCarter asked.

Price nodded. "When Nmosu split off from the group, he didn't go alone. Justin Mulumba and Daniel Lukwebo, each of whom has a war crimes file as long as my arm, went with him. Your briefing packets include pictures and bios on each of the men. For the moment, though, I wouldn't invest a lot of time into Lukwebo."

McCarter's brow furrowed. "Why not?"

"Apparently someone decided he needed another hole in his head," Price said. "So they shot him and dumped him in an alley."

"Are you sure another black ops agency isn't already taking these guys down?" James asked.

"Negative. We ran that through all the channels and every one pleaded ignorance. Whoever killed Nmosu and Lukwebo probably wanted to shut them up."

"We could just sit back and see if someone waxes Mulumba for us," Encizo said.

"I see your line of reasoning, Rafe. But that's not a good plan," Price said. "If someone's trying to cover tracks, we want to know who it is. Otherwise, they'll get away with killing one of our ambassadors."

Encizo nodded his understanding. "Point taken," he said.

"Send us the briefing packets," McCarter said. "We'll take it from there."

CHAPTER TWENTY-THREE

"Move your legs faster," Justin Mulumba shouted, "or I'll cut them off."

Mulumba patted the worn handle on his machete and barked out a harsh laugh.

The small group of women he was addressing—all younger than twenty, some many years younger—shot furtive glances in his direction, but quickly turned their attention back to their work. They were carrying weathered leather suitcases or cardboard boxes filled with Mulumba's possessions. Like a line of ants, they loaded the items into the back of one of his Toyota SUVs before turning away and looking for something else to move. Though young, some of the women struggled with the burdens they carried, their bodies rendered weak from lack of food and health care. Not to mention the frequent sexual assaults they suffered at the hands of Mulumba or his men. None wanted to catch his eye because they knew that with attention came exploitation and abuse.

Mulumba had collected the women during various raids on local villages over the past couple of years. He'd had a larger group six months ago, one that had included a few elderly men and a couple of babies. Disease and starvation had thinned the group down, which explained at least to some extent why only the young women had survived.

A group of Mulumba's guards stood nearby. All carried AK-74 or AKM rifles. A couple wore ragged camouflage fatigues, the same ones they'd owned when they'd deserted the DRC's army. Another man wore cut-off blue jeans and a tattered black T-shirt, while the fourth was dressed in cutoffs and a faded red shirt with the sleeves ripped off.

The women had spent the morning packing the contents of Mulumba's tent in preparation for his departure. Once they'd loaded the vehicles, he'd count off maybe half the women and take them along, though he'd make them walk alongside the vehicles and not allow them to ride inside.

The remaining women would be taken into a field and shot dead, like diseased livestock, except he wouldn't bother burying them. He'd heard a couple of the women who'd been with him the longest sob. They knew what was coming. If they didn't die, they'd have to bury the ones that did. After that, they'd walk several miles on empty stomachs before they stopped for the night, cooked dinner and satisfied whatever other hunger Mulumba experienced.

The afternoon was hot, the air thick with humidity. Mulumba, his shirt dark with sweat and clinging to his chest and back, turned away from the women and swigged from the bottle of water he carried. Fear fluttered in his stomach and constricted his breathing. He didn't like feeling scared and he certainly didn't want to look at his people when he felt afraid.

Yet he found himself unable to stop the sense of panic when it bubbled up inside him and seemed poised to consume him. Within the past twenty-four hours, everything had changed. He found himself in unfamiliar territory—living as prey rather than predator—and it unnerved him.

A former army captain, he'd deserted the military three years ago when he realized the rebel factions lived better than he did. Sure, he'd had a job, a title and a small but regular paycheck. He'd spent less time looking over his shoulder. Rebels lived on the run. But they also took what they wanted—took who they wanted. They lived comparatively well, no small feat in an impoverished country.

He'd started out with the M23 rebel group. But he quickly found himself at odds with the leadership. They'd wanted to effect some kind of change—or at least claimed they did. For his part, he just didn't care. He could mouth the words and the slogans. But, at the end of the day, he just wanted the perks. He wanted to invade a village and take its young women, its crops and whatever other meager valuables it had, and he wanted to keep as much as possible for himself.

In that way, he didn't consider himself any different than other rebel leaders—or politicians, for that matter. He was just willing to admit it, at least to himself.

Now all that was falling apart.

When Nmosu first had told him about their intention to work with the Iranians and Hezbollah, Mulumba had been wary. Most of the Western world—save for a few bleeding hearts at human rights organizations—ignored people like him so long as he and his fellow rebels left Western people and property alone.

But Jules Nmosu and Daniel Lukwebo, the founders of the group, had had a different take. Or at least they had after Iran and Hezbollah began waving big wads of U.S. dollars in their faces.

They'd signed on to the whole affair, spent months training for it and even pulled the whole damn thing off.

Now they were dead.

He guessed the Iranians had killed Nmosu. It'd happened too quickly for it to have been a reprisal for his actions. The way Mulumba figured it, the Iranians probably had killed Nmosu because he knew too much. Lukwebo was another matter. Maybe the Iranians had killed them; maybe the Americans had done it as a reprisal for the murders.

Regardless, it left Mulumba in charge and probably meant he also was a target—of somebody.

So he was packing up his belongings and his people and getting the hell away from the camp before someone came looking for him.

Once he drained the bottle of water, he crumpled it in his fist, tossed it aside and checked his watch. He wanted to have the camp torn down before nightfall. That gave him about three hours.

Mulumba stalked over to his Toyota and yanked open the rear driver's-side door. He stood six feet, eight inches. At three hundred pounds, his body was packed with muscle. A wide scar snaked his forehead before it cut a lumpy, purplish trail over the bridge of his nose and across his right cheek. A man of his size and with his combat background rarely found himself afraid of anything, at least not when it came to head-on confrontation.

But in Lukwebo's case, the dumb bastard had never seen it coming. He'd climbed into his pickup, started the engine and an instant later a bomb under the hood had vaporized him and everything else inside the cab. That was what scared Mulumba. If he couldn't see it coming, he couldn't fight it. That meant he was helpless; a feeling that was all but alien to him.

With some difficulty he maneuvered his large frame through the door. An olive-drab blanket neatly folded into a rectangle lay across one half of the backseat. Grabbing one corner, he flipped aside the blanket and exposed a Type 79 submachine gun. The gas-operated weapon, originally manufactured in China, fired 500 rounds a minute from a 20-round magazine. The weapon, which he'd won several years ago in a poker game, fired 7.62 mm ammunition.

Fisting the weapon and an ammo belt, he withdrew from the vehicle and slung the SMG's strap over his shoulder.

He heard something crash behind him. The sudden noise caused him to wheel around, his big hand wrapping around the Type 79's pistol grip. Though the vehicles obscured his vision, he heard one of his men shouting and cursing. A woman sobbed and apologized rapidly and repeatedly.

The corner of Mulumba's mouth curled up in a snarl. He slammed the SUV's door and wound his way between a couple of the vehicles, searching for the sources of the noise.

He saw one his fighters, a youth who just was barely eighteen, standing over the woman. He was holding his AK-74 up by his left ear, the rifle butt pointed at her. She was holding one hand up defensively, begging for him to stop. Tears trailed down her cheeks and glistened even in the fading sunlight.

A cardboard box lay on its side on the ground. Its contents, a few cans of food, were spread over the rocky ground. Glass jars of cherry jelly had shattered, spreading the glass and the contents everywhere.

"Hey!" Mulumba shouted.

The guard, who'd been ready to strike, hesitated and turned toward Mulumba. The woman also whipped her gaze in the big African's direction and, seeing him, began to sob even harder.

Bridging the distance in long strides, Mulumba closed in on the other two. He looked at the guard.

"What's the meaning of this?" he demanded.

The guard gestured at the cowering woman with the barrel of his AK-74.

"She dropped this box of food," the man said.

"And you would beat her for this? For dropping my things?"

The man opened his mouth to reply.

Mulumba gestured for silence and the guard shut up.

Mulumba looked down at the woman, who was shaking and pressing her body against the ground as though she wanted to melt into the earth for protection.

"You dropped my food, yes?"

The woman nodded vigorously. "I didn't…"

Again he waved a hand for silence.

"You shouldn't be beat for this," Mulumba said. He watched as her face morphed from terror to confusion to relief. She began to sob again, this time from relief.

"Thank you," she said. "Thank you."

Mulumba smiled coldly and nodded once.

He then turned the Type 79's muzzle in her direction. Terror immediately overtook her again and she threw up a hand to protect herself.

The Chinese gun ground out a half dozen rounds. The bullets pierced her chest and flayed the flesh of her shoulders, splattering the ground and the cardboard box.

Turning his gaze on the guard, he watched the young soldier fidget and cast his eyes at the ground.

"I'm sorry about the food," the guard said.

Mulumba shrugged and his expression suddenly turned bored. "Don't worry. We have plenty of food."

He turned and walked away. For a moment, at least, he felt a little more in control, a little less vulnerable to surprises. Perhaps he'd been overreacting. The other two men had been simple-minded fools. Only by the most generous definition were they warriors. Of course, they both were dead, their corpses rotting in a hole somewhere. They weren't real soldiers, real masters of the destinies, not like him.

He reached his tent. He had a flask of whiskey stashed inside. A drink sounded good. Besides, he needed to go online to check with the bank in Zurich. As best he could tell, the Iranians hadn't come through with the money they'd promised. So they'd brought all this trouble on themselves for nothing.

He grabbed the entrance flap, peeled it aside and ducked his head to enter the tent.

The sound of automatic weapons fire at his six caught his attention.

He turned.

HAWKINS KNELT NEXT to one of the dozen or so tents arrayed throughout Mulumba's camp. The smell of marijuana smoke and body odor registered with him, causing him to wrinkle his nose involuntarily. He peered around the edge of the tent and saw a guard standing there, taking a hit from a marijuana cigarette. Holding in a lungful of smoke, the guard stared at the sky for several seconds before he exhaled.

Several minutes ago Hawkins had crept out from a line of trees to the west of the camp and crawled over fifty yards of hard-packed earth until he'd reached the tents. McCarter had sent him and Encizo in to terminate the outer ring of guards with knives and sound-suppressed weapons. The idea was for the two American members of Phoenix Force to lead as many of Mulumba's prisoners to safety before they launched any major gun battles. Once they'd moved them off the line of fire, it would be open season on the rest of Mulumba's people.

The only thing saving the main man at the moment was that the Stony Man fighters needed any information Mulumba could provide. Once they'd milked him of anything useful, his chances of growing to a ripe old age dropped to almost nil.

Assuming, that is, Phoenix Force actually could take down the guy's small army of rebels and snag him before he tried to escape. Assuming that one or more members of Phoenix Force didn't end up dying out here. Like the other members of the group, Hawkins knew every time he walked into battle could be his last. If his number came up, he hoped he didn't let down his teammates in the process.

Hawkins straightened just a little before he stepped from cover. He crossed the space between himself and the pot-smoking hardman. Just as he got within a few feet of his target, some stones crunched under Hawkins's boot. Even high, the other guy heard the noise and began to turn in Hawkins's direction. The soldier surged forward and was on the hardman in an instant. He clamped a hand over the guard's mouth, could feel the scratch of his whiskers against his palm, and jerked his head to the left.

With his right hand, Hawkins dragged the blade across the other guard's throat and held on to him until his struggling body went still. The Stony Man fighter dragged the corpse to a nearby tent and thrust the body inside.

Before Phoenix Force had hit this location, the U.S. military had scrambled a Predator drone over the camp to shoot new video. As best as they'd been able to tell, Mulumba had maybe twenty armed men in the camp, probably a few of them barely eighteen, if that. Hawkins had spent enough time on Africa's killing fields to know that rebel movements in these countries often recruited cannon fodder by force, snatching underage boys and coercing them into becoming soldiers or turning them into murderous automatons with the help of drugs. Experience told Hawkins that at any time he might end up blowing the head off of an aggressor who turned out to be a thirteen-year-old kid. He'd accepted that fact, though by no means had he made peace with it.

Moving through the tents, he caught up with two more guards, taking down each with his blade. He was beginning to feel edgy. It had been about two minutes since he'd made his first kill. With each passing second, the chances of something going wrong increased. Someone might miss one of the dead guards or discover their bodies. Mulumba might climb into one of the vehicles and leave, forcing Phoenix Force into a vehicle pursuit.

Hawkins had no intention of letting a thug like Mulumba walk away. He knew Encizo felt the same.

The soldier continued to wind his way through the tents, occasionally halting at one long enough to check it for occupants. He came across a pair of women; one was kneeling next to a fire, the second stood over her, pointing and speaking rapidly in a language Hawkins didn't understand. A grilling rack was positioned over the fire, its metal blackened by flames. A similarly scarred pot stood on the rack, its contents bubbling audibly. Hawkins caught a whiff of some kind of meat cooking in the pot, though he couldn't recognize it.

He made a mental note of their location before he started moving again. Once they started evacuating the camp, he'd try to make sure the two women were moved, too.

Slipping out into the open just for a second, he was able to get past the women, who seemed engrossed in their work, and continue moving. Up ahead, he could see a couple of the Toyota SUVs that Mulumba seemed to prefer. He also saw several women, all dressed in worn clothing, their feet bare or shod in cheap flip-flops, milling around the vehicles and carrying armloads of canned goods, sacks of nuts and coffees, as well as portable stoves and other items.

Mulumba had obviously decided to pick up stakes and leave the area. Considering that two of his compatriots had been killed in the span of a couple of days, Hawkins had no trouble believing the African strongman wanted a change of scenery.

Hawkins knelt in the shadow cast by one of the tents and activated his throat mike.

"Rafe?"

"Go," Encizo replied.

"You have a visual on Mulumba yet?"

"Negative."

"You made any friends?"

"Four. You?"

"Three down."

"Only three? I didn't come all this way to carry you."

Hawkins grinned. "I'll try to do better."

An automatic weapon chattered from some distance away and Hawkins flinched. The sound of several terrified women screaming cut through the air.

"Damn," he said.

"So much," Encizo said, "for evacuating people before it gets too heavy."

"Yeah."

McCarter's voice broke in. "You lads okay?"

"Vertical," Hawkins replied.

"What happened?"

"Somebody fired a gun," Hawkins said.

"I figured that much, you bloody ignoramus."

"You know as much as I do then."

"Impressive bit of intel," McCarter said. "I guess it's time for me to come in and fix everything."

"Please do," Encizo said. "We're confused and scared."

"Smartass," McCarter replied. "Hawk, you see if you can isolate Mulumba. Encizo, you do what you can to get the civilians out of here."

"Not sure I can get them all."

"Understood. Just get as many of them away from Mulumba as you can. If they aren't on the firing line, we can operate more efficiently."

"Meaning kill more bad guys more quickly," Hawkins said.

"Exactly," McCarter said.

HAWKINS RAN TOWARD the sound of the autofire.

He emerged from the tents and spotted three females clustered together. The two women who looked the youngest stood next to one another. One, her hand covering her mouth, was staring wide-eyed at something while the second woman had her hand flat on her chest as though she was trying to keep her heart from bursting out. A third woman stood in front of the other two, her slender arms extended, her legs spread in a wide stance, offering up her frail form as a shield for the others.

Hawkins admired the lady's guts.

He sheathed his knife, drew the Beretta 92-F from his thigh holster and threaded in the sound suppressor with quick, practiced movements. He crept up to the line of SUVs, then passed between a couple of them. One of Mulumba's men was walking up to the women, motioning with the barrel of his rifle for them to move away.

His face was a mask of anger and he was shouting something at the women that Hawkins couldn't understand. The shielding woman didn't budge. The guard halted a couple of feet from her and raised his rifle, preparing to strike her with it. Hawkins raised the Beretta in a two-handed grip, lined up a shot and tapped the trigger. A single 9 mm round punched into the bridge of the guard's nose. The bullet's impact smacked the back of the hardman's skull and he spun a quarter of a turn before his legs went rubbery and his body crashed to the ground.

The gunshot had splattered the woman with flecks of blood, brain matter and bone fragments. While she didn't scream, she did back away from the fallen man and, with her fingertips, began to frantically brush away the bits of human matter from her clothes and skin. Her young friends screamed again.

Hawkins disappeared between the vehicles again, not wanting to attract attention. Part of him worried the sight of a heavily armed commando in their midst would only stoke panic among Mulumba's prisoners. But he also worried they would, in their search for protection, crowd around him and render him unable to fight without putting them in jeopardy.

He moved to the other side of the SUV and glided along it, keeping his head down. He rounded the vehicle's front end, ducked and hid between it another vehicle. Peering out from his cover, he saw two of Mulumba's grim-faced guards running toward their dead comrade from a couple dozen yards away, their eyes sweeping for the shooter as they moved.

Hawkins waited a second for the footsteps to grow louder before he rose and, using the SUV for cover, put one of the approaching hardmen in the Beretta's sights. He squeezed the trigger twice. The bullets cut across the distance. The first buried itself in the throat of the thug on the right, while the second drilled through his nose. Momentum carried the dead guard's body another step before he pitched face forward onto the ground. The second guard had covered a couple of yards before it registered with him that his comrade had disappeared. Even as the man was casting a quick look over his shoulder, Hawkins was bracketing the guy's torso in the Beretta's sights, knocking out two more rounds of Parabellum, both of which lanced into the guard's chest and cut his sprint short.

Hawkins moved out from between the parked vehicles. The women were staring at the fallen thugs. The two who were afraid a few seconds ago looked on the verge of panic. Their hands were clasped over open mouths, chests heaving, tears streaming down their cheeks. Even the third woman, who'd thrust herself between the guards and her companions, stood frozen, eyes fixed on the dead men.

Apparently sensing someone was standing behind her, she whirled in Hawkins's direction. Her eyes widened and her mouth opened.

He jerked his head in the direction of the helicopter they'd used to get close to the camp. "I'm a friend," he said, using what little French he knew. "Go. Get out of here while you can."

She kept her gaze fixed on him for several seconds, likely trying to figure out whether she could believe him. The other women—who Hawkins could tell were little more than teenagers—were grabbing at her arms and shoulders, trying to pull her away. She shrugged them off.

Hawkins again gestured for them to leave. "Go."

The woman licked her lips.

"You here for Mulumba?" she replied, also in French.

Hawkins nodded.

Her face became a mask of barely contained rage.

"Kill him." She spit.

"Consider it done," he said. "There's a truck that way. Less than a kilometer from here. Gather up anyone you can find, take them there. Get these girls out of here."

She eyed him, her wariness obvious. "Who are you?"

"Mulumba's death sentence," Hawkins said. He was starting to feel impatient, knowing that he was burning time. "You need to know more?"

She chewed on her lip a moment and considered the question. "No," she said finally.

"Good," Hawkins said before moving on.

CHAPTER TWENTY-FOUR

Crouched behind a boulder, Encizo stalked two of Mulumba's men. One was speaking into a two-way radio. From the smattering of French the Cuban understood and the urgency in the man's voice, he could tell the thug was trying unsuccessfully to reach one of his comrades. The guy had tried to contact others on his team and had failed each time. The second man, apparently alarmed, was pulling his rifle from his shoulder and looking around, as though the others would pop out from a bush and yell "Surprise!"

Encizo already had stowed his blade and exchanged it for a sound-suppressed Beretta. By his reckoning, he was one hundred yards or so from Mulumba's tent. Though he couldn't see it, a group of the warlord's prisoners was visible, each of them carrying boxes and other items out of the various tents and storage sheds that dotted the property.

The SUVs, along with a couple of rusted pickups and sedans covered in faded paint, were parked along the dirt road that wound through the camp. The roads had been scarred with deep ruts, probably created during the country's rainy season.

The Cuban had taken down six other hardmen at this point. He guessed Hawkins had terminated at least as many. He needed to take down these men and make his way to Mulumba.

He rose in a slight crouch from behind the boulder,

sighted on the man with the radio and squeezed the trigger. The bullet slammed into the man's chest and he wilted.

Seeing his comrade fold in front of him, the other guard brought up his weapon and wheeled toward Encizo. The Phoenix Force commando never let the man finish his assault. The Beretta chugged two more rounds. One slug whistled past the guard, while the second lanced into his temple and drilled through his head before bursting out the other side of his skull. The impact caused the man to stumble sideways even as his body went limp and he collapsed. The Kalashnikov in his grip suddenly erupted, letting loose a short burst. Jagged yellow flames flashed from the muzzle and the bullets chopped into the ground, kicking up a plume of rock fragments and dirt.

Encizo muttered an oath. Obviously he'd just tipped the opposition that he was there. The remaining guards would respond.

"Encizo," McCarter said. "Sitrep!"

"I'm okay," he said.

"I heard shots."

"Affirmative. Just took down two of their men. One of them had to fire his gun one last time before he went to hell."

"I think we lost the element of surprise," McCarter said dryly.

"Thanks for the heads-up."

"Glad to help. Now, keep going."

"Roger."

Encizo continued toward Mulumba's position. He followed the line of vehicles as long as he could, depending on them for cover. By the time he'd gotten within twenty yards or so of Mulumba's tent, Hawkins had fallen in with him. They put several yards between them but continued to move in the same direction. By now, both men realized trying to maintain stealth at the expense of power no longer served them well. Encizo had holstered his Beretta and instead was wielding his MP-5 with a 30-round magazine. Hawkins brandished a compact M-4 A-1 CQBR.

A ragged line of gunners sprinted into view, their Kalashnikov rifles unleashing punishing bursts in the direction of the Phoenix Force duo. Encizo's MP-5 rattled out a deadly response. He hosed down the attackers with an unrelenting volley of autofire that cut down two of them. Hawkins's rifle spit out a burst of its own that felled a third gunner by shredding his gut.

The rutted road leading to Mulumba's quarters was J-shaped. The Phoenix Force warriors had made their way along much of its length. But now they turned the corner and walked the short curve leading to his tent. Each man had stepped off the road and was walking along the dry drainage beds that ran on either side of the road.

As they closed in on Mulumba's tent, they crouched and surveyed before they passed the point of no return on the trail. From his vantage point, Hawkins could see more shooters had stationed themselves in various spots in front of his tent, finding cover behind parked ATVs, oil drums and waist-high walls made of concrete blocks. Several block walls had been erected around the large tent, several yards apart from one another. Hawkins guessed they'd been built to help protect him from head-on assaults.

Under other circumstances it probably would have worked, giving Mulumba's hardmen a place from which to hold people at bay for hours if not days.

Hawkins activated his com link. "McCarter?"

"Go."

"We're in position."

"No kidding you're in position," McCarter replied. "I

can see you from here. You might as well be wearing those bloody awful orange hunting caps."

"You have a count?"

"Five guys. Three in front, two in back. I'm surprised they had the presence of mind to cover the entire building."

"Can you help us?"

"Silly question. Give me a three count."

As they'd drawn most of the guards to one side of the camp, McCarter had been able to reach a slight rise that looked down on Mulumba's compound. He'd positioned himself with an M-91 A-2 sniper rifle, chambered in .300 Winchester Magnum. Constructed with a four-round magazine, the rifle used by the Navy SEALS boasted a muzzle velocity of more than 2,500 feet per second and a range of 1,000 meters.

Hawkins knew McCarter, a master marksman, would put that kind of power to deadly use.

The rifle pealed once and Hawkins heard an anguished cry burst from behind one of the concrete block walls. One of the men apparently panicked. He popped up from behind one of the barriers and began to fire his AK indiscriminately in the direction of Hawkins and Encizo. The barrage forced both men to press as hard as possible against the ground as the bullets slashed the air above them.

After what felt like forever, another rifle shot boomed and the autofire ceased. Hawkins looked up and saw the shooter's upper torso poking out from behind one of the block walls, on his back. The top part of his head was missing and blood had pumped out from his neck, darkening the bone-dry ground.

"Two more and I get a teddy bear," McCarter said into their earpieces.

The final shooter surged out from behind a big oil drum. Even as he moved he laid down a blistering trail of bul-

lets that smacked into the ground a few yards in front of
Hawkins, forcing him to again press his face down into the
hard ground. When a pause in the shooting came, Hawkins
looked up and saw the guy diving behind a nearby pickup.
The vehicle was a faded blue-green that reminded Hawkins
of the paint used on the bottoms of swimming pools. The
tires were long gone. Rust had eaten away the truck's quarter panels and had left a reddish-brown-rimmed hole on
the driver's door.

In the meantime Hawkins flashed a series of hand signals at Encizo, who replied with a nod.

The Cuban warrior switched out magazines on the
MP-5 and fired the weapon at the dilapidated truck, rak-
ing it with an unrelenting storm of 9 mm slugs. The bullets punched holes through the vehicle's steel body, lanced
through the windows and caused the glass to web. Mean-
while, Hawkins rose and ran in a zigzag motion for the vehicle. Moving around the vehicle's tail end, he found the
hardman crouched behind the engine block, presumably
using the big piece of steel to protect himself from the gunfire. The guy's face registered surprise as Hawkins moved
into view. He raised his AK to attack, but Hawkins had
the drop on him. Another burst from the M-4 dispatched
the guy to hell.

"He's down," Hawkins announced into his throat mike.

In the next instant he heard a rifle's thunderous report,
followed a few seconds later by another shot.

"Two more gone," McCarter growled.

"Hawk," Encizo said. "Cover me."

"Roger," Hawkins said.

Hawkins watched as Encizo broke from cover, ran up
to the tent and tossed something through the door before
sprinting away. A moment later a loud crack sounded from
within the structure, accompanied by a bright white light.

Hawkins moved up behind Encizo, who went through the door first, his MP-5 searching for a target. They found Mulumba standing there, hands clasped over his ears and staring at one of the walls. Encizo crossed the room in a heartbeat and hit the guy in the back of the head with the butt of his MP-5. The big African sagged, his body swaying for a stretched second before it crashed to the floor.

THEY'D SEATED MULUMBA in a folding steel chair and bound his wrists with plastic loop restraints.

Hawkins had seated himself on Mulumba's cot, where he tried to break into the guy's laptop with little success. Once they took it back to their hotel, he figured they could have the Farm's cyber team break into it remotely to see whether it contained anything useful.

Mulumba's back was to Hawkins. From his vantage point, the American could see the guy had a large bruise forming on the back of his skull where Encizo had struck him. After about forty-five minutes, Mulumba groaned and began to stir. As he realized his hands were immobilized he took in a sharp breath and began straining at his bonds.

McCarter had been shuffling through Mulumba's papers while he was unconscious. Once he heard Mulumba make a noise, he threw the papers on the floor and strode over to the prisoner. He stood in front of the murderous rebel leader, crossed his arms over his chest and smirked.

"Hello, lad," he said.

"You're British? Why would the British want me? I mean, why are you doing this?"

"Blah, blah, blah," McCarter said. "Shut the hell up and leave the questions to the professionals." He yanked his Browning from its holster and gave the guy a hard stare. "Otherwise," he said, "I might lose my patience. You don't want me to lose my patience."

Mulumba glared at him, but said nothing.

"So," McCarter said. "You were expecting someone, just not the British. Is that right?"

"I said no such thing."

"No need," McCarter said. "I'm pretty perceptive."

"You're mercenaries," Mulumba said. "You have to be. Otherwise, why would you be here?"

McCarter thought he detected a note of hope in the rebel leader's voice.

"Not mercenaries," he said, shaking his head. "You can't buy us off, if that's what you were thinking."

"We're big fans of your work," Hawkins said.

Mulumba straightened in his chair. He turned his head and tried to throw a defiant look at Hawkins, but he couldn't quite swivel his head far enough.

"My work is freedom," he said. "I am here to stand up against tyranny, the tyranny of this government."

McCarter snorted.

"Freedom?" he said. "Do you call it freedom when you kidnap small children from their families and turn them into your personal soldiers? The stable of women you were keeping here—how many of them had the freedom to come and go? Not too many, I'd venture to say. They looked scared to death."

"I am at war," the big African said. "I don't need to explain myself to you."

McCarter bent at the waist and positioned his face about a foot from Mulumba's.

"You're right," the Briton said. "You don't have to explain yourself to me. We both know what you are. This isn't some grand political movement you and your friends are running. You don't want to make things better for your country or your people. All you and your friends really want is to burn down villages, steal other peoples' shit and force women to have sex with you. All the political crap you and people like you spew is just a wild stab at making it all seem less insane than it really is."

"Cut me loose and say that to me."

McCarter laughed and held up both his hands, palms facing Mulumba. "I'd cut you loose, but my hands are shaking too much," he said. "Now let's get down to business. A U.S. ambassador was killed in this country. Your friend, Jules Nmosu, was involved in it. It seems like he got the short end of the stick on that deal, though, considering that someone shot and killed him after he made his big score. Awfully shabby treatment for one of the founders of your high-minded organization."

Mulumba said nothing.

"Unfortunately," McCarter said, "things being as they were, there was no footage of the shooting. So we're left to wonder—who killed poor Jules?"

"Like you care. He's just another dead African to you."

"Oh, we care," McCarter said. "Granted, we don't really give a crap about Jules, per se. Frankly, I'd go piss on his corpse if it was lying on the ground here. That said, he did kill some people who actually matter. That pissed off some other people who really matter. And here we are. So, for starters, why did you idiots actually think killing a U.S. ambassador might be a good idea? And why did the guy who did it end up dead immediately after? You guys didn't want to split the money?"

McCarter saw Mulumba tense just a little bit. He held McCarter's gaze, but licked his lips before speaking.

"Who said anything about money? Or about killing this man in the first place?"

McCarter straightened. His hand lashed out in a blur and he backhanded the thug in the cheek. He then stepped back and let a grin tug at the corners of his mouth.

"Not sure who you think you're dealing with," he said. "But, in case you weren't paying attention, we laid waste to a dozen or so of your men, and barely broke a sweat. Not sure why you think people who can do all that will fall for your line of bull. Maybe that works with the local cops and military. But we're not them."

"You don't scare me," Mulumba growled.

"Of course we don't," the Briton said. "If we cut those plastic ties, you're probably ready to jump out of the chair and tangle with us."

The African pursed his lips. He stared at McCarter, then flicked his eyes to Encizo and Hawkins.

"Who started all this?" McCarter said.

"Ahmadah," he replied. "Hossan Ahmadah."

"Means nothing to me."

"He's Iranian. The son of a high-ranking army general, one who was involved in taking over the U.S. Embassy back in the 1970s."

"Okay."

"He's not military, though. He's Hezbollah. But he also runs an import-export business in Kenya. It's mostly been a front for shipping counterfeit things."

"Sells it to raise money to pay for Hezbollah's operations?"

"Right."

"And why did he want the ambassador dead?"

Mulumba shrugged. "I don't know."

"Bullshit," Encizo said.

"I don't know," he said more emphatically. "I didn't make the original deal with them. Nmosu had dealt with Ahmadah. He'd bought some weapons from him. The Iranian approached him a few months ago about this whole thing, offered to pay him for doing it. I didn't want to do it. I knew it would bring us nothing but trouble, but they didn't listen to me. That's why they killed Nmosu. They wanted to make sure no one could trace it back to Hezbollah, back to Iran."

"Because it would cause a war."

"Yes."

"You know this for a fact?"

Mulumba shook his head. "It's a guess. But tell me I'm wrong. Tell me that's not why Lukwebo is dead."

McCarter blanked on the name, but tried to keep his expression flat so the guy didn't realize it. After a second he remembered who Lukwebo was and shook his head no.

"We didn't kill Daniel Lukwebo," he said. "We didn't know he was dead, for that matter."

"Wish we had killed him, though," Hawkins interjected. "He's nothing more than a butcher and a serial rapist. How many international charges had he been indicted on?"

"Go to hell," Mulumba said.

"If I go to hell," Hawkins said, "I hope they give me a room right next to yours."

McCarter continued, "So some bastard from Hezbollah paid your band of merry men to kill an ambassador. You have no idea why. Did your friends ever stop to think they'd end up with the U.S.A. breathing down their necks? What the hell was their end game?"

"Hezbollah offered them a million dollars to commit this murder. Need I tell you that's a lot of money?"

"More than I have in my pocket, that's for damn sure," McCarter replied. "Offered, but didn't pay up, right?"

Mulumba ducked his head and stared at the floor. "Right."

"So you guys signed up for this gig. You killed several men. And now, the whole group's destroyed. And you didn't get your money. Is that right?"

The rebel leader nodded.

"Well," McCarter said, "nothing wrong with trying to better yourself, right?"

Scowling, the creases in Mulumba's forehead deepened. He knew they couldn't leave a killer like him to hurt more people. He shot a glance at Hawkins, who smiled grimly as he thought of the woman he'd encountered. He'd send her and her group, armed with the machetes Mulumba was so fond of, back to exact revenge.

"Payback's a bitch, they say," Hawkins mused. He addressed Mulumba directly. "You just wait right there, my friend. There are some women I'm sure you're dying to see."

CHAPTER TWENTY-FIVE

Two hours later the members of Phoenix Force had returned to the Embassy. As they walked across the grounds and made their way toward the main building, McCarter again noticed the American flag outside the entrance was flying at half-mast. When they entered the lobby, he saw the framed portrait of Ambassador Pearson staring down at them from the wall. McCarter knew the guy had a wife and kids. He'd been young enough to still have a fulfilling career ahead of him. That Hezbollah and Iran had caused all that to be cut short galled McCarter. That he had no idea why they'd set these events in motion bothered him even more.

While the others went off to grab a shower or to watch some television, McCarter and Manning went to Richard Austin's office to ask him to let them into one of the secure conference rooms.

McCarter had earlier contacted the Farm via his secure sat phone to relay what Mulumba had told them about Hossan Ahmadah. Kurtzman had asked for a couple of hours to investigate and promised to call back with information. McCarter was expecting that call, so he really didn't have time for any of the niceties.

Manning was too much of a workaholic to take a break. Instead, under his arm, he carried Mulumba's laptop and his satellite phone. He figured he would let Kurtzman and his cyber team at the Farm work their magic and mine for information.

During the trip back to their helicopter, the Phoenix Force warriors had met up with the group of women they had freed from the terror experienced at the hands of Mulumba and his thugs. When informed that Mulumba was back in his tent, securely tied and helpless, the women swore to retrace their tracks and turn the tables on their depraved master.

At two minutes after the hour, the secure phone in the conference room rang. McCarter snatched it from its cradle and brought the receiver to his ear.

"You're late."

"Two minutes," Kurtzman said. "Ease up."

"Sorry, lad. It's almost a reflex. You find anything?"

"A little," he said. "Ahmadah's tried to keep a low profile, but he's been on a couple of radars."

"CIA?"

"Yeah. And the State Department and a couple other alphabet-soup agencies—NSA and DIA—have been tracking him. Hunt is mining Europol and a couple other international databases, too, for leads."

"Hunt" was Huntington Wethers, a professor of cybernetics who'd taught at UCLA before being recruited to Stony Man.

Manning had been scrolling through the numbers stored on their seized satellite phone. "Did the good professor find anythingt?"

"Not yet," Kurtzman replied. "He's trying the shared databases first, which don't have the juicy stuff. But it's a hell of a lot easier than hacking into the systems of foreign intelligence agencies. We also filed a formal request with MI6 and the Canadians."

"Lord help us," McCarter said, rolling his eyes to the ceiling. "The Canadians?"

Manning scowled at him and gestured with his middle finger, prompting a grin from the Briton.

"What did you find, Bear?" Manning asked.

"Well, the basics your warlord friend provided are accurate. He did come from a prestigious family in Iran. His father retired from the military as a general. Apparently he was a smart political player. He was in the army during the last couple of years of the shah's rule. But he was smart enough to know changes were coming. While he wasn't a terribly devout Muslim, he was smart enough to make friends with several people who were. Once the ayatollahs took over, a lot of those relationships served him well. Next thing he knew he was getting kicked upstairs every few years."

"So he knew the right ass to kiss," McCarter said.

"Yeah, but don't dismiss him as a mindless climber. The old man apparently was a good soldier and a good organizer. Though it's been hard to prove, the general belief is that he provided weapons training and advice to the people who stormed the Embassy. Later on, he was among those involved in supporting Hezbollah in its early years. He provided training and occasionally recruited for the organization."

"So junior comes by his shitty beliefs honestly," the Phoenix Force commander said.

"In a nutshell, yeah."

"This is an interesting history lesson," Manning said, "but it doesn't tell us much about our target."

"I'm getting there, cranky," Kurtzman said. "Telling you about the old man also tells you something about our friend Hossan."

"Because?"

"Because the old man is everything the kid isn't and vice versa. The old man was a pragmatist. If another secular strongman government had moved back into Iran, he'd have been right there, carrying suitcases and kissing ass. Hossan is the opposite. He really supports the Iranian theocracy and he thinks it's a good model for other Muslim countries, including Iraq. He hates Israel—doesn't consider it a legitimate state. He's a fervent supporter of Hezbollah, even if they are a bunch of thugs. It's what he knows."

"At least they're his thugs, right?" McCarter said.

"Right. And he's up to his neck with the group. He ships and sells a lot of the counterfeit crap that Hezbollah cranks out. He also fronts some of their real estate investments in Kenya—a couple of shopping centers and a couple of apartment buildings. He also smuggles ivory out of the country. He's their guy in that country and, according to the intelligence reports, he's pretty damn proud of it."

"Good on him," McCarter said. "Love it when a local lad makes something of himself."

"Does that mean he wants to be secretary general someday?" Manning interjected "Or is he happy hawking elephant tusks?"

"Not sure he's quite that ambitious," Kurtzman said. "If he is, he probably keeps it to himself. It's never a good idea to lobby for your boss's job. Of course, I've seen Hal's job. I'd sooner stick my arm into a meat grinder than volunteer for his gig."

"But when your bosses also are people willing to blow up buses, it's especially unwise to piss them off," McCarter said.

"Hey, speaking of Hal, the big guy is gesturing at me."

"The middle finger?" Manning asked.

"Ha," Kurtzman replied. "No, for some reason, the masochistic bastard wants to speak with you two. Hang on."

While they waited, McCarter leaned forward, clamped his hand over the top of a can of Coke standing on the table and pulled it toward him. Popping the top, he swigged from the can and set it back down.

"Gentlemen," Brognola said. "Nice work on tracking down the assassins."

"Not too hard," Manning said, "when someone else kills the perpetrator for you."

"No complaints here. Dead is dead. The Man's happy with how that turned out. You guys pulled it off without any civilian casualties. That's good news. Unfortunately it's the only thing he is happy about right now."

"Uh-oh," McCarter intoned.

"I told him that Iran and Hezbollah had a hand in this killing. You can imagine how happy that made him. He was even more thrilled when I couldn't tell him why they'd undertaken such a blatant provocation."

"Bad day at the office."

"Isn't it always? I've downed half a bottle of antacids. My stomach still feels like a witch's cauldron. Anyway, we need to know what they're up to. Able Team has also found Hezbollah thugs sniffing around this whole mess, too."

"They took care of them, right?" Manning asked.

"Negative. A load of them escaped by helicopter. We found the chopper a few hours later, abandoned in an airfield in Argentina. They torched the interior. Our best guess is they piled into another aircraft and headed out of the country. But it's only a guess right now. So we have a trained group of terrorists heading for God knows where. Able Team is looking over Escobar's facility, trying to piece together what the group was training for. But right now, we don't have much to go on. At the same time, the Man has to weigh whether to go to war over this. I think he'd pull the trigger on it if he had to. But I don't think an all-out war is an outcome he wants. So I'm having a bad day. He's having an absolute shitstorm of a day. And we all know what direction it rolls, right?"

"Understood," McCarter said.

"Based on everything we're seeing, we're thinking the attack in the Congo was the beginning of something, not the end. And, if something that brazen was the opening salvo, what comes later probably will be big and awful."

"Are we sure it's the Iranians?" Manning asked.

"We've got Hezbollah there," Brognola said. "And we've got some high-ranking Iranian officials linked to it. Am I missing something?"

"Look," Manning said, "it's very possible the Iranian government is stirring the pot. And Hezbollah's not exactly subtle in its attacks. So I wouldn't put it past them. All I'm saying is, maybe the people pulling the strings don't have the support of the Iranian leadership."

Brognola paused. "So you're saying it's a rogue operation?"

Manning shrugged, though Brognola couldn't see him. "Possible rogue operation. That's what I'm saying."

"And you base that on?"

"Just a hunch," Manning said. "A hypothesis."

"I won't dismiss it," Brognola said. "But I'm also not sold on it."

"Understood," Manning said. "Regardless, it doesn't change our next move. Right, David?"

"Right," McCarter confirmed.

"Good," Brognola said. "Bear is going to send you more information on the target. I'll make sure there's a plane waiting to transport the team. Give us a couple of hours to pull it together."

CHAPTER TWENTY-SIX

Argentina

Daniel Ben-Shahar strode toward his apartment building. In his left arm he carried a brown paper sack filled with a bottle of Pinot Noir, a loaf of bread and two kosher chicken breasts wrapped in white butcher paper. In his right hand he gripped the handle of a beat-up brown valise stuffed with the day's receipts from his bookstore.

When he got home, he'd break open the bottle of wine, cook up the chicken and pore over his bookkeeping work. He always left the number crunching for the evenings. It was his least favorite part of running a business and the easiest thing to put off. Maybe once he sucked down a couple of glasses of wine, he'd enjoy the work a little more.

Maybe he'd sprout wings and fly, too, he thought.

He'd spent too damn many years in the thick of the action to ever, ever enjoy the mundane tasks of running a business. That much he knew of himself. You didn't spend twenty years running operations for Mossad and playing dirty tricks on radical Islamists if you weren't a damn adrenaline junkie. You just didn't.

It wasn't a life for a sane man, feeling your breath stop every time you started the car, hoping this wasn't the day someone had hooked a bomb into your ignition. Trailing a trained assassin into a dark alley so you could slit his throat, then stopping by the toy store to buy your son a fire truck for his fifth birthday twenty minutes later. No normal man would do that kind of work. He'd become an accountant or an attorney.

Ben-Shahar had never been drawn to those professions, though. Instead, as a young man, he'd signed up for his compulsory military service, but stayed on for a decade after that. A natural athlete and a man who liked to push himself, Ben-Shahar had become a commando with the Israeli army. It had suited him to a point, though he'd always chafed at being told what to do. He'd often been dressed down by his superiors for questioning orders or—almost as bad—for suggesting ways to improve on orders. And, while he didn't enjoy the punishments, he did take a certain satisfaction from bucking authority.

It had eventually cost him his military career. In the 1990s, he'd been part of a small unit sent into Lebanon to find Israeli soldiers who'd disappeared. It was there that he'd first encountered Hezbollah, after they'd kidnapped a pair of Israeli army privates who'd been stupid enough to venture out of the barracks after dark to look for hookers. A group of Lebanese men had grabbed the soldiers and moved them to an empty warehouse in Beirut. Given enough time, the Hezbollah crew probably would have killed the men or maybe demanded that Israel trade some of its prisoners for the two soldiers. Ben-Shahar had seen enough of these incidents play out over the years to know the two soldiers were as good as dead.

When they'd received a tip about the soldiers' whereabouts, Ben-Shahar had, against his commander's orders, followed a tip that had led them to the two privates. During a short firefight, a bullet had ripped through his arm, but he and his team had succeeded in freeing the hostages.

Right after that, he'd been shown the door for his insubordination.

He'd assumed he'd lost everything at that point. Instead, two days later, a Mossad recruiter had showed up at his door and asked him if he still wanted to fight for his country. The young Israeli had known he wanted to fight. Fighting for something was just a fringe benefit.

Once he'd finished his training, he almost immediately was sent into Lebanon, where he could track Hezbollah and its Iranian masters.

Over the years he'd hopped around the globe doing similar work in the Middle East, Europe, Africa and South America. Then two years ago, the powers that be had yanked him off the prime operations. Instead they'd stuck him in Argentina, where there was a significant population of Israelis, set him up with the bookstore, and put him on inactive status. They hadn't said it was an age issue, but he knew better. He'd started to move into his late forties. He still was in good shape, better than most men ten years his junior. But he wasn't in good enough shape for the commando operations he craved. At least that was the viewpoint of some of the men and women in charge of Mossad.

He considered fighting it, but decided against it. Terrorists shooting at him, he could handle. Bureaucrats armed with pens and stacks of paper? Not so much. So he'd traveled to Argentina where he could serve long enough to score a pension. Then he'd start working in the private sector as a security consultant or something.

He first sensed danger when the small hairs on the back of his neck stood up. He took a few more steps before he stopped in front of a pet store window and looked inside at two white kittens and a calico kitten wrestling on shredded newspaper. Staring into the window for several seconds, he noticed a young man in jeans, a white T-shirt and a red windbreaker walking toward him. The young man quickly averted his gaze the moment Ben-Shahar looked in his direction, which only stoked the Israeli's suspicions. Most people would smile, nod or return the stare with one of their own before they looked away.

Ben-Shahar turned and walked away from the display window. The thoughts began to tumble through his mind. He had plenty of enemies sprinkled throughout the world, including here in Argentina. Though he'd adopted a new name, dyed his hair black and wore colored contact lenses, it still was possible he'd been identified by Hezbollah members, Iranian diplomats or someone else who wanted him dead.

If they'd identified him, that was a problem, too. His cover wasn't flawless, but it was good. If he'd been outed, he'd have to at least consider the possibility that someone in Tel Aviv or at the Israeli embassy had sold him out. It certainly wouldn't be the first time Mossad—or any spy agency, for that matter—had blown the cover of one of its own agents.

He could try to figure it out. Or he could get his new friend to explain it all to him.

The latter option made the most sense.

He kept walking and two blocks later, an alley opened up to his right. He quickly turned into the alley and walked several paces inside. By the time he turned around, the young man in the red windbreaker was standing in the alley entrance. In his right hand he gripped a knife that he waved menacingly at Ben-Shahar.

"Your money, old man!" the guy said. "Give it now!"

Ben-Shahar sized the man up. His accent marked him as a local. His feet were spread the same width as his shoulders. He looked balanced and Ben-Shahar saw no signs of nervousness in his body. Nor did he detect any emotional strain in his voice. He obviously wasn't a neophyte mugger, but it was unclear whether the guy was a skilled assassin or a spy.

"Sorry," Ben-Shahar said. "My hands are full. I can't reach my wallet."

"I don't want your wallet," the mugger said, his voice level. "You own the bookstore. You carry that bag home with you every night. You drop off an envelope in the night deposit drawer at the bank before you go home to your apartment."

"How do you know all this?" Ben-Shahar asked. He purposely tried to inject some fear into his voice to give the other man a false sense of confidence.

"You ask too damn many questions. Just give me the valise. Maybe I'll let you go home."

"Of course."

Ben-Shahar took a couple of steps forward and threw the valise on the ground between them.

The guy looked at it, then at him. He threw a glance over his shoulder to make sure no one was behind him.

"Pick it up and hand it to me."

Nodding, Ben-Shahar set his bag of groceries on the ground. He took a couple of steps forward, scooped up his valise by the handle, and moved toward the man. The mugger threw out his hand and gestured for the former Mossad officer to stop. Ben-Shahar ignored him, stepped forward once more and swung the valise. One corner of the case's bottom hit the other man in the temple, knocking his head to the side and throwing him off balance. Ben-Shahar swung the case again in an arc and brought it down hard on the man's spine. He belched out air and dropped to the ground on all fours, only to receive a punishing kick to his body, snapping several ribs in the process. He collapsed to the ground, rolled onto his back and gasped for air.

Ben-Shahar walked over to the man and set the sole

of his shoe on his throat. The mugger bucked his torso wildly and grabbed at his ankle. He tried in vain to push his leg away. Ben-Shahar had too much leverage for that to work. He continued to push his foot down until he felt the man's neck give way under the pressure, saw the man's eyes change from wide with terror to dull, unseeing.

Ben-Shahar retracted his foot, stepped back and studied the newly dead man for several moments. He walked away, retrieved his bag of groceries and his valise, and headed out of the alley. He was just a few blocks from the apartment, where a night of wine and accounting awaited him.

BEN-SHAHAR SHUT THE front door of his apartment behind him, carried his things to the dining table and set them on top of it. Moving to the kitchen sink, he started water from the tap and let it run for several seconds. While he waited for the water to warm, he studied the dried blood staining his knuckles. Not bad for an old man, he told himself. I haven't lost a thing.

As he washed his hands, he thought about the fight. He'd walked away uninjured, barely even winded. He'd had half-inch-thick blocks of steel sewn into the bottom of the valise. The modification had made the case heavy as hell, but it also gave it lethal striking power, like a blackjack.

Ben-Shahar had held back when he'd hit the guy in the head. Judging by the thug's cool demeanor, he guessed the guy was a career predator. No doubt, Buenos Aires would be better off without the bastard stalking its citizens.

Still, he didn't need the headache of a murder charge. He didn't need the publicity that came with it, either, especially since he was living under an assumed name.

He laid the towel on the counter, opened a drawer and rummaged around for a bottle opener for a few seconds until his phone chirped, announcing a text message. Retrieving the phone, he looked at the message and scowled. The message consisted of a five-digit sequence of numbers.

Pocketing the cell phone, he went to his landline, picked up the receiver and dialed a number. He heard several clicks as the call was patched through a series of cutout numbers. On the third ring, a man answered.

"Yes?" It was Eitan Chertok, his former commander.

"It's me," Ben-Shahar said. "Daniel."

"Daniel," Chertok said. "Good to hear your voice."

"You, too, my friend?" Ben-Shahar asked. "I assume this isn't a friendly call."

"It's not. I have bad news for you."

"Okay."

"Abaigael Katz. I'm afraid she's dead."

Ben-Shahar felt as though someone had punched him in the gut.

"Abbey? Dead? What happened?"

"She died in the field. She was shot."

"Damn."

"I know you two were close…"

"Close? I entered the military with her father. I held her when she was a baby. I watched her grow up. She was like a daughter for me."

"I'm sorry. But that's why I called you. I knew you'd want to know."

Ben-Shahar's throat ached and his eyes squeezed shut. "Thank you for the call." He sucked in a deep breath to steady himself. "Who did it?"

"I can't tell you."

"You can't *not* tell me. You know that."

"It's classified."

"I need to know."

"Daniel…"

"I made her father a promise. He never wanted her to

join Mossad. But there was no talking her out of it. I made a promise…"

"I know…"

"A promise that nothing would happen to her."

"You can't make those kinds of promises, my friend. Not in this business."

"Who did this?"

"Seif Escobar. You know him."

"Al-Jaballah's toady in Mexico?"

"Yes."

"Was she tracking him?"

Chertok hesitated for a couple of seconds. "No. She was undercover. She infiltrated his organization a while ago. It seemed like she was fitting in just fine. When she missed her check-in, we knew something was wrong. Then the Americans told us she'd been killed."

"The Americans? What's their role in all this?"

"You heard about the assassination of the U.S. ambassador?"

"In Africa? Of course."

"Apparently, Escobar and al-Jaballah were involved somehow."

"Which means the Circle is involved."

"I didn't say that."

"You didn't need to. Why would they do this?"

"We're not sure. They're a bunch of blasted fanatics. Whatever their reason, it won't be good."

"It also won't be good for Israel."

"Forget about it, Daniel. I know where you're going. Just forget about it."

"You know I can't do that."

"I can order you to stand down."

"You can't order me to do anything. I was retired, remember?"

Chertok again fell silent.

"Have I made my point?" Ben-Shahar asked.

"Damn it, I'm telling you to leave it alone."

"Thanks for the call, old friend."

"Daniel…"

The former Mossad agent hung up the phone. A minute later, it began to ring. He grabbed the cord, yanked it from the wall and went to his room to pack a suitcase.

CHAPTER TWENTY-SEVEN

"Hey," McCarter said. "He's here."

Manning, who'd been pouring coffee from a thermos into a foam cup, stopped and shot his friend a look. The pair had been camped out in a building next to Ahmadah's offices for about two hours while Encizo and Hawkins watched his apartment. McCarter was standing next to a window, peering outside, his eyes intensely focused on something.

Hawkins set down the thermos and moved next to the Phoenix Force commander, careful to keep his bulky frame away from the window.

"What do you see?" Manning asked.

"Black sedan. Pulled up to the back door. Two—no, three—guys just climbed out. None are Ahmadah."

"Must be the muscle."

"They're looking around, hands in their jackets. So, yeah, either they all have heartburn or they're the security detail. And now we have a fourth guy climbing out of the back. It's Ahmadah."

"So, three security guards and the main target."

"Assuming they have no one inside the building."

"I wouldn't take that bet."

"Me, either."

"Because we're seasoned combat professionals."

McCarter grabbed a duffel bag from the floor and fitted the strap over his shoulder. It was unzipped. He dropped his right hand inside and wrapped his fingers around the grip of an MP-5. He also carried a pair of Browning Hi-Powers, one in a shoulder holster, the other in the small of his back, both hidden by a light windbreaker.

The big Canadian had stowed an MP-5 in a shoulder rig; he carried extra magazines for it in a black duffel bag similar to the one McCarter was toting. A .357 Desert Eagle rode on his hip in a fast-draw holster clipped to his belt. The warrior also had stowed a pair of flash-bang grenades in the duffel bag.

As they moved down the stairs, McCarter sent the others a text to let them know the Iranian had surfaced at his office.

"Should we wait until they get here?" Manning asked.

McCarter shook his head.

"They're at least fifteen minutes away. Most likely Ahmadah is here for a while. But if he just stopped in to grab something, I don't want to be standing around all slack-jawed if he turns around and leaves in five minutes."

"Good point," Manning said.

"Like I said, combat professional."

Nairobi, Kenya

IT HAD BEEN years since Ben-Shahar had visited Kenya. However, he still had contacts in the country; former Mossad agents like himself who kept one foot in the spy game even as they'd moved on to other professions.

He'd arrived at the Jomo Kenyatta International Airport several hours ago. He'd taken a taxi to the hotel, where he'd showered, eaten a half decent meal and changed clothes. From there, he'd met with a former Mossad agent who sold wildlife tours to Israelis and other foreigners. The guy had been happy to pass him a .380 Beretta, no questions asked, along with a couple of spare magazines.

He'd come to Kenya to find Hossan Ahmadah. They'd never met. However he'd learned of the man during his career with Israeli intelligence and had followed Ahmadah's career as much as possible. Ahmadah had his hands in all kinds of operations and ran logistics for Hezbollah, the Circle and other related groups. If anyone knew about the location of Escobar and al-Jaballah, it was him.

Standing across from Ahmadah's office building, Ben-Shahar saw the Iranian's black Mercedes sedan roll past the building and turn right into an alley next to it. He crossed the street, waited a minute and followed the sedan into the alley. When he heard car doors slam, he backed up against the exterior wall of Ahmadah's building and let another minute pass, figuring that was enough time for the Iranian to get inside.

Before he could start down the alley again, he saw a pair of men step into view from behind the neighboring structure. Both were Caucasians; one tall, the other bulky like a weightlifter or an American football player. He noticed the tall one had a duffel bag looped over his shoulder, the straps pulled taut by the bag's heavy contents. His hand was buried inside the bag. The Israeli's gut told him the man was carrying a gun inside the bag.

If that was true, who the hell were these guys? Since Ahmadah was part of a group that had killed a Mossad agent, it was possible the two men were from the Israeli secret service. Maybe they'd come here to interrogate him or even to kill him. If it was the latter option, it could end up being a damn awkward situation for Ben-Shahar, especially if he went in there, guns blazing.

It also was possible they were Americans who were looking to terminate some Hezbollah operatives. Again, that could be a problem if they took the Iranian out before Ben-Shahar had a chance to speak with him.

He glided along the edge of the building, ducking under the occasional window, his eyes searching for security cameras or alarm sensors. It felt good to be doing this. He hadn't realized how much he'd missed being in the field, missed the excitement.

Then he remembered why he was here and the rush dissipated, replaced first by a creeping guilt, then by a cold rage that dulled everything else. Other than an ex-wife who hated him, Katz and her parents had been the closest things to family that Ben-Shahar had. With them gone and his spy career reduced to nothing more than a sideshow, the Israeli carried a profound sense of emptiness. It had surfaced several times since he'd first received the phone call from his former Mossad commander. It was a feeling he only could acknowledge in brief flashes before he switched his mind back to the task at hand.

At this moment, that was a good thing. He needed to focus. He was about to thrust himself into the jaws of the reaper.

MCCARTER TOOK THE lead as he and Manning rolled up on the building. One of Ahmadah's thugs had remained outside to guard the door. Lighting a cigarette, he was leaning against the Mercedes, his rump resting against the driver's-side quarter panel. As he shook the match in his right hand to extinguish it, he turned toward the Phoenix Force commandos. Pushing himself off from the car, he turned to face them, his cigarette pinched between his lips. He slid his right hand behind his back and gestured for them to halt with his left hand. He barked in French for them to stop.

McCarter yanked the MP-5 from inside the duffel bag and squeezed the trigger. The SMG cut a ragged line across the man's torso, killing him. The Briton jogged over, knelt next to the man and began sifting through his pockets while Manning scoped out their surroundings for other threats.

Pulling a ring of keys from one of the man's jacket pockets, McCarter used the key fob to unlock the Mercedes and pop open the trunk. Looping his arms underneath those of the dead man, he dragged the thug around to the back of the sedan. He dumped his torso in first, then grabbed the man's ankles and folded his legs, stuffing them inside the trunk. He wiped his hands clean on the man's pant leg and slammed the lid closed.

He moved to the door and tried three keys from the dead man's key ring before he found one that worked. Manning stood behind McCarter, his MP-5 held snug at his hip. As the door swung open, Manning went through it with McCarter a couple of steps behind him.

The first room they entered was filled with cardboard file boxes. McCarter closed the door behind them before they moved deeper into the building. They split up and quickly searched the first floor and found it was empty.

McCarter found a set of stairs leading to the second floor and he paused there, waiting for Manning to catch up. The big Canadian emerged from a hallway and moved to his friend's side.

The former SAS commando stepped onto the stairs first while Manning covered his six.

As McCarter reached the last couple of steps, he paused and signaled for Manning to follow. Manning was up the steps in seconds. A steel security door with a small rectangular window led from the stairs into the second floor. Manning turned and watched behind them while McCarter pushed down on the release bar and eased the door open.

The Phoenix Force commander bulled his way through

the door, sweeping the muzzle of his MP-5 over his surroundings in search of a target. Manning did likewise.

They'd stepped into a long hall with a white-tiled floor that made every sound seem several times louder than it was. From up ahead, they could hear male voices speaking in Arabic. Neither of the warriors understood more than a few words that they'd picked up during various missions in the Middle East over the years.

McCarter and Manning moved down the corridor. The voices grew louder as they got closer to the source. They had passed a couple other doors as they'd traveled the corridor, but the rooms had been empty. In one they had found a Hezbollah flag hanging on the wall and a spot on the floor had been marked as facing Mecca, presumably for praying. Another of the rooms included a conference table and a couple of white boards, while a third was furnished with three desks with phones and computers.

The conversation between the men down the hall stopped. McCarter halted and he gestured with a hand for Manning to do likewise. Had Ahmadah heard them? McCarter strained his ears for any sign the Iranians had heard them and planned to attack.

He dropped to one knee and aimed the MP-5 at the door. Manning remained on his feet, but also kept his H&K trained in the same direction as McCarter.

After a few seconds the men started conversing again. Perhaps it'd been a natural pause? McCarter ran his eyes over the corridor to double check for motion detectors, cameras or other devices that might betray the Stony Man fighters' approach, but saw nothing.

In the meantime Manning heard something at his six and turned to look. The stairwell door was opening and he saw one of Ahmadah's gunners coming through it.

Apparently the gunner was not surprised to find them as he was already drawing a bead on Manning.

The Canadian swung the MP-5 and began hosing down the hallway with a storm of 9 mm rounds. The barrage cut a path toward Ahmadah's shooter and spurred him to dive to the ground. The Iranian's SMG was chugging out flames and hot lead.

Manning had gained a head start of less than a second. It made all the difference. The bullets from Manning's SMG caught his opponent in midair.

Once it became clear to McCarter that a quiet approach was impossible, he decided to try another tack. The Briton surged down the corridor, toward the room where the voices had been coming from. He palmed a flash-bang grenade, pulled the pin and tossed it through the door. The occupants of the room began shouting and a commotion was audible from the room. The grenade let out a sharp, disorienting crack and a heartbeat later McCarter was through the door.

In the room he saw Ahmadah, hands clamped over his ears. A guard, holding a submachine gun, was turning toward the door, though his motions were slow, as though he didn't have his bearings.

The MP-5 chattered. The guard caught a blast in the torso and dropped to the floor. The crackle of autofire registered with Ahmadah, who shoved a hand inside his jacket and clawed for hardware. With a couple of long strides, McCarter was on him. He jabbed the MP-5's muzzle into the guy's chest.

"Wouldn't do it, lad," he said.

The Iranian swore under his breath but withdrew his hand from inside his jacket and raised his arms.

A COUPLE MINUTES later Ahmadah was seated on the couch. McCarter had relieved him of a pistol and a folding knife.

He'd emptied the magazine from the pistol, a Makarov PM, set the weapon on a coffee table in front of Ahmadah, and pocketed the knife. Manning had bound the guy's hands behind his back with plastic handcuffs.

McCarter, arms crossed over his chest, stood over the Iranian and stared down at him. Ahmadah returned the stare. McCarter saw plenty of rage and defiance in the Iranian's eyes, but little fear. They were in for a long day, unless the Briton got control of the situation quickly.

"I won't tell you a thing."

"Shit, lad, at least let me ask the question," McCarter said.

"Burn in hell," the Iranian replied.

McCarter kept his eyes locked on Ahmadah and nodded his head slowly. "So, it's going to be like that, eh?" He turned to Manning. "Guess we might as well just go home."

The Canadian nodded his head in agreement. "Looks like it," he said.

"You want to cut his throat?" McCarter asked.

Manning shook his head emphatically. He grabbed a piece of his shirt and tugged at the fabric. "Brand new," he said. "Hate to get it bloody the first day."

"You're a dandy," McCarter said. "Guess it's best left to the real men to handle the dirty work."

"I guess. You know, we could take him back to the United States."

"What? You heard the man. He wants someone to kill him."

"Wait, how about that black site in Bulgaria? The CIA still has that."

"We don't talk about the black sites."

Manning grinned. "He's not going to be telling anyone."

"Fair enough."

McCarter turned his head back in Ahmadah's direction. Though his gaze still looked steely, McCarter noticed a film of perspiration glistening on his forehead. He swallowed hard as the Phoenix Force fighters studied him.

"What do you say?" McCarter asked. "You Hezbollah types like Bulgaria, don't you? Blew up a bus or some crazy crap there, right?"

Ahmadah spit on the floor between him and McCarter.

"You don't scare me," he said.

A smile ghosted McCarter's lips. "Famous last words, son." He turned to Manning. "They still doing the experiments at that place?"

"The place in Bulgaria?" Manning pretended to think about it for a few seconds. "Just the stuff with the genitals."

"Genitals?" Ahmadah cried.

McCarter smirked. "Genitals. You know what those are, right? Your bloody twig and berries. Your wedding tackle."

"I know what they are!"

"Hey, easy. Don't lose it. Look, it's some human endurance thing. See how much pain you can take before your heart bursts or some heady crap like that. Don't worry. A sturdy fellow like you won't miss his naughty bits if some scientist chops them off, right?"

"No country's going to let you do that on their soil," the Iranian said, some of the certainty gone from his voice.

"You keep telling yourself that," Manning said, "while some witch doctor works his magic on you. All they need is a house with a soundproof basement."

"You are bastards!" Ahmadah yelled. "If something happens to me, my friends will make sure you never rest. They'll hunt you relentlessly, kill your families, everyone you love. They'll attack your country!"

McCarter guffawed. "Families? Do we look like we go

home to houses with white picket fences in the suburbs?"
He jerked a thumb at Manning and then himself. "As far
as the world's concerned, we don't exist. We're way off the
books. Here's my life. I slither out of a damn hole somewhere and burn people like you down so Bob the insurance
salesman in Idaho can get drunk at the office Christmas
party, feel up his receptionist and beg forgiveness for it on
Sunday. That's my life. You want to rob me of a normal life?
Good luck with that, lad. The people I work for would burn
the last six generations of the fetid gene pool you crawled
from. Spare me the empty threats."

McCarter shook his head in disgust and looked over at
Manning. "This jackass is wasting our time. I'm thinking
Bulgaria."

Manning shrugged. "I don't know," he said. "If we're
going to take him to Bulgaria, we have to listen to him during the whole flight."

"True."

"How long is the flight?"

"Hell if I know. Hours."

"Long time."

"Right. Too bloody long to listen to this idiot. Of course,
he's pissed me off. Enough that I'd like to see him dumped
in a nameless prison somewhere."

"Sure."

McCarter turned back to Ahmadah. The Iranian was
clenching and unclenching his jaw, making his cheek muscles ripple.

"What do you think?" McCarter asked. "Ready to get
away from it all?"

Ahmadah licked his lips. "You two are insane."

"What's your point?"

Ahmadah stared down at the floor. "It doesn't have to
go this way," he said.

BEN-SHAHAR CREPT THROUGH the first floor, taking in the bloody wake created by the other two men.

He hadn't seen them kill the guard outside. But they hadn't bothered to clean up the blood on the sidewalk. Considering who they were targeting, he was half tempted to hose down the concrete himself to prevent the local police from seeing the mess and investigating. He guessed they'd have a cleanup crew of some kind following up quickly behind them.

Ascending the stairs, he slipped onto the second floor, the Beretta poised in front of him. He saw another corpse sprawled on the floor. A pool of blood had spread beneath the man. His weapon still lay on the floor a few feet from his curled fingers. The smell of gun smoke lingered in the air.

From up ahead he heard people speaking. He moved past the dead man and made his way toward the voices. When he reached the doorway, he stood outside the jamb and listened to the conversation. He recognized Ahmadah's voice from recordings he'd heard during his time with Mossad. The other man's accent was unmistakably British. The third guy, he couldn't quite place. Canadian, maybe?

He felt an urge to surge into the room and force the Iranian to speak, but checked himself. He still had no ID on the other two men. All he knew at this point was that they were deadly. They may be just as willing to kill him, too. His thoughts began to whirl. Had he made a bad decision coming here without any backup? Beating down a mugger in an alley was one thing. Now he'd walked right into a shadow war, one where he didn't know all the players. It was an amateurish move, one he'd made out of emotion instead of cold logic.

Part of him hoped it wouldn't prove to be a fatal mistake on his part, while another part of him wondered what he'd lose by dying. He'd already lost what little family he'd had and his career likely was over. Maybe a final descent into blackness would provide a welcome relief.

Maybe.

He'd know soon enough.

"MAYBE IT DOES need to go this way," McCarter said.

"No, it doesn't," Ahmadah whined.

"You willing to talk?" McCarter asked.

"Yes."

McCarter nodded slowly. He studied the Iranian's face and his body language for clues about his sudden change of heart. Had they scared him enough to get him to turn on his country? Maybe. For some people the threat of brutal treatment was enough to soften them up; for others, it took a real beating, physically or mentally, to get them to cave. McCarter had taken Ahmadah as the latter type, a dead-ender who'd need more than tough talk aimed at him before he spilled secrets.

Maybe you were wrong, McCarter told himself. His gut told him otherwise.

"Why the change of heart?" he asked.

Ahmadah licked his lips. "I don't want to go to Bulgaria," he said. "I don't want anyone cutting on me."

McCarter scowled. "Little freak like you? I figured you'd enjoy that stuff."

"No, you're wrong."

McCarter nodded his head slowly. "Good," he said.

"Why did you hit the U.S. ambassador?"

"Because he's an agent of the great Satan," Ahmadah replied. "He, like all Americans, wants nothing more than to enslave all Muslim lands, to suck away our resources, kill our children, so America can grow richer. He was just another agent trying to further America's agenda and that of the illegitimate state of Israel."

McCarter looked over his shoulder, then back at Ahmadah. "You read that off a cue card?"

Reaching into his pocket, the Phoenix Force commander pulled out the folding knife he'd taken earlier from Ahmadah. He opened it and walked to Ahmadah, the blade gleaming under the light. For the first time, he saw real fear register in the bastard's eyes as he moved the blade toward Ahmadah's crotch.

"Paradise and all your virgins won't be the same without the crown jewels," McCarter teased as he moved the knife even closer, slicing the fabric of Ahmadah's clothing. McCarter smiled cruelly as their prisoner began to scream.

"You save that crap for your next YouTube video," McCarter said. "My friend and I are here for real information. You want to spew propaganda, I'll kill you here and save us the trip to Bulgaria.

"Why did you kill the ambassador? More important, why did you hire local yokels to do it? Hezbollah and Iranian intelligence have the juice to get it done themselves. Why bring in outsiders?"

"Deniability." Ahmadah spit out the word. "We wanted him dead. We didn't want it tracked back to us."

"Why were you worried about the killings being traced back to Hezbollah or Iran?"

"Isn't it obvious? We wanted him gone."

"Because?"

"Because he had strong ties in Iraq. People in the government there respected him—the Sunnis, the Shiites, both respected him. They trusted him."

"So you wanted him gone," Manning said, "because he had strong ties with Iraq? That would make sense if he still was the ambassador there. But he was working in Africa."

"You would've sent him back," Ahmadah said. "Once it happened."

"Once what happened?" McCarter asked.

"The attack in Iraq. Once we hit your Embassy there."

McCarter took a step forward and wagged the knife blade at their prisoner.

"Hit our Embassy? What the hell are you talking about?"

"The U.S. Embassy," he said. "We're going to hit it."

"Who? Iran or Hezbollah?"

"Neither. Not exactly."

"Damn it," McCarter said.

"When?" Manning asked.

Ahmadah tried to shift his weight in the chair, but the effort caused him to wince in pain. "A day," he said. "Maybe two."

McCarter noticed the Iranian's stare flicker past him. It had not registered before, but he'd done this a couple other times, too. McCarter turned to look behind him and saw a digital clock fixed to the wall.

"You got a date, lad? A bus to catch? What're you looking at?"

"Give me a minute," he said. "I can tell you the exact time the attack will occur."

McCarter gestured for him to stop. "Hold it," the Briton said. "Answer my question. Why are you so damn fixated on the clock? What's going to happen?"

Manning peeled away and headed for the door. He'd only taken a couple of steps when gunshots roared in the hallway outside.

BEN-SHAHAR HAD BEEN listening as the Iranian danced around the questions. The Israeli knew why Ahmadah was being so cagey. He didn't want to tell his interrogators about the Circle, but he also got the sense something else was at work.

He listened for another minute or so as the Westerners tried in vain to get usable information.

The small hairs on the back of his neck rose, telling him something was wrong. Acting on instinct, he whirled around and retraced his steps, heading for the stairwell. Before he reached the door, it swung open. A black-haired man with a thick, black beard came through the door. The guy swung a pistol at Ben-Shahar and squeezed off a shot. The bullet whizzed past Ben-Shahar's head. He raised the Beretta and fired it twice. His shots found their target, drilling into the shooter's heart. At the same time, a second guy came through the door.

Ben-Shahar was moving his pistol to fire at the man but before he could fire, the other man's pistol cracked. He felt something sear his shoulder and spin him around. A similar sensation burned through his abdomen. The gun had fallen from his grip. He twisted at the waist back in the direction of the shooter. The man was walking toward him, the pistol raised, lining up another shot.

Damn, he thought, so it does end here.

An instant later the shooter seized up as a pair of holes opened his chest. He crumpled.

Ben-Shahar started to turn around, but he felt a big hand grab his collar and yank hard, causing him to stumble. The fabric rubbed against the entrance wound on his shoulder and he moaned with pain.

"Come on," the Westerner he'd pegged as Canadian said. "Apparently today's just full of surprises."

It took Manning a couple of minutes to tear away the guy's jacket and shirt so he could see the wounds. He applied dressings to the bullet holes to staunch the flow of blood.

He looked up at McCarter and the other members of Phoenix Force, all of whom had arrived in the past few minutes.

"This guy is losing blood," he said. "Lots of it. We need to get him to a hospital."

McCarter nodded. The guy tried to sit up. Manning put a hand on his good shoulder to keep him down. "Stay still," he said.

The man waved him off. "I'm Mossad," he said. "And that son of a bitch is lying to you."

"Lying? What the hell?"

"Ask him about the Circle. That's who he really represents. They're the ones crazy enough to attack our ambassador. They're the ones willing to attack the Embassy. Ask him about that."

McCarter made eye contact with Manning. "You deal with secret agent man," he said. "Apparently my friend and I still have catching up to do."

McCarter turned and walked over to Ahmadah, who was staring at him with wide eyes as McCarter again withdrew the knife.

"What's the Circle?" he asked.

The Mossad agent grabbed hold of Manning's shoulder and used it to pull himself forward. The effort caused him to grimace.

"It's a group of men in the Iranian government," Ben-Shahar disclosed. "They answer only to the ayatollahs."

McCarter looked at the Israeli and then at Ahmadah. "He's stealing all your best lines," McCarter said. "You'd better start talking or I'm going to put two in your damn head, call it a day and go for a pint."

Ahmadah shot Ben-Shahar a murderous look, which transformed to a wide smirk.

"It's like he said. It's a group of men answerable only to

a few clerics. Most people don't know about it. The group provides a counterbalance to the Qods Force and the IRG. Some of the clerics worried that these groups were becoming too strong."

"Makes sense," McCarter said. "They have their own guns and money. Autocrats don't much like that kind of unchecked power."

"They're not autocrats—they're holy men."

McCarter wagged the Browning's barrel. "Stray off point again, and we're back at the whole me-shooting-you-in-the-head conversation. Our Israeli friend is making me a hell of a lot happier."

"Idiot," Ahmadah snapped. "The group operates well behind the scenes. It's much smaller than the others—a couple hundred loyal fighters and supporters."

"Including you."

"Yes, though they also borrow from Hezbollah on occasion. That's where they first recruited me."

"And the ayatollahs are good with this group?"

He shook his head no. "They were. But that changed for the most part. In the last couple of years, there started to be a lot of friction."

"Because?"

"Because the ayatollahs were so conservative."

"Surprise. That's sort of their gig, isn't it?"

"When the U.S. invaded Iraq, we wanted to make it unbearable for them to stay. We were allowed to do some things, like train fighters and smuggle weapons across the border. But that was all we could make happen."

"You wanted more?" McCarter asked.

"We wanted the Americans out of the country altogether. Some of us would've been just as glad to see you Brits leaving on the same boat. But to make that happen, we would've needed to ship more fighters, provide better weapons. Perhaps secure support from countries like China and Russia. Most of the country's leaders weren't willing to do it. If we went too big, they were afraid the U.S. would have no choice but to retaliate."

"Impressive restraint on their part."

"Rank cowardice!"

"All right, true believer, keep telling yourself that. Here in the real world, your little plan likely would have ignited a regional war. It would've made your war with Iraq look like a skirmish."

Ahmadah shrugged. "Sometimes you must spill blood to cleanse the earth of vermin."

McCarter gave the guy a cold smile. "Finally we agree on something, mate. And you killed Ambassador Pearson because he maybe could've helped cool tensions."

"Yes, and he also knew about the Circle, or at least knew many of the players. He might have pieced things together before we could pull the trigger."

"And, when you pull the trigger, what's that going to look like?"

"You'll see soon enough. They want to drive the United States out of Iraq. They want them to go away, and the only way to make it happen is to attack the Embassy."

"A suicide bomb. Like al Qaeda did here in Kenya."

"No, you small-minded bastard. They're going to hit with a UAV."

"A drone?"

"A drone. They built a damn drone and they're going to use it."

McCarter nodded. Able Team had heard rumors that Escobar was shipping parts for a drone to Iran. And, from what he understood, Blancanales had almost lost his life checking out those rumors. It made perfect sense. The for-

mer British commando stared down at Ahmadah, lifted
his head again and looked McCarter dead in the eye.

"The one you want is Ahmed al-Jaballah," the Iranian
said. "He's the one behind all this."

McCarter memorized the name.

"I'll look him up."

"He'll kill you," Ahmadah said. "I wish I could see it!"

CHAPTER TWENTY-EIGHT

McCarter made a call to Stony Man Farm and, in less than a half hour, the local CIA station chief showed up at Ahmadah's warehouse. He identified himself as Stephen Clark. McCarter pegged him as in his thirties. He was dressed in a navy-blue suit that looked tailored and expensive. His black shoes gleamed, as did his white teeth. Hawkins had remained behind while the others had driven Ben-Shahar to the hospital.

"You sure you're not a politician?" McCarter asked.

"You sure you're not an asshole?" Clark replied.

They were standing on the second floor of Ahmadah's office building and Clark was surveying the carnage. He'd been able to wrangle several Marines from the Embassy grounds to pick up Ahmadah.

"Thanks for the heads-up," Clark said. "Always good to know when Washington dispatches outsiders to shoot up my area of responsibility."

McCarter already was on a hair trigger. Worried about what Ahmadah had told him, even more worried about how to stop it, he had no patience. He turned to Clark.

"What you'll do," he said, "is get a clean-up crew in here five minutes ago. Burn the place down, throw the bodies into a river, send the Mercedes back home to New Jersey. I don't care what you do. Make all of this go away. And, as for that piece of shit, Ahmadah, you'll get him on a military transport back to the United States as soon as possible.

We're taking his laptop and tablet. Grab the servers, take them back to the Embassy. Our tech guy will call yours, so we can tap into all that data. My boss is already on the phone, ironing out any other particulars with your boss."

Clark scowled. "Yeah, I already heard you guys called Langley."

"Yeah," McCarter said. "Nothing personal. We're on a tight schedule and need to keep things moving."

"Got that impression. Who are you guys, anyway?"

"A figment of your imagination," McCarter said. "You never saw us here."

"I get that a lot," he said, his tone weary.

Clark turned and headed for a small knot of CIA employees who'd accompanied him to the scene and started gesturing and barking orders.

"Bloody hell," McCarter said. He walked to a table where they'd stowed Ahmadah's computers. He slipped the laptop under his arm and handed the tablet to Hawkins. McCarter had a rental car parked a couple of blocks away from Ahmadah's office. The Stony Man commandos exited the building and headed for the vehicle.

"What do you think, chief?" Hawkins asked.

McCarter shook his head.

"I think there's a storm bearing down on us," he replied.

"Ahmadah gave you no specific times?"

"No, I don't think he knew."

"You think what he's saying is credible?"

McCarter shrugged. "I think we have to act as if it is credible. Sitting on our hands, doing nothing, is unacceptable."

"Right."

They reached the car. McCarter unlocked the doors. They climbed in and headed for the hospital where the rest of the team had taken the Israeli.

"It's always possible the military interrogators will get more out of Ahmadah," Hawkins offered.

McCarter nodded his agreement.

"Given enough time," he said, "I'm sure they'd get something out of him. It's the time factor that worries me on this. Once he disappears, these bastards may go to ground or they may accelerate their timetable. I'd rather they did the former than the latter. Ideally, I'd rather they did neither."

"How often do we get the ideal situation?"

"Thanks," McCarter said. "That helps."

"Just making a point."

"Your point sucks."

Hawkins shot him a lopsided grin.

"Glad I could set your mind at ease."

"For now, we can ask our new best friend with Mossad—if he told the truth about that—for more information. In the meantime, the cyber team at Stony Man Farm is going to break into the laptop and the tablet remotely to see what they can nail down. Grimaldi was going to prepare the plane for a trip to Baghdad."

"So, for now, we wait."

"For now."

KURTZMAN STARED AT his monitor and clicked through several windows, scouring through the information from Ahmadah's computers.

The guy had kept detailed notes on everything related to the strike in Iraq. It was poor tradecraft, Kurtzman thought, but understandable. The Iranian had outfitted his computer with an encryption system that would stump more than ninety-nine percent of the cyber experts in the intelligence world and the private sector. And, to a guy who didn't know jack about computers, like Ahmadah, it probably had seemed like putting a digital Fort Knox around his information.

But Kurtzman and his team obviously were in the other one percent in that department. Kurtzman had encountered the encryption package before and knew that, if he hit certain triggers, it would erase the computer's hard drive. He'd managed to get past the software and now, along with Wethers, was perusing the contents.

Barbara Price glided up behind him and put a hand on his shoulder.

"You find anything?" she asked.

"Silly question," he said. "I found lots of stuff."

"Okay, tell me the right question."

"The question is do I understand what I've found."

"Okay, do you?"

He ran his fingers through his hair. "Not sure," he said.

She gave him a playful slap on his arm. "You could've just told me that."

"You didn't ask the right question."

"You're an idiot."

Resting his palms on either side of the keyboard, Kurtzman pushed his chair back a few inches from his workstation and screwed his eyes shut. "Sorry, I've been staring at this thing for hours. Here's what I'm trying to say. A lot of the stuff on his system is written in Persian. Some of it seems to be using some weird little code. There's probably enough material here to keep the NSA's code breakers and Persian linguists busy for years."

She nodded.

"That said, I did find some information about the drone."

"That's great."

"I found several pictures of the MQM-107 drone. Familiar?"

She shook her head.

"It was made by Beech Aircraft in the 1970s. Has a wingspan of just less than ten feet. Stands around five feet tall. Single turbojet. Beech made a couple thousand for the U.S. Army and Air Force. Some of those ended up overseas. Within the last year, it was reported that North Korea had purchased some from Syria and planned to use them as a building block for attack drones."

"Okay."

"I've only finished some cursory research," he said, "but, according to the intelligence reports out there, they had limited success with it. I'm guessing part of it for the North Koreans was a money problem. But along the way, I also found some other interesting intel about a group of Iranian and Syrian scientists who were working on a similar project for a couple of decades."

"What'd you find out?"

"According to the reports, they were a lot more successful with it than North Korea. They had at least a little more money to spend—economies of scale and all that crap. And they had some pretty good scientists behind the effort. It's not clear where the whole thing ended up or if it's ended, for that matter. The U.S. never found evidence of a finished product. Of course, we were kind of busy fighting two wars and trying to monitor Iran's nuclear program at the time.

"But I looked at the pictures. Some were stock photos of the original drone. But there were a few pictures of a sleek-looking little number that looked similar to the Streaker."

Price cocked an eyebrow and smiled. "Streaker?"

"Yes, Streaker. That's what the original drone was called. Don't go there."

"Fine, I won't."

"Good. This new craft looks similar to the original. Unfortunately it had one key alteration—a missile on each wing."

"Damn."

"Who knows whether they were functional? I mean, this is the same country that faked pictures of its Qahar 313 fighter jet flying over some mountains, right? Apparently they're not above it. But here's what makes the whole thing scary. There's a network of companies located in Iran, Qatar, Bahrain, and until a couple of years ago, Syria. U.S. and British intelligence had been tracking them for at least a decade, if not longer. The theory was they were purchasing weapons-related technology through front companies in Europe and the United Arab Emirates and shipping it back to Iran and Syria. Syria was definitely the junior partner in all of this. When things started to go south there, it looks like Iran cut them out of the loop. Who can you trust these days?"

"So who was running the companies?"

Kurtzman smiled and clapped his hands together. "You're stealing my punch lines, Barb. There's nothing on the official documents, of course. But all the intelligence reporting indicates that al-Jaballah was the guy pulling the strings at Sky Death Inc."

"Sky Death Inc.?"

"A little artistic license on my part. The English translation for the company is Shamsir Industries."

"Shamsir. As in the curved swords?"

"Bingo. Proving once again you're not just another pretty face."

She punched him in the shoulder, but grinned. "What else do you have for me?"

"After all that? I'm spent."

She nodded her understanding. "Keep digging," she said. "I need to talk to Hal."

"We STILL DON'T know whether these clowns have a working model of the aircraft?" McCarter asked. He was speaking to Brognola and Price through an encrypted line.

"No," Brognola replied.

When he'd received the call from Stony Man Farm, he'd excused himself from Ben-Shahar's room and locked himself in a neighboring room. Though they were speaking through a secure connection, he knew most of what he said could be heard easily through the door or walls, if someone wanted badly enough to listen to it.

"The general consensus," Brognola said, "is that they do have the craft. We sent the videos and images to Langley and Fort Meade, and they saw no signs that the things were frauds. And your guy seemed pretty confident that the strike was going to come down, right?"

"Yes," McCarter said.

"Not great evidence," Brognola said. "But probably enough to assume it's true. At least enough that we shouldn't ignore it."

"Not a chance," McCarter said. "We need to deal with it and I think I know how."

CHAPTER TWENTY-NINE

"We've got a couple of hours before we reach our destination," Manning said.

James, Grimaldi and Encizo, both of whom were assembling their M-4 rifles, looked up from their work and nodded their understanding. The three warriors were hiding in the back of an Iranian military truck that had been snatched by dissidents and turned over to the CIA for a small bounty.

The driver of the truck, Saied, was a fighter with the MEK—Mojahedin-e-Khalq. He was a low-level guy unlikely to trigger alarms with the border guards, but familiar enough with the territory and the language to get them through the country. If the guards hassled Saied, the Americans had handed him several stacks of Iranian currency and ordered him to buy cooperation from the Iranian border guards.

If that didn't work, well, it was going to be a bloody trip into the country, Manning thought grimly.

The road they were taking into Iran was pocked with potholes. The truck jerked and shuddered every time it crossed over one of the holes, setting Manning's teeth on edge. Finally, to distract himself from the rough ride, he shut his eyes and ran through their plans in his mind.

The control center was a small facility about twenty miles over the border. It had been an army outpost when the shah had ruled the country. After the ayatollahs took over, they'd kept it as an early warning post in case the Iraqis decided to rush the border. And over the decades they'd outfitted it to sweep up bits of military and other transmissions from their hostile neighbor. It had a small airstrip, a portable air traffic control tower and a handful of other buildings, including a hangar.

U.S. intelligence had nailed down what it believed was the most likely site for the UAV control center.

Now the Phoenix Force warriors just had to blast their way through a dozen or so guards, destroy the control center, all before they got the bird in the air.

But first they had to drive twenty miles into hostile territory without getting caught.

No worries, he told himself. Just another day at the office.

MANNING CHECKED his watch.

"We should be stopping soon," he said.

"Good thing," Encizo said. "All this bouncing and jostling around is killing me."

"Hard trip," Manning said. "Especially for an old guy."

"This old guy's going to kick your ass," the Cuban said.

"Sure, right after your nap," Manning said.

"And prune juice cocktail," Grimaldi added.

Encizo turned to James. "How about you? You want to pile on, too?"

"Hell, no," James said. "I respect my elders."

"Bastards," Encizo said, grinning.

A tablet sat on Manning's lap. He powered it up and checked their GPS coordinates. They had another mile to travel before they reached their target. Each man began gathering his weapons and other equipment.

The truck slowed to a crawl before the engine's growl grew louder and it launched into a turn. Manning heard the pop of tires rolling over gravel as the vehicle moved for another minute before it stopped completely. After a few seconds, the driver's door opened and closed and the warriors heard the crunch of footsteps moving alongside the truck.

Encizo and James moved to either side of the truck's interior, crouched into kneeling positions and trained their M-4 rifles on the door. Manning slipped his fingers around the pistol grip of his weapon and laid it across his lap, while Grimaldi pointed the muzzle of his M-4 at the door.

Manning heard someone working the door release before it was rolled upward.

Saied was the only one standing in the doorway. If staring down the barrel of four guns bothered him, he gave no outward sign of it.

"We're here," he said.

James climbed down from the truck, followed by Encizo. Both men surveyed the area while the others disembarked from the truck. Other than the ribbon of road stretching past them a couple dozen yards away, there was nothing.

Saied gestured to the north with his chin. "The base is that way," he said.

Manning nodded, walked around the side of the truck and spotted a smudge that he assumed was the control center.

By the time he returned, Saied had walked away from the others. He had grabbed two handfuls of a large tarp covered with digitized camouflage patterns, and was pulling it down, revealing a beat-up white compact car. He tossed aside the tarp, which rippled in the breeze and skittered over the hard-packed earth. He climbed into the car, turned over the engine and gunned it. The car lurched forward. Saied guided it to the nearby road.

James, Grimaldi and Encizo quickly pulled camouflaged tarps from inside the truck and used them to shroud the truck. Manning looked at the vehicle and decided that, while the covering wouldn't fool anyone up close, it would be good enough to obscure it from anyone at the target site, at least for a while.

If all went to plan, they wouldn't need much time.

If...

The big Canadian knew better than to expect things to unfold easily. In combat, plans had a way of becoming obsolete once the first shots were fired. They'd gotten this far without a problem, which Manning considered a minor miracle. But he also knew their luck wouldn't hold forever. So they'd better move.

"All right, ladies," he said. "It's clobbering time."

SEVERAL MINUTES LATER Grimaldi was lying on the ground, on his stomach. He'd set up a Barrett sniper rifle on a tripod and was staring through the scope at the front gate. James was about seventy-five yards away, also hunkered down in a depression in the ground, sizing up the opposition through a rifle scope.

A large gate protected the entrance to the UAV control center facility. A gravel road snaked through the gate. Four men, all wearing olive-drab fatigues and black combat boots, all carrying assault rifles, stood outside the gate. One of the men was scanning his surroundings, while two more were talking. The fourth had a handheld radio of some kind pressed to his ear. Grimaldi settled the scope on the guy's face and noted his concerned expression.

The Stony Man pilot activated his throat mike. "Cal?"

"Yeah?"

"You see our friend on the radio?"

"Guy who looks like he caught the clap from a sheep?"

"That's him."

"Yeah. What about it?"

"If he's not happy," Grimaldi said, "maybe we shouldn't be happy, either."

"Do I sound happy?"

"Point taken."

"Yours, too. What's bugging him?"

"Hell if I know. Try reading his lips."

"Good idea," James said. "Except I don't read lips or speak Farsi."

Before Grimaldi could reply, he heard the rumble of an engine to his left. He whipped his head in that direction and spotted a red pickup, clouds of dust rising up around it as it rolled along the gravel road leading into the camp. Turning the rifle in that direction, he trained the scope on the approaching vehicle's windshield. Other than the driver, he thought he saw two others inside the truck cab, though the sun's glare reflecting from the windshield made it hard to get a clear look.

"We have two maybe three people in that truck," Grimaldi said.

Manning's voice buzzed in the pilot's earpiece. "Sitrep."

"Truck. Undetermined number of occupants. No ID on them."

"Roger that. Let them go to the gate. The reception they get should tell us something."

"Roger."

Swiveling the rifle, Grimaldi tracked the truck through his scope. When the truck reached the gate, and came to a stop, one of the guards walked up to the driver's side of the vehicle and spoke to someone inside the cab for several seconds. Two of the guards circled the truck, though each kept his rifle slung over a shoulder. Obviously neither considered the truck's occupants a threat, Grimaldi thought. The guard who'd been speaking with the driver stepped back from the truck window and waved them through. A couple of seconds later the gate began to roll back. The driver goosed the accelerator and the vehicle rolled through the gate, which slid closed behind it.

Grimaldi followed the truck for several seconds before it stopped again, this time next to a low-slung building made of concrete brick that had been painted white.

His scowl deepened. Who the hell was in the truck?

The driver's door swung open. A tall, skinny man clad in the same olive-drab fatigues as the guards at the gate slid from inside the cab. He dragged his forearm across his brow, squinted at the sun and spit on the ground before turning back toward the vehicle. Stabbing his hands inside, his legs and back muscles tensed as he tried to drag something out only to have it yank his torso inside.

Finally the driver broke free, stepped back from the vehicle, yanked something from his hip and aimed the weapon in his hand inside the truck. At the same time another guard came around the front of the truck and stood next to the first guy. The truck driver stepped forward and reached inside the truck again. This time the second man squeezed through the door, too, and they both pulled, bringing a third man into view, his body limp.

Grimaldi cursed. The guy was dressed in a short-sleeved shirt and faded blue jeans. The pilot focused on the face to confirm his suspicions, even though he already knew the answer.

He keyed his throat mike.

"They've got our driver," he said.

"You sure?" Encizo asked.

"He's sure," James said. "I'm seeing the same thing."

"He alive?" Manning asked.

"Affirmative," Grimaldi said. "Looked like he was trying to fight them. I think the driver zapped him with a stun gun or something. He's looking pretty docile right now."

"You can bet," James said, "they already know we're here."

"If not, they will soon enough," the Canadian said.

"Right," Manning said.

"So we hit them now?" James asked.

"Yeah."

"I've got the creeps who nabbed our driver," Grimaldi said. "Cal?"

"I'll handle the guards at the front."

The tall, skinny guy with the stun gun had stepped away from Saied and was hammering him in the ribs and head with a series of fast, vicious kicks with his booted foot. The other guard stood by, arms crossed over his chest, watching his comrade.

Grimaldi lined up the shot. None of the men he'd observed so far seemed to be wearing body armor. His target had his back turned to Grimaldi, giving him a wider area to hit, especially at a distance of several hundred yards.

Curling his finger around the Barrett's trigger, Grimaldi took up the slack, exhaled about half the contents of his lungs, and squeezed off a shot. The slug drilled into the Iranian's back, snapping his spine before it exploded out the front of his chest in a spray of crimson and gore.

The second guy had knelt next to Saied and was looping his arms underneath the MEK fighter's arms when the first shot rang out. The soldier shoved Saied away, rose in a crouch, his hand scrambling for the grip of the Kalashnikov rifle while his eyes swept the surroundings for a target.

Grimaldi swung the Barrett's muzzle toward the other hardman, aimed for the center mass and triggered the big gun. The round slammed into the man's shoulder, the impact spinning him 180 degrees as he corkscrewed to the ground, blood springing from his shoulder. The guy was writhing on the ground, prompting Grimaldi to line up another shot at the man's torso. The round punched through the guy's rib cage and his body jerked up once before it went still.

The roar of another large-bore round was dying down. He looked in the direction of the gate and saw that James had taken down two of the guards. A third was crouched at the rear of the guard shack and was sweeping the muzzle of his Kalashnikov around, in tandem with his eyes, as he sought the source of the gunshots that had taken out four of his comrades.

"I've got this one," Grimaldi said into his throat mike.

Locking the guy in his sights, he caressed the trigger. The rifle thundered and the man's head disappeared in a spray of red.

"Front door's open," Grimaldi said.

MANNING SPRINTED FOR the stretch of fence that ran along the rear of the Circle's facility. Encizo, lying prone on the ground, covered his teammate with his M-4 rifle. Manning guessed the fence stood well over ten feet high. Razor wire ran along the top edge of the fence.

Once the demolitions expert reached the barrier, he dropped into a crouch and studied his surroundings for threats. Encizo uncoiled from the ground and sprinted to Manning's position and knelt next to him.

A couple dozen yards from the fence stood a prefabricated air traffic control tower. The windows of the elevated control room overlooked the whole property. An airstrip ran along the front of the tower. The tower's roof bristled with radio antennae and satellite dishes. An unmarked military helicopter sat on a patch of asphalt north of the tower.

Once the first big-bore rifle shot shattered the silence, the chatter of submachine gunfire erupted in response, only to again be sporadically drowned out by more .50-caliber rounds.

Manning brought around a pair of wire cutters and began working on the fence, while Encizo watched over both of them. With the gunfire up front, the Cuban hoped most of the gunners would press toward the gates. That would buy Manning and him enough time to penetrate the fence so they could undertake their respective tasks.

Things seemed to be unfolding that way for maybe thirty seconds. Manning had just finished cutting a long vertical line through the fence when a Kalashnikov-wielding man surged out from the tower's control room and opened fire. The first wave of gunfire went wide and slapped into the hard-packed earth a few yards behind the Phoenix Force commandos.

Encizo whipped the M-4 toward the shooter and squeezed off a fast burst. The bullets sparked against the catwalk railing and careened away. Encizo's opponent fired another burst that pounded into the ground just in front of their feet. Manning by now had dropped the wire cutters and was scrambling for his own rifle. The M-4 in Encizo's hands spit a more sustained burst and some of the rounds flew at upward angles into the torso of the shooter. The guy suddenly seized up, staggered and pitched forward. His body folded over the railing before his weight dragged him over the side and he plummeted headfirst to the ground.

The brief gun battle earned the Stony Man commandos more unwanted attention.

Three more gunners surged from behind the communications building. They moved in a staggered line, their weapons spitting muzzle-flashes and bullets. Another shooter hung back, crouched next to one corner of the building and squeezed off more autofire. Rounds pounded into the ground or whistled just past the ears of Encizo and Manning.

The Cuban darted away from his teammate. Running along the fence, he snapped off quick bursts at the line of gunners moving in their direction. Manning took his cue and sprinted in the other direction, his own weapon firing. If nothing else, they'd split the attention of their attackers and make it more difficult for the Iranians to take them out as a single target.

At least two of the shooters were tracking on Encizo and he was feeling the heat. Bullets were drilling into the ground around him as he ran in a zigzag pattern.

He knew his luck would run out any second. He twisted at the waist, angled the M-4 up and fired the grenade launcher on the run. A fragmentation round hissed out of the tube, arced over the fence and sent the shooters scrambling as it descended. When it hit the ground, it unleashed an explosion that rent the air, sending swarms of razor-sharp shrapnel flying in all directions. The bits of metal shredded clothing and chewed into the flesh of the fleeing Iranian gunners. The concussive force of the rounds knocked them from their feet and sent their ravaged bodies crashing to the ground.

The communications building had shielded the fourth gunner. He came around the building, his assault rifle looking for a target. Manning spotted him first and hosed the guy down with a torrent of autofire from his M-4.

Several tense seconds passed as they waited for more hardmen to show up. When none came, Manning located the wire cutters, returned to the fence and finished the hole he'd been cutting before the gunfight had erupted. Once he finished, he looked up at Encizo who gestured with the barrel of his M-4 to go ahead through the opening. Manning squeezed his big frame through the hole. Once he was on the other side, he took up his rifle and watched for any more Iranian soldiers or intelligence agents. Gunfire crackled elsewhere and Manning figured the other Phoenix Force warriors still were fighting.

Manning rose to his full height, flashed his old friend a thumbs-up and headed for the communications building.

Encizo ran for the nearest building. The intelligence they had was sparse, but it was believed to be a barracks or a mess hall. He glided along the side of the building, using it to cover his approach. His real target was the building they believed housed the control center for the UAV. When he reached the edge of the building, he knelt and chanced a look around the corner.

Like the other buildings here, the control center was a stubby concrete-block building. A heavyset guard, his round face covered with a thick, black beard, stood next to the door. A second man was crouched on top of the building.

Encizo raised the M-4 to his shoulder, drew a bead on the guy on the roof and curled his finger around the trigger. Just as he prepared to squeeze it, he heard the scuff of a shoe sole striking against the ground.

He spun around and spotted an Iranian coming up on his six. The guard clasped a large pistol in both hands and was aiming it at Encizo's head.

ENCIZO THREW HIMSELF to the right. The M-4 rattled out a quick volley of rounds that drilled into the hardman's chest. By the time the Cuban warrior struck the ground, his attacker had fallen. At the same time, gunshots erupted at Encizo's six as the shooters at the control center took advantage of their reprieve from the reaper.

Encizo rolled onto his back. Bullets sliced through the air inches above him as his opponents began unloading their weapons at him. He dragged his M-4 in a horizontal arc, discharging the weapon at the shooters. If nothing else, he hoped the barrage would send them to ground and buy him a second of breathing room. Encizo saw the door guard spin on his heel and sprint for a black pickup parked a few yards from the building. The man on the roof flattened himself and waited for the storm of lead to pass.

Encizo rolled onto his feet and sprinted for the barracks, legs pumping furiously to propel him forward. The two guards had begun to empty their weapons in his direction. Bullets chewed up the ground as the shooters tried to burn Encizo down with a twin attack.

Picking up speed as he closed in on the barracks, he fired the M-4 at a window and the glass pane disintegrated. With fluid movements, he bent at the knees and launched himself through the opening. Bullets whizzed through the window, tugging at his clothes and whistling past an ear.

ENCIZO STRUCK THE ground, grunted as his chest and stomach collided with the concrete floor, rolled and came up in a crouch. He looked around and knew he was indeed in a barracks—an empty one, fortunately.

It was a long, open room populated by several beds. He noticed most of the beds were made. But blankets, sheets and pillows scattered on the floor suggested some of the guards had been asleep when Phoenix Force first attacked. Lockers lined a wall; doors on a couple of them hung open and stray pieces of clothing lay in front of them, pulled out as the sleeping soldiers hurriedly dressed for battle.

Encizo noticed the gunfire outside the barracks had stopped. His scowl deepened. That meant the guards who'd just been shooting at him were probably closing in on the building. Or they assumed he was trapped and they were waiting for reinforcements.

He was up and moving to the nearest window, the one he'd just thrown himself through. He wanted to have a look and assess what was happening outside. He wished he had one of the small barbell-shaped robots with built-in cameras to throw out. Or at least a stick with a mirror. As it was, he'd just have to risk a glance out the window and hope he didn't catch a bullet in the face.

Hell of a plan.

As he drew up on the window, glass shards crunched softly under his feet. Autofire crackled outside the building. He tensed for an instant before realizing that it was coming from somewhere else in the compound.

He broke open his grenade launcher, fed a high-explosive round into it and snapped the launcher closed as he reached the wall below the window. He rose slowly from his crouch, back brushing against the wall. When he reached his full height, he peered around the window frame in time to see one guy, his body hunched low, sneaking toward the window. Encizo poked the M-4's barrel through the window and squeezed off a quick burst. The murderous fusillade ripped open a ragged line in the man's throat and jaw, a pained cry dying inside him as his body crashed to the ground.

As the guy wilted to the ground, more shots rang out from behind him. The torrent of slugs lashed the building's exterior. A few lanced through the window and buzzed past Encizo's face as he jerked back from view.

In the same instant something thudded against the door. It exploded inward, slapped the wall and bounced off it. Encizo steeled himself. Experience told him that a flash-bang grenade may come rolling into the room. And, while he'd trained to handle exposure to them, he first needed to be ready for one when it flew through the door.

Instead a behemoth of a man rolled through the door.

The AK-47 the giant clutched against his body would have looked comical if he wasn't sporting such a murderous look. The guy was pissed, probably murderously angry, and making no attempt to hide it.

Encizo helped out by stroking the trigger of his M-4. The burst from the little rifle tore into the man's face as he took a third step into the barracks. A second guard was dumb enough to bull his way through the doorway after the first guy went down. Encizo spared the guard the facial, but instead ventilated his chest.

Reloading his rifle, Encizo locked the muzzle on the door and took a couple of steps toward it.

Something thudded against the floor behind him.

Encizo whipped his head in the direction of the sound. He spotted an egg-shaped metal object bouncing across the floor. Grenade! And he had maybe two seconds before it exploded.

He turned toward the door and surged forward. It was exactly the move his attackers would expect. It also was the only option at hand. So he was going to sprint like a scalded cat for the door.

His legs pumped furiously, propelling him across the floor. His heart, fueled by fear and adrenaline, thudded hard in his chest. It seemed like forever before he reached the exit. He threw himself through the door and rolled across the ground, putting precious distance between him and the blast.

The concrete-block exterior of the building muffled the initial blast only slightly. Windows shattered and shards of glass slashed their way through the air.

As the blast died down, Encizo pulled himself from the ground, eyes searching for other threats. His ears were ringing. His elbows and knees, which had taken the brunt of the impact when he struck the ground, hurt like hell. He came around the building in time to encounter a hardman peering in the side window, apparently looking for the warrior.

Encizo cleared his throat. The guy spun in his direction. He was bringing up his Kalashnikov, ready to fire it with one hand at the Cuban.

Encizo's M-4 chugged out a fast burst. The 5.56 mm rounds slammed into the thug, rent flesh, drilled through bone and sent him tumbling backward.

Encizo spun on his heel and headed for the control center.

BOUDRI, SEATED IN the control room, dragged a forearm over his brow to wipe away the sweat. He knew the whole mission had gone to hell. He'd thrown everybody he had at the Americans, but they'd kept coming.

At this point he had one last option. He stared at the monitors and double-checked the drone's position. He'd hoped to fire missiles from the craft, to show the Americans what it was capable of. Unfortunately he was running out of time. Time to switch to the contingency plan, which was less flashy but equally deadly.

Fingers racing over the keyboard, he punched in the autopilot program that would crash the drone directly into the Embassy. If he destroyed this symbol of American aggression and killed some of its people, he'd still consider it a victory.

Once the codes were entered, he rose from his chair and headed for the door. He needed to buy some time. He grabbed an AK-47 that was leaning against the wall, aimed it at the computer stations, squeezed the trigger and hosed down his workstation with bullets. The bullets crashed through the monitors and chewed through the plastic computer towers. Muzzle-flashes lit the room with strobelike effect. Smoke filled the air, stinging his eyes.

When he'd destroyed the last piece of equipment, he set the AK on a nearby table, pulled a Makarov from his hip, pushed the barrel into his mouth and squeezed the trigger.

ENCIZO THUMBED A switch on the detonator and was rewarded with the thunderous peal of C-4 charges. The explosions tore the lock from the control center door and caused it to swing open.

Pushing through the smoke, he stepped into the small building and swore. A man lay curled up on the floor, most of his head missing. A Makarov lay on the floor near him, several inches from his hand. Brash shell casings were spread all over the floor.

Encizo surveyed the equipment inside and saw that it all had been ruined, rent by bullets.

There was no way they could try to control the UAV from here. It was up to McCarter and Hawkins to stop it now.

CHAPTER THIRTY

Baghdad, Iraq

Muqtada al-Abuddin stood in front of his bedroom mirror, tightened the knot of his necktie and thanked his God for the chance to make history. With the fingertips of his right hand, he smoothed the silken fabric of the tie, studied his freshly shaved features and knew a freedom fighter was looking back at him. He wasn't sure how the day was to end for him, whether he'd wind up a conquering hero or a martyr. Regardless, he was at peace with the outcome.

He turned away from the mirror and crossed the room to where his suit jacket was folded over the back of a wooden chair. While he shrugged on the jacket, his mind traveled back to the day before, when he'd met with some of his brothers to film his video. In the already stifling hot warehouse, he'd sat under a bank of lights and read his statement, cursing the U.S. for its presence in Iraq and calling on his Shiite brothers to rise up and fight against the crusaders. At any other time, he knew the Americans would ignore such rants. After today, though, they'd listen to his every word, study his every gesture and wonder how he'd succeeded.

He checked his watch and realized he was late. Exiting his bedroom, he made his way through his cramped apartment to the front door. The Interior Ministry was sending a car to pick him up and shuttle him to the Embassy. He didn't want to keep them waiting. He was always punctual, sometimes obsessively so. Being late today could make his superiors suspicious. He'd spent untold hours working hard to gain their trust. Maybe he was being overly cautious, but he didn't want to do anything that'd draw suspicion.

When he walked outside his apartment building, he didn't see the car. Good. The sun already was hot and he immediately felt sweat gather underneath his shirt. He guessed it might be one of the last times he'd feel the sun warm his scalp and shoulders. Deciding that he should enjoy it while he could, he shut his eyes and stared directly at it, marveling at its intensity.

Al-Abuddin had been born in Baghdad, the son of an Iraqi father and an Iranian mother, both Shiites. He'd been raised in the Thawra district of Baghdad, also known as Sadr City, in one of the tenements there. When Muqtada was ten, his father'd had a stroke, which forced his family to move to Tehran, to live with his grandparents. In Iraq, under the grinding poverty in Sadr City, his parents had focused much of their anger at Saddam Hussein. Once they moved to Iran, however, his grandfather and his friends had spent hours railing against the deposed shah and against the Americans who'd supported his regime. The men in his life had taught him early that the Americans were the cause of ills not just in Iran, but throughout the Middle East.

His grandfather's friends had sons and even grandsons who were involved in the IRG and Hezbollah. With his own father incapacitated, al-Abuddin found himself spending more and more time with this group, absorbing their wisdom and adopting their views as his own. Eventually he'd found himself attending their schools and learning combat skills at their camps.

When the U.S. had invaded Iraq, he'd been glad to see Saddam Hussein deposed from power. Hussein's execution had been one of the few moments al-Abuddin could recall having experienced joy. That had quickly faded once he returned to his homeland and saw America's reach everywhere he looked. American soldiers ran checkpoints throughout the city. Their vehicles, bristling with guns, had driven through his streets. A wellspring of rage seemed to open up every time he saw such things. For years he'd felt powerless to do anything about it. That was before he'd met Ahmed al-Jaballah and men associated with the shadowy parts of the Iranian government. These were men and women who'd shared his alarm and disgust as they'd watched America's imperialist tentacles seize neighboring Iraq.

Fortunately they also were well connected.

Al-Abuddin knew that al-Jaballah had recognized something special in him. Not that the older man had said as much, but al-Abuddin could tell just the same. Al-Jaballah had been able to secure a job for him with the Interior Ministry, providing security for various members of the Iraqi government, including its lawmakers.

Having that job gave him access to sensitive information, including intelligence reports about his fellow operatives at work in Iraq and any steps by the government to foil them. And, on days like today, it allowed him to get close to national leaders and gain access to sensitive spots like the U.S. Embassy. He was indeed a lucky man.

A black SUV pulled up to the curb in front of him, stopped and waited for him to climb inside. Al-Abuddin exchanged pleasantries with others from the Interior Ministry even as the driver guided the vehicle back into traffic. He stared out his window, his mind only vaguely aware of the streetscape zipping past. His thoughts were focused on fire and blood and the history he'd make today.

OMAR HASSAN SAT in the back of his air-conditioned limousine, reading through the advance notes his aides had prepared for his meeting at the Embassy.

He had already met the ambassador on more than one occasion and had found the woman easy to speak with and knowledgeable about his country. Karen Wallace, the ambassador, had been a professor of Middle Eastern studies—and, from what Hassan understood, the daughter of an aerospace tycoon—before she'd been appointed ambassador. Those conversations had occurred at black-tie events at the Embassy, where courtesy was the norm.

Today, however, they were supposed to discuss ongoing problems with al Qaeda cells operating in Iraq. Her country thought the Iraqi government was turning a blind eye to the problem. While sympathetic to their concerns, he thought the U.S. was expecting overnight miracles where none were possible. Whether the two sides ever would agree on that or other issues, remained to be seen. Hassan hoped they'd at least continue to find some common ground.

Unlike some of his fellow countrymen, he thought there were benefits to having the Americans in Iraq at this stage. Not that he approved of the way they'd handled many things—from the invasion to the occupation and reconstruction and beyond. He'd lost friends and relatives, not just in the initial war, but also through horrific attacks perpetrated by Saddam loyalists, al Qaeda and others jockeying for power after the dictator had fallen.

Still, with its resources and its interest in the region, he thought the U.S. could provide a powerful ally for his homeland. That wasn't a position that made him popular with many of his countrymen, but he hoped it would help move the country forward over the long term. Hassan knew his promises of a stronger economy and a better infrastructure were what had fueled his win in the last election. Making that promise happen would be the thing that helped him win again—at least he hoped so.

Slipping a cigarette between his lips, he brought out his stainless-steel lighter, lit the tip of the smoke and puffed it to life. He forced the smoke through his nostrils and snapped the cover closed on the lighter before he pocketed it.

Though a Shiite, he worried about Iran's interest in his country. Without a doubt, the two states had common interests and he thought they could work together. However, he also believed Iran had an agenda for its neighbor that went beyond policy issues such as border security and trade. Many of its top officials wanted real influence in the state, which worried him greatly. It was hard enough to build and maintain a functioning government without another country trying to pull the strings.

Just as the limo approached the Embassy, he realized his cigarette was almost gone. He remembered lighting it, but not smoking it. His lips curved into a smile. Whenever he thought about politics, the world around him faded away and he became absent-minded. His wife often teased that he should have studied political science instead of engineering. But then, what use would he have gotten from a political science degree under Saddam?

The limousine wheeled up to the Embassy gates. Six men, all dressed in black T-shirts, cargo pants and combat boots stood at the gate. They all cradled submachine guns of some type. He guessed they were contractors of some sort since they weren't wearing military uniforms.

Hassan's driver stopped the limo and lowered his window as one of the guards lumbered up to the vehicle.

"Omar Hassan," the driver said.

The guard peered inside the vehicle and, when he saw Hassan, greeted him with a curt nod.

"Welcome, sir," the guard said.

"Thank you, my friend. Six guards? That's more than usual."

"Yes, sir," the contractor said.

"Is there a problem?"

"They just tell me when and where to be, sir. They rarely tell me why."

"So typical," Hassan said.

"Yes, sir. You are cleared to enter the complex." He stepped away from the vehicle and gestured with his hand and the gates began to pull back. The limo rolled onto the Embassy grounds and wound its way to the main building.

The limo stopped and Hassan emerged from the backseat, at first squinting against the sun until his eyes began to adjust to its brilliance.

Ambassador Wallace, flanked by an entourage of aides, stood several yards away. Once she spotted Hassan, she broke from her group and walked toward him, spurring her security and aides into a rush to catch up. She came to a halt a foot or so from him and extended her hand.

"Mr. Prime Minister," she said, smiling. "It's an honor."

"The honor is mine, Madame Ambassador," he said. As he took her hand, his eyes drifted past her to the two men standing a few feet behind her. One man was tall, with a face that reminded Hassan of a fox, while the other was bulky. The grim-faced men carried rifles of some sort. Their eyes were hidden behind mirrored aviator shades, but Hassan swore they were appraising him.

Hassan switched his attention back to Wallace.

"Security seems tight today," he said.

Her smile faltered for an instant. "Our intelligence agencies have reported increased chatter among certain terrorist groups."

"Increased chatter about…?" he asked, cocking an eyebrow.

"We don't have a specific threat," she said. "Just a lot of talk. We didn't want to dismiss it out of hand, though. In America, we have a saying—better safe than sorry."

"Of course," he said.

"We did give your security team a heads-up on this," she said. "Apparently they decided not to tell you."

That surprised him, but he tried to play it off.

"I'm sure they made the right decision," he said.

She gently touched his forearm. "This is one of the most secure places in Iraq," she said. "Nothing bad could happen here."

I'VE GOT A bad feeling about this, McCarter thought. He swept his eyes over the crowd and looked for anything amiss. He saw a bunch of strangers, some armed to the teeth, some of questionable loyalty, milling around an Embassy compound while a couple of VIPs stood out in the open jawing.

"See anything?" Hawkins asked.

"A huge cluster in the making," McCarter said.

"Thank God," Hawkins replied, his lips curling into a tight grin. "I thought it was just me."

McCarter shook his head. "I see about a million reasons this could go wrong."

"Yeah."

"But I'm a pessimist by nature."

Gordon Schafer, the Embassy's security chief, walked up behind Wallace, tapped her on the shoulder and leaned in to speak in her ear. When he pulled away, she nodded, said something to Hassan, and started for the Embassy.

Hawkins jabbed McCarter in the ribs with his elbow. "Train's leaving," he said. "We'd better get on board."

AL-ABUDDIN FLOWED WITH the rest of the crowd into the building. His laminated credentials were clipped to the breast pocket of his suit jacket. As the group entered the lobby, he glanced at one of the security cameras that hung overhead and made no attempt to hide from it. When it was over, he guessed the footage of him walking through the lobby, glancing up at the camera, would be played over and over by the news networks.

The group was led into a large conference room filled with several small tables and chairs, while the ambassador and the prime minister adjourned to a smaller room where they could speak privately. Al-Abuddin had been inside the Embassy once before and he knew this room was a place for additional security personnel and aides to wait for their leaders to conclude their business.

Setting his briefcase on a table, he opened one of the outside pockets, slipped a hand inside and fished around until he found a set of keys that lay on the bottom. He withdrew them and slid them into his pocket.

He walked up to a blond woman who worked for the Embassy and asked for directions to a restroom. Even though he knew the Embassy's general layout, he smiled and listened patiently as she explained how to find the first-floor restroom. She offered to escort him, but he declined. It was in a public area. Since he was a credentialed visitor, he didn't need a chaperone.

He stopped in the restroom briefly, just in case the woman had watched him, before heading back out. He made his way through a series of corridors until he reached a door marked Private. Using the key from his bag, he unlocked the door, slipped inside and sealed the room shut again.

The room was large, with the concrete floors and the overhead steel beams exposed. A tool bench ran along two-thirds of the back wall butting up against a maintenance elevator. Crossing the room, he lifted the freight elevator's gate, stepped inside and closed the gate behind him. With his index finger, he punched the button for the second floor and rode the elevator to that level. Exiting the elevator, he found himself inside a small maintenance room. He wound his way around a stack of crates and found a steel locker on the floor. Kneeling, he unlocked it, raised the lid and shoved aside a pile of shop rags and newspapers. Underneath those items lay a folded green blanket. He lifted the blanket and found an Uzi, four magazines, along with a plastic key card that would open most of the doors in the building. He pocketed the card.

Picking up the Uzi, he snapped in a magazine, chambered a round and stood, a grim expression on his face. He was about to undertake a dark deed, but it would bring light soon enough.

McCarter stood along one wall inside the conference room and watched the various diplomats, politicians and aides assembled there. Two Kevlar-clad DSS agents guarded the door. Schafer, the security chief, stood next to him while Hawkins stood on the other side of the room, watching the proceedings unfold.

Fifteen minutes had passed since the group had sealed itself in this room, and the former SAS soldier felt his unease growing with each passing second.

With Ahmadah out of circulation, would al-Jaballah proceed with his plans? There was no way to know for sure. On the one hand, he might have decided to go to ground as his operation was rolled up. Or, with his people disappearing, his network unraveling, the guy might decide to go for broke. McCarter had seen it happen too many times: corner evil and, like a rabid animal, it turns and attacks.

So bring it on, he thought grimly.

McCarter leaned over to ask Schafer a question. The security chief held up a hand, gesturing for him to wait, cocked his head to the right and pressed his earbud with the first two fingers of his right hand. The creases in his forehead deepened, along with his bulldog-like scowl. Occasionally he'd whisper a reply.

Here it comes, McCarter thought.

Schafer's fingers dropped from his ear. Grim as hell, he turned to face McCarter, jerked a thumb at the door and rolled toward it. McCarter fell in behind him and gestured for Hawkins to follow. The three huddled just outside the door.

"One of my guys just radioed me on a private channel," Schaeffer said. "A member of the Iraqi delegation is roaming the upstairs. They saw him on one of the security monitors. Guy's armed."

McCarter nodded.

"Other information on him?" he asked. "How'd he get in here?"

"His name is Muqtada al-Abuddin. He works for Iraq's Interior Ministry. Apparently he's trusted and has a fairly high clearance level."

"High enough to come in here," McCarter said.

"Right," Schafer said.

"You want me to go after him?" Hawkins asked.

"Negative," McCarter said. "I want you in there, in case someone makes a play for the high rollers. I'll take care of the stray."

CHAPTER THIRTY-ONE

Manning had just finished planting the packet of Semtex at the base of the satellite dish when a scraping noise to his left caught his attention. He froze and strained his ears. A second or two passed while he waited, then the murmur of hushed voices reached him.

Reaching down to his thigh holster, he drew his sound-suppressed Beretta and turned his whole body in the direction of the noise. He was crouched behind one of the satellite dishes, which gave him some cover. He craned his head around the edge of the dish in time to see two men walking toward his position.

Around him was a pair of large satellite dishes, one of which was covered with a radome, a cover that looked like a huge golf ball and was designed to protect satellite dishes from the elements and to obscure the direction it was pointing. It wouldn't shield the dish from the load of Semtex he had planted on the neighboring dish. In his jacket pocket, he carried a detonator that could be used to fire off the charges from a distance. First, though, he needed to get away from the satellite dishes.

The two men crept past his position. One was dressed in the same olive-drab fatigues as many of the other thugs on al-Jaballah's payroll. The other man wore jeans, a black windbreaker and brown hiking boots. The guy in fatigues was carrying some model of the Kalashnikov rifle. The man with the leather jacket, an autoloading pistol in his grip, cast a glance at the satellite dishes. Manning felt himself tense. His hold on his rifle tightened and he thought things were about to explode, but the guy looked away and kept moving.

Manning waited for them to pass before he worked his way out from among all the gear. He wanted to take out the communications system for a couple of reasons. First, since they were miles into Iran, the last thing Phoenix Force needed was a distress call going out to nearby military bases. They had a lot of fig in them, but shooting their way through ten miles of broken highways before the opposition could overwhelm them with sheer numbers or pound them with missiles from combat jets was beyond Phoenix Force's capabilities.

Manning didn't mind dying behind enemy lines—and he had no doubt Iran was an enemy. But he had no interest in spending even a minute in an Iranian jail. He knew all too well that the U.S. government wouldn't try to get him out. It wouldn't even acknowledge his existence. His homeland of Canada would do the same.

So he'd spend his last days rotting in a hole, probably beating the hell out of the guards when they weren't beating him. At least until his body became too injured or weak to do it. After that, he could almost guarantee he'd endure horrible torture at the hands of the Iranians or witness his fellow teammates going through the same thing. Regardless, he had no interest in walking that path.

The way he saw it, his best bet was to fight like hell until someone got the best of him.

And if they didn't, hell, he'd live to fight another day.

Right now, though, he had to fight today.

Still in a crouch, he wound his way around the exposed satellite dish and crept up to the radome covering the second dish. He rounded the large, ball-shaped cover just as the two hardmen moved past. The guy in the blue jeans apparently sensed something. He spun around, his pistol in target-acquisition mode. His actions spurred the guy in the fatigues to move, too.

Manning's M-4 ground out a punishing burst. The slugs ripped a ragged line over Mr. Blue Jeans's chest. His companion triggered his rifle. Jagged flames erupted from the AK's muzzle. The bullets sliced through the air just to Manning's left.

But the Canadian still was sweeping the M-4 in the other guy's direction. The slugs from his compact weapon lanced into his opponent's torso, stitching the guy from left hip to right shoulder.

Manning jogged away from the bloody scene. He wanted to blow the charges he'd planted, but needed to put more space between him and them. He'd covered a couple dozen yards when a line of three shooters emerged from behind the hangar. Manning hosed them down with a withering hail from the M-4, the weapon showering the ground with brass shell casings.

He ejected the magazine from his weapon and reached for another from his belt. Just as he started to feed the fresh magazine, something big registered in his peripheral vision. Before he could turn his head to look, he felt something slam into his side and knock him from his feet.

The M-4 slipped from his fingers and he heard it thud against the ground. He struck the dirt, one arm pinned beneath him. One of al-Jaballah's thugs had knocked him over and was now straddling him. The guy's fist was drawn back by his ear, poised to rock Manning with a blow to the head. The punch rocketed forward. Manning threw up an arm to block it. The man's fist collided with Manning's forearm. Bolts of pain burst out from the point of impact. Manning belched a lungful of air through his gritted teeth.

The guy on top of him was big. Something was tattooed in a black script that Manning didn't recognize on the dome of the man's shaved head. The Phoenix Force warrior chopped down on his opponent's collar bone and heard a snapping noise, like a stick breaking. The thug's jaw dropped open and his eyes widened. Manning struck the guy in the same spot, eliciting a scream from him. He threw another punch at Manning, striking the Phoenix Force commando in the jaw and snapping his head to the right.

The Iranian had shifted his weight enough that Manning was able to maneuver off his right hip and free his trapped arm. As he pulled his arm free, he snatched the Gerber knife on his belt from its holster and drove the blade into the other man's thigh until it skittered off the man's femur. Manning gave the blade a hard pull, and the razor-sharp steel sliced through muscles and tendons. An agonized scream erupted from his opponent's mouth. The Iranian rolled off Manning and lay on the ground, writhing in pain, even as one hand slapped around on his hip for his pistol.

Manning drew his Beretta and squeezed off a single round. The bullet punched into the other man's forehead, leaving a ragged, dime-size hole before punching through the back of his skull.

Manning climbed to his feet and gathered the M-4.

Then he slipped his hand into his jacket pocket. When he located the detonator, he pulled it out. With his thumb, he flicked two switches, one right after the other. He was rewarded with twin peals of thunder, followed by columns of roiling, orange-yellow flames shooting into the sky. Within minutes the satellite dishes were engulfed in flames.

He activated his throat mike.

"Control center gone," he said.

"Not to be a killjoy," Grimaldi said, "but we need to get

in the air and over the border. If they don't have reinforcements on the way, they will soon."

"Roger that," Manning said. "I'm heading your way. Everyone else should do the same."

The other Stony Man warriors voiced their understanding and the radio fell silent. Manning turned to have one last look at the fire before starting for the helipad.

He spotted a man lumbering toward him. The guy was clutching a pistol in his hand and lining up a shot at Manning.

The Canadian whipped forward the assault rifle's muzzle. Jagged muzzle-flashes spit from the weapon. Bullets crossed the distance between the two men, tearing into the gut of Manning's opponent and driving the man to the ground.

Baghdad, Iraq

AL-ABUDDIN BYPASSED THE elevator and moved for the nearest stairwell. The last thing he wanted at this stage was to be cooped up in a box, where the security teams could hit the emergency stop on the elevator and leave him stuck.

Shutting the stairwell door behind him, he reached his hand under his jacket and wrapped his fingers around the grip of the Uzi hidden beneath his specially tailored jacket. In his other hand he carried a suitcase filled with a sound suppressor and several clips of ammunition. He surged up the stairs, taking two steps at a time.

When he reached the top floor, he was barely winded. He'd spent months training his mind and body for this moment. And, though the arrival of the American and the mouthy Briton was unwelcome, it wasn't totally unexpected, especially after they'd burned through operations in Mexico, Africa and now the Middle East.

He tried to shake it off. There was nothing he could do but stick to the plan and hope it worked.

He pulled the Uzi from the rig under his jacket and lowered himself to one knee. From inside the briefcase he pulled out the sound suppressor, threaded it onto the SMG's muzzle and set the weapon aside. Next he pulled additional magazines from the case and stuffed them into his pockets. Grabbing the Uzi, he rose, pressed the release bar on the security door and moved through it. He'd taken maybe a half dozen steps when a U.S. Marine in camouflage fatigues stepped into view. One hand was resting on the grip of his sidearm and he held up the other hand, palm forward, gesturing for al-Abuddin to halt. When the Marine's eyes lighted on al-Abuddin's weapon, it was too late. The Iranian raised the Uzi and had it at hip level before the other Marine could clear his holster. The Uzi coughed out a short burst that savaged the man's torso before he collapsed to the floor in a dead heap.

Al-Abuddin stepped up to the fallen American. Kneeling next to the Marine, he grabbed the security card that hung from an olive-green lanyard around the man's neck and pulled it free. Before al-Abuddin could get to his feet, a second Marine stepped into the corridor. The Beretta 92 cracked twice. The slugs slashed through the air just over al-Abuddin's head. Holding his ground, he fired off another fast burst from the Uzi that chewed into the American's thighs. The guy let out an agonized scream and dropped to his knees. Al-Abuddin cut loose with another burst from the Uzi. This time, the bullets cored through the man's torso and killed him.

Al-Abuddin rose to standing and raced down the corridor.

He heard no signs that sounds from the brief firefight

had reached the individuals on the rooftop, though he couldn't be sure.

Another stairwell, this one accessible through a sealed door, led to the Embassy roof and the anti-aircraft batteries there. Swiping the card, he pulled the door open and swept the Uzi's muzzle over the narrow corridor, but found it empty.

He surged up the stairs to a second door at the top. He unlocked it, slipped out onto the roof and ran in a crouch to one of the rooftop air conditioners. Kneeling next to the big machine, he peered around the corner at a pair of Marines. Both stood at the edge of the roof, one guzzling from a plastic bottle of water, the other checking the horizon through a pair of binoculars. Three MANPADS— Man Portable Air Defense Systems—were arranged on the ground. The shoulder-to-air missiles were within easy reach of the Americans.

Al-Abuddin aimed the Uzi at the unsuspecting men. His finger curled around the trigger.

McCARTER BURST THROUGH the stairwell door and saw the carnage the Iraqi had left in his wake. Two Marines, their bodies ravaged by bullets, lay on the ground, each in a pool of blood. Instinct and experience told him both men were dead. He saw no signs that either man was breathing. The former SAS commando muttered an oath and keyed his throat mike.

"I have two men down," he said.

"Roger," Hawkins replied. "Al-Abuddin?"

"Nowhere to be seen."

"Damn. You need me up there?"

"Negative," McCarter said. He was gliding along the wall, moving for the doors leading to the roof. "Just make sure the rest of the riffraff stays downstairs."

"Good luck," Hawkins said before signing off.

As McCarter passed by the fallen warriors, a cold rage overtook him. He felt at once detached from the bloodshed, as though he just was observing it, even as it focused his mind and sparked a rush of adrenaline that coursed through his body.

The Iranian had left the door to the roof ajar. McCarter moved up next to it, stole a glance around the jamb and verified that the stairwell was empty. Moving up the stairs, he kept the MP-5's muzzle trained on the door, even as he threw an occasional glance over his shoulder to make sure his six was clear of threats.

When he was about halfway up the stairs, he heard someone cry out in surprise and pain from the rooftop. Biting off an angry curse, he surged up the remaining steps to the rooftop door, which had been left open.

Pausing, he chanced a look through the doorway before darting onto the roof. The Iraqi sun was brilliant, glinting off the steel housings of the multiple air-conditioning units arrayed on the rooftop, each one emitting a loud hum. He slipped on his sunglasses and exited the Embassy. The heat struck him immediately, warming the top of his head, his shoulders, snatching the sweat from his skin as soon as it exited his pores.

After the initial blast of heat, McCarter was only vaguely aware of it. Finding his target consumed his attention. Crossing the roof, he slid into the narrow passage that lay between the AC units and traversed its length, stopping just before he ran out of cover. He peered out from cover and saw the Iranian, the tricked-out Uzi in his hand, muzzle pointed skyward, standing a couple dozen yards away. Though the guy was facing McCarter, he was looking down at the corpses at his feet, likely admiring his handiwork. Shell casings lay on the ground just a few feet from where the Phoenix Force commando now was crouched. He guessed the bastard had stepped from hiding and scythed the two men down in a merciless storm of lead.

The Briton eased himself to standing and leveled the MP-5. He watched as, with his free hand, his target plucked a phone from his belt.

"Afraid the call will have to wait," McCarter said, stepping from cover.

The guy's head snapped up, his face a mask of shock. He already was bringing his Uzi down and sprinting to his right.

McCarter stroked the MP-5's trigger. Jagged yellow muzzle-flashes lashed out from the weapon. The heavy spray of bullets savaged the guy's chest and stomach, caused the killer's body to jerk under the barrage before his shredded form dropped to the rooftop.

McCarter rolled up on the guy and kicked the fallen Uzi away from his hand.

Kneeling next to him, McCarter saw the phone in the man's grip. Peeling open his fingers, he picked up the phone and started to examine the screen. Before his eyes could focus, a cold sensation raced down his spine in spite of the desert heat. He jerked his head up in time to see another man, this one armed with a grease gun of some sort, trying to line up a shot at McCarter.

He squeezed off a quick burst that sent the other guy scrambling. McCarter tossed aside the phone, figuring he could pick it up later, and moved across the rooftop, eyes searching for the other man. He moved into the maze of exposed ductwork winding its way around the rooftop. Motion to his right caught his attention. He spun in time to see his opponent burst into view from behind one of the AC units, his SMG spitting bullets.

Rounds tore into the rooftop a few yards in front of

McCarter. He spun toward his opponent, the H&K chattering through the contents of its magazine. The fusillade of bullets went low, chewing into the guy's thighs. He jerked crazily under the onslaught for a stretched second before falling to the rooftop. McCarter moved in on the shooter, changing out magazines as he did. The man was in motion, his hand scrambling to free a pistol from its holster. The MP-5 rattled again and the man was dead.

Manning's voice buzzed in his ear.

"The UAV is gone," he said.

"What?" McCarter said.

"It's in the air."

"On its way here?"

"What do you think?"

"Damn it," McCarter replied. "Can you get to the pilots?"

"Working on it. What if I can't, though? Can you bring it down?"

McCarter scowled. "Sure," he said. "I'll throw a bloody rock at it and pray."

"I'll take that as a maybe."

"Just deal with the pilots. Hawkins and I will handle things on our end. Right, T.J.?"

"Right," Hawkins replied.

McCARTER BEGAN WALKING across the Embassy roof toward the Stinger missiles the Marines had stockpiled.

As he moved, he keyed his throat mike again. "Hawkins, where the hell are you?"

A second passed, then two. McCarter muttered a curse, but kept moving. He was worried as hell about Hawkins, worried the guy might be captured or injured somewhere inside the building below. Hell, his American friend might be dying, for all McCarter knew.

The Briton shoved those thoughts from his mind. He was worried, yeah. But he needed to focus on the mission first. It was the only choice a soldier could make. He'd expect—hell, demand—that the other Phoenix Force warriors would do the same.

Which didn't make him feel a damn bit better about it.

Kneeling next to one of the dead Marines, he reached for the guy's binoculars, which had fallen to the roof. Apparently one of the bullets that had pierced the guy's chest had torn apart the strap on his binoculars.

Now I'm stealing equipment from dead Marines, McCarter chided himself. Aren't I a bloody prize?

"Sorry, lad," he muttered.

And the Marine was just that. McCarter guessed he was eighteen, old enough to serve his country but too damn young to die like this. The Stony Man warrior felt a flash of anger burn hot before he squelched it. He'd deal with this later. He'd killed the shooter, yeah. But given the chance, he'd burn down the man who'd started all this carnage.

First, he needed to make sure the bastards failed, though. Then came the nasty part.

Peering through the binoculars, he swept them over the sky. A small black dot hovered on the horizon, invisible at that distance to the unaided eye. He guessed it was the UAV, but he couldn't be sure.

Setting aside the binoculars, he switched the channel on his com link and via satellite contacted Stony Man Farm through an encrypted channel.

"Go, David," Barbara Price said.

"I have control of the roof," McCarter said. "I have a visual on a bogey, but I can't identify it. If it's not a friendly, I need to take it down. Can you advise?"

"I'll patch us into U.S. Central Command. Someone's

monitoring the airspace. They probably already have seen it and can advise. Give me a minute."

"Don't have a minute," McCarter growled.

"Give me what you can," Price said. "Stand by."

While he waited, McCarter hefted the Stinger, which weighed more than thirty pounds, onto his shoulder, rose to his full height and activated the targeting apparatus. By now he could see the craft without the help of the binoculars. Some primitive part of his brain knew he was at ground zero; that he was seconds away from death. A surge of adrenaline rushed through him, caused his jaw to clench and his muscles to tense. He sucked in a deep breath; exhaled to override it. The last thing he could afford right now was to act out of self-preservation and risk shooting down a friendly aircraft.

At the same time, the craft had drawn closer and he knew it didn't have to be on top of him to unleash its deadly payload.

After what seemed like an eternity, Price came back on the line. "It's not one of ours," she said. "They're checking with the Iraqis."

"Damn it," he growled.

"I know, David. Sorry."

He turned on the targeting mechanism and began to line up his shot.

A few seconds later Price said, "Confirmed as unauthorized."

"Roger."

A high-pitched whine began to emanate from the Stinger's targeting system, telling McCarter that he had a clear shot. He triggered the weapon. The missile hissed out from the tube and sliced a path across the sky. McCarter could follow its exhaust trail without the binoculars.

The missile slammed into the UAV. The Briton heard a

muffled explosion as flames engulfed the craft. The fire ignited the fuel tank and sparked a second explosion that disintegrated the drone. McCarter set the launcher on the rooftop and made his way back into the Embassy.

As he descended the stairs, he activated his throat mike and summoned Manning.

"Sitrep," McCarter said.

"We have the facility under control," Manning said.

"Boudri?"

"Dead."

"You have any guests?"

"Negative. We didn't find anyone in the surrendering mood today."

"Understood."

"Grabbed a couple of laptops and mobile phones from anyone we identified as a high-value target. Those may have some information value to us. Why?"

"We still need to find al-Jaballah. Otherwise, we've only done half the job."

"Agreed."

"Since we don't have anyone to interview, we should get Kurtzman and his people to access the data on the computers and phones as soon as possible. Come back here and we'll start shoveling that stuff back to Wonderland as soon as possible."

CHAPTER THIRTY-TWO

Ajunta, Nigeria

Al-Jaballah heard a sharp cracking sound from outside his villa. Gunshot! Without thinking, he spun toward the door. His hand dropped to the grip of the Walther .380 holstered on his right hip, his heart hammered in his chest and he stared at the door, expecting it to burst inward.

It took a stretched second for his mind to interpret and recognize the noise for what it was—the backfire from a passing car's exhaust. His face and neck flushed hot with embarrassment. He snapped a look at two of his guards. They stared at him with stony expressions.

"What are you looking at?" he snapped.

One of the guards muttered an apology, and both turned their eyes from al-Jaballah. A toxic mix of fear and anger swirled in the Iranian. He was losing their respect. He saw it in their eyes. Once he lost their respect, could treason be far behind? Without fear—of him, of the ayatollahs, of something greater than themselves—why listen to him? Take a bullet for him?

He gestured at his luggage. "Idiots," he said. "Make yourselves useful and move my things to my room."

He turned from the security men and headed up the stairs. Entering the study, he slammed the door behind him, dropped into a leather armchair, yanked a half-empty pack of cigarettes from his shirt pocket and shook one into his hand.

It had been a week since everything had fallen apart in Baghdad. Since then, he'd moved three times, this small villa being the third place in a matter of days. The place was owned by a British oilman who several times had sold embargoed machinery and parts to the Iranian government. Over the years the guy also had made available to Iran some of his best engineers and metallurgists, all of whom had unwittingly helped the country in its pursuit of a nuclear program. Aside from the access to top engineers and technicians, Iran also had gained the ability to blackmail the oilman when it suited Tehran's purposes. With a couple of calls, al-Jaballah had been given access to the place for as long as he wanted. That could be a week, a month or a year.

Judging by his luck over the past several days, though, he doubted he was going to stay here long. He'd spent four days in Uganda before the commandoes had found him. A half dozen of his best men had died in a brief battle, though he and a few advisers had escaped. His time in Sudan had been even shorter, though the results no less deadly.

He stepped to the door and grasped the knob.

"It's about time you got here with my things," he said.

Twisting the knob, he swung the door open and poked his head into the corridor outside. What he saw caused him to take a sharp breath. The suitcases stood in the hallway, a few feet apart from one another. One of his guards lay on the floor between the suitcases, facedown on the carpet.

A small red hole was visible between his shoulder blades.

Al-Jaballah slid the Walther from its holster, cocked back the hammer and stepped into the hallway. Grabbing the dead guard by the collar of his black sport coat, the Iranian dragged the corpse into the study and slammed the door.

Holstering the Walther, he rolled the dead guy onto his

back. The ragged exit wound in the guy's chest, the gleam from the light striking the man's blood-soaked skin, barely registered with al-Jaballah. Instead, he threw the guy's jacket open and grabbed the micro Uzi from the shoulder rigging under his arm.

He slid two more of the short magazines into his pants' pocket.

Even as he acted, his mind raced. They were here—in the house! How did they even find him so quickly? It had been less than twenty-four hours since he'd decided to come here, but already they'd found him.

He tried to shove those questions from his mind. Calm down, he thought. Use your head and you can get out of this.

He'd have time later on to figure out how they had found him. First, he needed to get out of this house alive, even if it meant ditching his entourage. If he left them to get chopped to bits by the Americans while he found another place to hide, he'd consider that a victory.

He wiped his blood-soaked hands on the carpet. The move left two dark red swaths on the flooring.

Picking up the Uzi, he stood to his full height. His mind was already planning his next move. He could hire mercenaries to stand in as guards. He still had cash he'd siphoned over the years from various arms and drug deals, criminal transactions ostensibly undertaken to help his country, but that had also lined his pockets.

But first he had to escape.

Fortunately he had a contact in town, an IRG commander who on paper had retired but who also would supply forged documents, weapons and other necessities.

He took a quick inventory. A money belt stuffed with currency was looped around his waist. He didn't have keys to either of the cars. No matter, he told himself. He'd learned a long time ago how to hotwire a car. In less than a minute he could have one of their cars started without a key. Or… He was in a small, gated community populated by army officers, corporate executives and high-ranking government officials. So even in a country as poor as Nigeria, most of the neighbors had nice cars worth stealing. One of them would be stupid enough to leave a vehicle parked outside where he could access it.

He moved to the door and put an ear to it. Someone had shot his guard right outside his door. So where was he?

Letting several more seconds pass, al-Jaballah convinced himself that he heard nothing in the corridor outside. He lowered his hand onto the knob, gently wrapped his fingers around it and started to turn it.

An explosion outside the building shattered the silence. Forgetting about the door, he whipped his head toward the windows and saw one of the cars, its interior engulfed in flames, the hood and the trunk both thrust open, flying into the air as though it'd been dropped on a landmine.

He tried to think of a prayer, but his mind had gone blank. Instead he thrust open the door and stepped into the hallway. Sweeping his Uzi over his surroundings, al-Jaballah saw no one. A second explosion roared outside the house and a jolt of fear rocked him. Plaster dust fell from the ceiling like a light snowfall. From outside his line of sight, he heard glass shatter.

Go!

Hugging the wall, he moved to the stairwell and crept down it, willing himself to move slowly.

When he reached the last step, he swept his gaze around the first floor. The concussive force from the blast had shattered windows. The front door hung open. The light from the fires consuming the cars danced in the doorway. The other guard's limp form was folded over the back of a chair, his arms curled up like the gnarled branches of a diseased tree. Al-Jaballah saw the tan upholstery on the seatback had been soaked with blood. There was a ragged gap where the guy's jaw should have been.

A man's voice sounded from behind him.

"We gave your men the night off."

Al-Jaballah started to twist at the waist so he could look at the speaker.

"Slow it down, lad," the man said. "Set the Uzi down. Kick it away. Then turn around. Slowly."

Al-Jaballah hesitated for the span of a heartbeat, but then bent forward at the waist and set the Uzi on the floor. He straightened to standing, kicked the SMG and it skidded across the floor, stopping when it collided with a table leg. I still have the pistol, he thought. From outside the building, he heard the whirring of helicopter blades.

"Is that yours?" he asked.

"Yes," the other man said.

"So you think you can take me with you? You sound English. You want to render me back to England? Why would they want me?"

The Englishman snorted. "You think I'm here to render you? What, knock you out and transport you somewhere?"

"You aren't here to extract me?"

"No." The man paused. "See, I have a problem with sticking a bag over someone's head, kidnapping him and taking him to another country in the dead of the night."

A note of amusement crept into al-Jaballah's voice. "Really? You're squeamish about such things?"

"No, not squeamish. More of a philosophical hang-up. Something an old soldier like me just can't reconcile."

"And that would be?"

"You killed a lot of people. Maybe you didn't pull the trigger, but you gave the orders that left a lot of people dead. You've got all kinds of blood on your hands.

Innocent blood. And I'm guessing it doesn't bother you one damn bit."

Al-Jaballah said nothing.

"And here's the thing about that, lad," the man continued. "If we took you somewhere, you're technically a high-level Iranian official. We couldn't drop you at some kind of black site. You know, drop you down the rabbit hole, never to be seen again, right? Your country would howl and cry over the great Satan, demand you be returned. Maybe Iran wouldn't do it in the open, but they'd do it. Pretty soon Russia and China would start pissing down the West's leg, too, demanding you be let go."

Al-Jaballah gave a slight shrug. "Perhaps," he said.

"Oh, don't sell yourself short, mate. I'm sure you're a big bleeding deal in Tehran. The mullahs would want you back. They'd wring their hands, piss and moan about the raw deal they were getting. And maybe—*maybe*—someone would give in to all their whining and send you back."

"Perhaps," al-Jaballah said. He noticed the thumping of the helicopter rotors was much louder as though the craft was right overhead. He cast a quick glance at the door.

The Englishman shook his head. "Forget it, mate, that's my ride. No one's coming to save you. Anyway, here's my issue. Hell, I'm not the most educated guy or even the smartest. But even an oaf like me knows if you kill a bunch of innocent people, you shouldn't walk free."

A chill raced down al-Jaballah's spine. "What should happen then?"

A smile ghosted the other man's lips.

"You've still got a gun under your jacket. You didn't think I missed that, did you? C'mon, I'm a pro. You've got that pistol. So drop your hands and—as the Yanks like to say—make your play."

It took a moment for the words to sink in. But when

they did al-Jaballah didn't hesitate. His hand was a blur as it disappeared under his jacket. He fisted the Walther, wheeled around and maneuvered the pistol so he could acquire a target.

As he turned, he glimpsed his opponent. The man stood just a few yards away. He was dressed from head to toe in black. Black combat paint was smeared over his cheeks, nose, forehead and chin. He held a Browning Hi-Power, similar to one al-Jaballah owned, in his right hand.

His finger tightened on the trigger.

McCARTER WAITED FOR him to spin around. His sound-suppressed Browning coughed once and a bullet drilled into the man's heart. Al-Jaballah stumbled back a couple of steps before he collided with the wall, streaking it with blood as he slid to the ground. His Walther cracked once and a bullet drilled into the floor.

The Briton pulled a thermite grenade from one of the pockets of his combat vest. He walked to the doorway, paused when he reached it, turned and looked at the body sprawled on the floor, wondering for a moment if unseen demons from hell had sprung up to drag al-Jaballah's soul to hell. McCarter wasn't a particularly religious man, but he occasionally hoped the justice he and his partners dispensed wasn't the final accounting for the mass murderers and psychopaths they chased.

Yanking the pin from the device, he tossed it onto the floor near al-Jaballah's corpse and ran from the house.

He found Manning and James standing outside, each dressed head to toe in black and bristling with weapons.

Grudgingly, the Nigerian government had agreed to let them enter the country to take out al-Jaballah.

McCarter and the others watched as the first orange-yellow bursts of flame flashed in the window.

"The locals know you were going to burn the house down?" James asked.

McCarter shook his head.

"Not that they deserve it, but I'm doing these bastards a favor," he said. "Iran will know this bastard was murdered."

"But they'll have a hell of a time proving it with everything burned down, right?"

"Hard, but not impossible. You took the other bodies, his security team, et cetera, and tossed them into the house?"

"Done and done," Manning said.

"Good," McCarter said.

The fire by now had engulfed the first floor, blocking the front door. Through the door and on the curtains, McCarter could see flames undulating.

Stony Man Farm had planned the whole operation out. Officials would blame the destruction on a wiring problem. Brognola had already placed a crew on standby to swoop in, secure the scene and clean up any signs that the commandos ever had been on the property. They'd sift the dirt for shell casings and make sure any remains had been vaporized or removed. A CIA front company planned, with the Nigerian government's help, to buy the property and raze the house. The front company's executives would promise new development on the property that never would materialize, all to stymie efforts by Iran to investigate the deaths.

McCarter wheeled around and started for the helicopter. "C'mon, lads," he said. "Let's get some shut-eye. We'll probably have to save the bloody world again tomorrow."

* * * * *

The
Don Pendleton's
Executioner®
NIGERIA MELTDOWN

Nigeria hinges on the verge of a revolution after a secret terror group is discovered

When Washington learns a secret military brotherhood is plotting a revolution in Nigeria, they know they need to act quickly. Mack Bolan is teamed up with a few men from the Nigerian military, but not only is he dodging bullets from the terror group, someone on his team has been hired to kill him. Closing in on the brotherhood in the heart of the jungle, he'll have to rely on his instincts to take down the leaders and disarm the traitor when he strikes.

GOLD
EAGLE®

Available January wherever
books and ebooks are sold.

TAKE 'EM FREE

2 action-packed novels plus a mystery bonus

NO RISK
NO OBLIGATION TO BUY

AleX Archer
TREASURE OF LIMA

A myth of the past holds the promise of wealth…and death.

Costa Rica's white beaches and coral reefs should have been adventure-proof. But naturally, archaeologist and TV show host Annja Creed's peace is interrupted by a mysterious woman with a strange tale. Her husband has disappeared after leading an expedition in search of the "Lost Loot of Lima." The treasure was lost in the late nineteenth century, when a Peruvian ship captain had gone mad with greed. Now Annja has been asked to lead a fateful sojourn for the lost loot. But where treasures are lost, danger will always be found….

Available January wherever books and ebooks are sold.